VAMPIRE'S MATE

GUARDIANS

VALERIE TWOMBLY

DEDICATION

For my fans. Thank you for sticking with me.

INTRODUCTION

Vampire Guardian, Marcus Dagotto is sworn to safeguard humanity. With the death of his mate, and a curse that will soon catapult him into bloodlust, he focuses on protecting his king and surviving each day. When the gods interfere, it's never a good thing and this time they destine him a new mate. He tries to resist the woman fated to be his, but when she ends up in trouble, instinct demands he protect her.

In the darkness, she may be the sliver of light that will save his soul.

After the love of Cassandra Jensen's life ditches her at the altar, she swears off men forever. But when a sexy stranger visits her nightly dreams and seduction plays a starring role, she reconsiders her current situation. Problem is, he's a figment of her wild imagination, at least until he steps into her life for real. His world is full of things that go bump in the night, and something evil is coming to claim him. To protect herself means losing him. To save him will mean the ultimate sacrifice.

A single kiss will change her life forever.

PROLOGUE

1712

Tears stung Marcus's cheeks when he raised his sword. "I am so sorry, love. I have failed you. It should be I who dies this day."

Eliza's cocoa eyes looked at him but didn't see him. Dead inside, her soul lost. She would never again be the woman he loved. He sucked in a breath and flexed his arms, the sword swung, slicing across her neck. The blade tore through sinew and bone and sent her head rolling across the stone floor. Reality nearly sent him to his knees, but there wasn't time to mourn the death of his mate. The fighting outside echoed in his ears, the demons were strong and put up one hell of a fight.

Marcus advanced down the corridor of the abandoned castle. The scene played out the same in every direction. Blood bathed the floors, and his brethren's heartsick screams echoed off the walls as they killed their mates. A demon jumped out from behind a door. Its claws tearing the flesh on Marcus's arm. He wielded his sword and sent another head flying across the room. Out of the corner of his eye, he caught a Draki dispatching another demon. The shifter, a friend who also searched for his mate. Not even the dragons were immune to Drayos and his fucking misery.

The dragon turned his head. "Be careful, my friend. My brethren will soon be setting this place on fire." Caleb's cerulean body shimmered as he shifted back to human form.

"Have you found your mate yet?" Marcus asked as he searched the adjoining room. Empty.

"Not yet, you?"

He stepped beside his friend. "I killed her."

Caleb laid a hand on his shoulder. "I am sorry, my friend. Drayos will die for what he has done."

Marcus nodded and moved forward in his search for the demon Drayos. He opened up the psychic path leading to his prince. *Aidyn.*

Marcus, did you find my sister?

He closed his eyes, so many hearts broken today. *She is dead, I am sorry, my lord.*

I will kill Drayos with my bare hands.

Aidyn had already lost his brother and father in this battle. The prince's pain ripped through Marcus and there was no doubt the other guardians felt it. It was a blessing and a curse to be connected to each other. He tried to pinpoint Aidyn's position, but something blocked him.

Aidyn, where are you? Do not engage Drayos.

The prince would die as well if he tried to kill the Demon Overlord. Aidyn was far too young; his two hundred years were no match against a thousand-year-old demon.

He took our women, used them to carry his spawn. He has killed everyone I love.

With weary muscles, Marcus took the stairs. He stormed from room to room, kicking in locked doors only to find them empty. *I know, my lord, and he will pay, but it is not wise for you to confront him.* He knew Aidyn wouldn't listen. Perhaps the gods would help.

"Zarek!" Marcus summoned the god. Nothing. No surprise.

After all, the gods could have stepped in and saved the women, but they had all been left to fate. Fuck fate, he was sick to death of it.

The sound of clashing swords filtered in from the hallway. He flashed into the room, not caring what he stumbled across. His vision filled with Aidyn and Drayos, they were face to face.

Drayos had morphed into a full demon and stood at least three feet taller than Aidyn. Blood seeped from the wounds that covered the demons blackened skin. Marcus tried to run toward them but found himself behind an invisible barrier. "What the fuck?"

He balled his hands and banged on the wall. "Aidyn!" The prince ignored him. Marcus was stuck, helpless as he watched the events unfold in front of him. Thoughts of telling Daria, his queen, she had lost her entire family in this battle sat like a balled-up knot in his stomach. He pressed his palms against his prison. *Aidyn, my friend, I can't bear another loss today.*

The air behind him shifted, a cool breeze lifted his hair. He looked over his shoulder and found Zarek towering over him in a Scottish kilt rather than his beloved Egyptian shendyt. His raven hair held a beaded braid on one side. *So this is why he ignores us? He is busy playing dress-up with the goddess Quadira.*

"Get me out of here!" Marcus demanded.

"You will not interfere, my son."

Marcus growled, his fangs elongated and he wanted blood. Yes, he would take the blood of his god if it ended the pain and suffering of his brethren. "You would let the prince die?" He tried to lunge toward Zarek but found his feet pinned to the floor. *You are our creator, we your warriors. Why would you do this to us?*

Zarek gave him a leveled gaze. "What makes you think the prince will die this day?"

Marcus looked back toward the fight. Aidyn had lost his sword; a small dagger was clutched in his hand. Both the demon and the vampire bore bloody wounds. Turning back to Zarek, Marcus dropped to his knees, he would beg the god if he had to. "The prince is too young to fight one as strong as Drayos. Send me in his place...please." He was three hundred years older than Aidyn and could defeat the demon. "We have lost so much today." Death haunted him like a fucking plague. He was a healer, but today, he healed no one. The anguished cries of his brethren still echoed in his ears. They had slain their mates, and then turned on each other to end their misery. Marcus would like to end his suffering as well, but he would continue on, his skills needed.

Zarek laid a hand on Marcus's shoulder. "I am sorry, my son, for all the pain you will encounter this day. However, today must shape the future." With those words, he vanished.

The future? Aidyn was their future, the line that tied them all together. They all hoped the prince would persuade the gods to find a cure for the curse Drayos had placed upon them. The curse would devour them, creating an imbalance that darkened their souls. When Zarek created his vampires, he used light and dark, good and evil. The light fueled the guardian of humanity, the darkness the warrior. A perfect balance, but once Drayos's curse took full effect, the light faded, the darkness turned them into pure evil destined to destroy everything in their path. Not even the humans they guarded would be safe.

He jumped to his feet but found the shield still erected around him. Aidyn's body lie still on the floor, and Drayos stood over him, sword poised for the fatal blow. Marcus beat on the invisible wall. "Aidyn!" He sucked in a breath, his heart trapped in a vice that squeezed the life out of him. He could do nothing but watch his prince die. A tear slid down his cheek for the death of his mate, his brethren and now his prince, his best friend. *I am no guardian. I am a failure. I have failed them all.*

Drayos swung his sword. Everything moved in slow motion as Marcus waited for the blade to connect with Aidyn's neck. Lightning sizzled from the sky and sent debris flying in different directions. The room crumbled around them as the earth shook. Drayos's head rolled across the floor. Marcus sensed the shield that encased him drop, and he rushed forward to where Aidyn now stood.

"What the hell just happened? Are you all right?" Marcus asked.

"I am not exactly sure. I think I caused the lightning."

"You?" Marcus looked over at the prince, his pants torn and his shirt missing. Dust from the debris covered bleeding wounds. There was something different about the prince. He appeared stronger. Marcus noticed a dark marking on Aidyn's chest and reached out to wipe away the dirt so he could get a better look. "Sweet deity!" He jumped back.

"What?" Aidyn looked at his chest, his jaw dropped. "I never felt it."

Like many of the other guardians, Aidyn had been given his mark. An indication of his position and abilities. Marcus bore the Ankh, a pair of angel wings spread out over the top. The ancient symbol meant life or living. A healer, able to repair the sick or injured with his energy. Now, the naked skin over Aidyn's left breast bore the mark chosen by the gods. The eye of Ra, the symbol of protection and power, sat atop a pyramid encased by a blazing sun. This could only mean...

Marcus.

His thoughts interrupted by the almost unrecognizable voice. *Father?*

Come to me, son.

Aidyn touched his shoulder. "I am fine, let us go help your father."

Together they flashed to the location his father communicated. When Marcus arrived, his father was on his knees holding the bloody, headless body of his wife, Marcus's mother. His sword lay beside him covered in blood. Marcus knew what had happened. His mother's belly was heavy with child. Drayos's demon spawn had been growing inside her, and like the other women, her soul had darkened. There was no cure. Marcus had tried to heal Eliza, but it had proved fruitless. Like him, his father had taken the head of the woman he loved.

"Father." Marcus knelt next to the frail man and placed an arm around his shoulder, pulling him in tight. "I am so very sorry." Tears welled in his eyes, he refused them escape. He would remain strong for the man beside him.

His father looked at him with red-rimmed eyes. "You will do the honorable thing."

Marcus closed his eyes, again. He would have to mourn later. "Yes," he whispered. How much more destruction could he take before he crumbled? Somewhere, he would find the strength needed to end his father's misery and begin his own.

"Take care of your sister." It was the last command his father would ever give him.

"I will. I love you." He kissed the man on the cheek then stood, his sword flashed through the smoke-filled sky and sliced through his father's neck. Marcus dropped to his knees, the heartache so severe he nearly passed out. His lungs contracted as he screamed to the heavens. Another failure, so many broken hearts he was unable to heal. Why couldn't he heal the broken hearts?

Strong arms circled him from behind and held him tight. "I have you, my friend," Aidyn whispered.

CHAPTER ONE

CURRENT TIME

"When do you suppose the bastard will show up?" Marcus asked, tired of waiting. He and Baal had staked out the stucco house for weeks, waiting for the ring leaders to show. They'd even rented a house across the street and worked in shifts. He'd just sent Garin and Lucan home for the night when Baal arrived.

The demon beside him stared out the curtained window before turning to answer. "My sources think it will be soon."

"I sure the hell hope so. I'm ready to burn that fucking hole to the ground." He wasn't sure how much more he could take. While they waited for the man in charge to show his face, the girls were paraded up and down the sidewalk like cheap streetwalkers. His jaw clenched so hard he thought his fangs would snap. Marcus wanted to move the women to safety, but they were forced to wait. If they showed their hand now, they might never catch the slave traders who were busy kidnapping Kothar demons to use in the prostitution market.

Baal's back went rigid. "That's a human woman."

Marcus's frame shadowed the window in two steps. "Damn it." Sure enough, there was a petite blonde, wearing a skin-tight red dress and heels to match being escorted down the sidewalk. Her shoulders slumped, and her head hung low. She looked to be either American or European. Her looks stood out considering they were in the middle of bum-fuck Egypt, literally. He had no idea humans were being taken and sold into slavery as well. "I take back my previous comment. Before I burn the house down, I will gut every one of the motherfuckers responsible. I may even heal them then gut them again for fun."

Baal slapped him on the back. "I will enjoy helping you."

Marcus didn't doubt it. Baal was a Kothar demon, and his younger sister Lileta had gone missing years ago. Hell, she might even be in the very house they staked out. He felt a twinge of pain in the center of his forehead. *What the hell?* He reached up and rubbed his temples.

Baal gave him a look of concern. "What's wrong? I didn't think vampires got headaches."

"We don't."

Marcus, I need you…now! Shit, his prince's voice slammed into his brain.

"I have to go. Aidyn is calling me. Something's wrong," Marcus said.

"Do you need my assistance?"

"No, stay here and watch that house. I'll send reinforcements as soon as I can." Before Baal could respond, Marcus flashed from the house to a remote location in the desert. He hadn't dared open a portal to Vandeldor back at the house. The demons in the area would sense it and run.

When he arrived in the forests of Vandeldor, storm clouds boiled in the sky. "Aidyn?" Debris flew at his face, causing him to squint. Movement caught his attention, and he ran toward it. When he drew closer, he realized Aidyn sat on the ground, cradling his mother, the queen, in his lap.

"What the hell happened?"

"She was attacked. You need to heal her," Aidyn replied.

"Attacked by whom?" Her neck was nearly sliced clean through, and blood pooled under her head. *Your majesty, who did this to you?*

Odage.

Marcus placed his palms on her neck, and energy flowed through his fingertips. Within seconds, her wound closed. He moved his hands down to her abdomen, searching for internal injuries. *Oh gods! How could this happen?*

He bowed his head. "I am sorry, my lady." He stood and looked at Aidyn. "There is nothing else I can do. Her life force has been taken. She will die." It was the only thing besides beheading that would kill an immortal. He touched the prince's shoulder. "Make your goodbyes quick."

Daria's hand trembled when she reached up to touch Aidyn's cheek. "Aidyn," she whispered. "It is time for you to take the crown and become king." Tears rolled down her cheeks. "I sense darkness descending upon the world. Evil not seen for many centuries will close in around you. Stay true to your course, my son."

Her gaze moved to Marcus. "Marcus, move closer to me." Her voice hardly a whisper.

He knelt next to her and gently grasped her hand. "Yes, Your Majesty?"

"You are like a brother to Aidyn. Promise you will stand by him." The once vibrant woman, who held the guardians together through a war with Drayos, now looked weak and fragile. Visions of his own father shifted through his memories. Moisture caught in the corner of his eye as he bent to kiss her hand. "I swear it on my life."

Daria turned back to Aidyn. "I love you, son. May the gods have mercy on you." She grew silent and her eyes slid shut.

The queen was dead.

Aidyn kissed the top of her head. "I love you, Mother." Marcus reached out and gripped Aidyn's shoulders as the new king wept over his mother's body.

"I'm so sorry. I have you, my friend."

"Why would Odage do this?"

Marcus sensed anger building up in the king. It wouldn't be long before Aidyn's fury unleashed itself. "I wish I had the answers, but I will find out. I promise you." He didn't understand either. Odage was an ally. This was out of character for the shape shifter or any of the Draki.

Lightning streaked through the sky and struck the ground. One of the most powerful guardians had just had his heart ripped out, and Marcus was standing in the middle of a shit storm.

"Aidyn, pull yourself together, or you will destroy us both." He prayed he didn't anger Aidyn further. The king's control over the elements would create a danger to everyone in their world. Hell, if he let Aidyn's temper continue to grow, it might reach the human realm as well. Lightning struck so close electricity sizzled across his skin. Smoke swirled from the crater left behind him. *Shit!* He pursed his lips and squeezed the prince tighter against his chest.

"Aidyn, I know how much you're hurting, but you must regain control."

"Marcus, help me. Talk me down from my rage."

"You can't bring her back, but you can avenge her death."

"Yes, I will kill Odage. How do we torture a Draki?" Another flash of lightning snapped over their heads.

"I don't know, perhaps we slit his belly open? In the meantime, think of how guilty you'll feel should your anger accidentally hurt the ones we protect." Marcus closed his eyes and let his energy merge with Aidyn's. While he couldn't heal a broken heart, he was able to help the king focus and surround him with a calming aura.

Some of the tension left Aidyn's body. "You're right. I will fight the urge I have to kill everything in sight. You're a good and loyal friend."

Marcus released Aidyn and the king stood, lifting the queen's body in his arms. "We need to take my mother home. I could use your help with the preparations."

"I would be honored to assist you."

After helping Aidyn prepare the queen's soul for departure the two men now stood on the beach watching her body burn. This had been Daria's favorite place. The beauty of it never ceased to astound him. Waves swirled in various shades of turquoise, and the beach itself resembled freshly fallen snow, dusted with diamonds. As beautiful as it appeared, it also haunted him. Three hundred years ago, they stood in this exact spot and cremated their loved ones remains. Marcus's mate, mother and father, not to mention, his king, as well as thirty warriors along with their mates.

"What are you thinking, my friend?" Aidyn asked.

"I can't help but recall the last time we did this."

"Yes, we have both suffered many losses in our lives. Today, we suffer another." He turned to face Marcus. "Make sure you tell your sister how much she means to you."

He dropped his gaze to the sand. "I probably don't do so enough."

"She is all you have left of your family. Cherish her, being alone holds no merit."

He touched Aidyn's shoulder. "You are never alone, Aidyn. Remember that."

Aidyn nodded. "Tomorrow, the gods will come."

The next day, Aidyn would be crowned king. No doubt Zarek would show up for the coronation, as was his duty. Marcus looked over at his friend. "Are you ready for this?"

Aidyn stared into the distance." I am left with no choice. My mother was a remarkable woman. I can only hope to lead our people as well as she did."

"You certainly have your work cut out for you, but I don't doubt you'll do well."

CASSIE SWUNG her feet over the edge of the bed and sucked in slow, deep breaths. Sweat trickled between her breasts, tickling as it formed intricate patterns on her skin. These dreams were driving her batty.

She dropped her face in her hands. "What's wrong with me?"

It always started the same, with her lying in bed naked, sleeping. A man slipped in beside her and caressed her arm. He started at the shoulder and ended at her fingertips. His lips brushed a light kiss on hers, then another until he suckled her lower lip. His tongue flicked out and demanded entrance, and she submitted, parted her lips, allowing their tongues to caress each other. The kiss deepened, became desperate until he pulled away and left her gasping for air.

He traced his tongue down her neck and stopped at her shoulder, giving a playful nip before he proceeded to her left breast. Warm lips wrapped around her pink bud, pulled until it hardened and she arched her back.

"Don't stop," she whimpered. He never listened. Instead, his tongue glided down her belly until he reached her pelvic bone.

Silver eyes flashed at her as he smiled. "Cassie, my love, I will worship your body until you beg me to stop."

Stop? No, she'd never ask him to stop. At a pace that was sheer torture, he started to nibble down her thigh while reaching to insert a finger deep into her sex. Her body shuddered with pleasure as her orgasm built. His tongue flicked out around her soft folds and lapped at her wetness. Her head thrashed side to side, while her body bucked wildly. It had been a long time since a man touched her, and no man had touched her like he did. Her body burned, and when she could take no more he inserted another finger and began sliding them in and out. His hand found her nipple and pinched the pink bud between his thumb and forefinger. She crashed over the edge, falling into an eternal flame of pleasure. Her screams filled the room. When her climax subsided, another took hold, sending her soaring. Tears rolled down her cheeks from the intensity. He was true to his word. She begged him to stop, not sure she could take anymore.

When he pulled away he smiled, white fangs flashed in the moonlight. "You are mine forever." Then he sunk his fangs deep into her neck, taking heavy pulls of blood that sent her body crashing into another wave of ecstasy.

She lifted her head, closed her eyes. "Men that handsome don't exist." Her active imagination still saw him. He was lean and muscular, every inch of him toned. His gray eyes were flecked with silver that flashed when aroused. Her fingers itched to slide through his dark brown waves. He was perfection, built only for her.

She laughed. "How fucked up and lonely I must be. I need to stop reading all those paranormal romance novels. They're showing up in my dreams."

CHAPTER TWO

MARCUS STRAIGHTENED, hands clasped behind his back and scanned the room. The throne was located in the west wing of Aidyn's home in Vandeldor. The windows on both sides were covered in heavy black damask in a show of mourning. The single gold throne glistened in the sunlight that somehow managed to sneak in, while twin onyx statues of Horus stood guard on either side.

Taking his position at the head, Marcus's men fell in, forming a line on both sides of the room. Attire for this function was a traditional black linen shendyt, an ancient Egyptian kilt that wrapped around the waist. A medallion crafted from gold depicting the sun fastened to the front. Feathers of emerald green, trimmed in gold, formed a collar around his neck, and each bicep bore a gold band. He longed for jeans and a T-shirt and right now, he could only think of his privates and how the boys were not happy at being exposed to a draft.

The doors swung open, and the king strode through, bearing the same manner of dress as them except his eyes were lined in kohl and the bands on his biceps were studded in emeralds. Aidyn made his way down the long, red carpet until he stopped in front of the throne.

He hesitated...waiting. Power crackled in the air and Marcus watched as one by one several of the gods and goddesses appeared in order of importance.

Dusaro, god of recollection, was first since he ranked at the bottom of those in attendance. Then Quadira, the goddess of fire, Ranis, god of darkness, Ediva, goddess of lightning and Argathos, god of vision. The last to appear was Zarek, the supreme god. Everyone, including the other gods and goddesses, dropped to one knee. Marcus liked to think he had forgiven his god, but upon seeing Zarek, realized he still wanted his god's blood.

Zarek's voice echoed across the room. "It is my duty to provide the guardians with a new leader. Aidyn Santiago is the last remaining member of his family." Zarek placed both hands on Aidyn's head, surrounding him in a bright, white light. Marcus knew the god transferred power to Aidyn from both of his parents. At their coronation, it was customary for the king or queen to receive their parents' power. He could only guess how lethal Aidyn would become after this.

"The deed is done. You will follow your new king in the quest to safeguard the human realm from evil. You will help him keep the peace among the other immortals. Should you waver in your loyalty to him..." Zarek cast a lethal glare around the room. "Then you will accept the punishment of death." His baritone voice lowered another octave with this final pronouncement.

Zarek looked down at Aidyn. "Rise, my son." Aidyn did as commanded then held out his wrist to the god. It was Marcus's cue to step in beside the king. Zarek extended his fangs and sank them into Aidyn's wrist. He would drain the king to the brink of death. It would be Aidyn's sacrifice to the gods. As the king's second-in-command, Marcus would be first to give of his blood to Aidyn. The rest of the guardians lined up behind him by rank. Each would give his blood until the king regained his strength. Every warrior would be tied to their leader.

With the coronation now over, and Aidyn at full strength, Marcus milled around the room. There were several guardians there he hadn't seen in person in many years. Communications lately were done via video conference so he could remain on top of the world's events. He stopped to chat with his third commanding officer, Lucan. "What are you hearing among the others?"

"There is concern about the increase in missing female demons. It seems the slave traders have been busy."

He scratched his chin. "Yes. While Baal and I were on a stakeout in Egypt, we saw a human female being escorted by a demon. I wonder if this was an unusual circumstance or if they are kidnapping humans now."

Lucan's eyes shimmered. "I'll ask around. We cannot allow our wards to be treated in such a way."

"No, we can't. Let me know what you find."

As soon as Lucan slipped away, Zarek slid in next to him.

"Do not blame yourself for the queen's death."

"What good is it to be a healer if I'm unable to help those I love?" He gazed across the room at Aidyn. He'd let his friend down once again.

Zarek directed his gaze toward Aidyn. "He does not blame you. He places the blame with us."

"As well he should," he replied through clenched teeth. "Haven't you done enough damage? You could have aided us. Instead, you left us to perish." He realized his anger hadn't abated even after three hundred years. He doubted three hundred more would be enough.

Zarek placed his hand on Marcus's arm. Sharp prickles penetrated deep into his bones, and the scent of spiced honey filled his senses. The sensation confused him, but he was jerked from his thoughts when the god spoke. "Someday, you will understand." Then he vanished.

"What the hell?"

Aidyn came up behind him. "What's the matter?"

He shook his head. "Nothing."

"You know you can't hold a grudge against him forever."

He crossed his arms over his chest. "Like hell I can't."

Aidyn sighed. "I know you blame the gods for taking everyone we love. I do, as well. However, this will destroy you if you let it." Aidyn slapped him on the back. "Now, let's get out of these fucking skirts before my balls disappear forever."

"Best idea you've had all day, and while you're at it, wash off that damn makeup before someone mistakes you for a female."

Aidyn cast him a dirty glance then flashed away. Marcus closed his eyes and pictured his home deep in the forest, on the other side of Vandeldor. His body sucked into a vortex as he flashed to his bedroom where he stripped, taking exceptional care to fold and return the clothing back to the cedar chest at the foot of the bed. Hopefully, he wouldn't need the traditional attire again for many years. He quickly redressed in a pair of jeans and tee, then made his way to the kitchen, popping open the fridge. An array of containers stared back at him, but he decided not to open any, or risk releasing some kind of toxic waste.

"Guess I'd better throw those out." *Tomorrow*, he thought. He wasn't hungry anyway, so he grabbed a beer then sat at the kitchen table. Since there was time to kill before heading back to the royal estate, he reached for his Glock. Caressed it with a chamois like a treasured female before he began to dismantle it. Laying each piece on a thick, soft towel. He raised his head when he sensed his sister approaching and seconds later, his front door was whipped open. Gwen swept into the room.

"Marcus, I need to speak with you." Stress filled her voice.

He grabbed a dagger off the table and jumped to his feet. "What's wrong?" He scanned the still open door for intruders. The murder of the queen had made him edgy.

"Zarek, he touched you, didn't he?"

He pinched the bridge of his nose. "What the hell, Gwen? You come in here like Hades himself is chasing you, only to inquire if the god touched me?" He rubbed a hand through his hair and tossed the dagger on the table. "What? Did he give me the plague or something?"

She grabbed him by the arms, her body trembled. "Zarek has blessed you."

"You're not making sense. What do you mean blessed me?"

She released him and wrung her hands together, took a step back and sucked in a breath.

"What is it? What are you afraid to tell me?" He leaned closer. *What has the bastard done to me now?*

"I had a vision. She came to me."

He scrubbed a hand across his face. "Who came to you?"

She folded in her bottom lip and chewed. "Your mate, I have seen her."

He knocked over a chair when he stormed across the room, his muscles flexed. *No. No. No!* "You're mistaken. I have no mate, remember? I killed her!" His heart burned at the thought of Eliza. Her laughter still rang in his mind as he recalled their walks on the beach. She always loved the waves lapping over her toes. *Blood bathed his vision as he walked through the castle. Eliza's eyes looking at him when he sliced off her head.* Why was Gwen doing this to him? He didn't want to remember.

"Marcus?"

"Huh?" She jostled him, and he shook free of the visions.

"I never meant to hurt you." Her palm caressed his cheek. "She came to me in a vision right after the ceremony. Zarek has blessed you with another mate."

His jaw ratcheted several inches. The gods were giving him another chance. "Who is she? We have so few females left now. I can't believe I haven't sensed her presence." Could she have been living in the human realm all this time? Possibly. There could have been children born that he was unaware of. It certainly would explain why he hadn't known about her.

She lowered her gaze. "She is human."

"What? What kind of fucked up shit is this? Do the gods despise me so much they would torture me with a human mate?"

"I don't understand, I thought you'd be happy with the news. What's wrong with a human mate?"

"Well, let's start with the fact I have to watch my wife grow old and die. Not to mention how the hell I explain what I am. 'Oh by the way, dear, I'm a vampire. I help a bunch of gods protect humanity from things that go bump in the night.' Did I mention the growing old and dying part?"

"Yes, yes, you did." She kissed his cheek. "I have faith it will work. Perhaps you can turn her into one of us." Her eyes glowed with excitement. "I will help you find a way to turn her, there must be a way."

"Gwen, I'm not sure how to do it, or if it can even be done. Not to mention we have never had human mates before." He snapped his fingers. "Maybe she's the daughter of a Chosen one." The Chosen were humans who had helped the guardians for centuries. The duty passed down from generation to generation. In exchange for their loyalty, the guardians made sure they were well cared for.

"Maybe you're right, which would certainly solve one problem." He hugged his sister. He loved her more than his own life, and she meant well. "Go on back to the meeting, I'll follow shortly."

Gwen nodded and flashed from the room. After she left, he balled his fist and slammed it into the wall. He wanted to kill someone. His mate was dead, damn it!

After several deep breaths and much more swearing, Marcus flashed back to Aidyn's home. His mood was sour, but he did his best to push it deep into the recesses of his mind. *No reason to darken everyone else's mood with my own.* Several warriors were already seated at the large oak table while others flashed or walked in. He strolled over and took a seat next to Garin. "What's up?"

"I think your sister is about to dish out a can of whoop ass." Garin inclined his head to the other side of the room.

Marcus focused his gaze to the powerful warrior who towered over his sister. The man wore a thick braid of golden hair that hung down his back. He recognized Quinlan, an ancient who had lived the last eight hundred years in Ireland.

"'Tis no place fer a woman," Quinlan stated.

A grin formed on his lips. "Shall we wager who wins this fight?"

Garin snorted. "I'm afraid that we'd both be betting for the same side. Undoubtedly, your sister will emerge the victor. I'm afraid the poor bastard doesn't stand a chance."

"Looks like the show's about to start." He pointed to his sister who had produced two daggers. The room grew quiet as many of the men stepped aside to view the growing feud.

Gwen took a fighter's stance, her legs slightly bent and arms in front of her. "You still want to make comments about a female warrior? I am a guardian, it matters not what my sex is."

The male warrior chortled. "It matters a great deal ta me what your sex is. I prefer me women naked and squirming beneath me. Come now, lass, let me show you what you've been missing." He waved his hands up and down over his groin.

She moved so fast she was barely visible. Tossing a dagger with deadly accuracy, it embedded in the vampire's abdomen. Gwen then flashed behind him, grabbed his braid and pulled his head back, shoving the other deep into his kidney. With a forceful shove, he landed on the floor with a grunt.

"I want my daggers back when you're done with them," she spat.

Garin leaned into Marcus. "You teach her that move?"

He grinned. "Yes, and she was an exceptional student."

Clapping came from the doorway and all the attention was moved in the other direction. When everyone spotted Aidyn, they dropped to one knee, their heads bowed in honor of their new king.

"Gwen, are these men bothering you?"

She threw him a smile as she knelt. "Nothing I can't take care of, my lord."

He snorted. "Indeed. I think you have also succeeded in scaring the rest of the men into submission." He walked to the fallen warrior and gave him a shove with his boot. "Quinlan, I suggest you behave, or I'll consider putting Gwen in charge of your missions."

Quinlan coughed. "Yes, my lord. My apologies."

Aidyn glanced around. "Please rise." He waited for everyone to stand before he continued. "I am a warrior, the same as you. I will not hide behind my crown and ask you to fight my battles." With hands clasped behind his back, he glided across the room, making eye contact with every warrior as he walked past them. Marcus sensed Aidyn's heightened power, it rolled off him in waves, crashing across the room. There was no doubt their king had gained an extra boost.

"The last words the queen spoke were of a descending darkness. I've heard from many of you that you've seen an increase in demon activity. Mainly the slave rings." He stopped mid-stride, turned to face the warriors. "I've also heard that humans are now being spotted among the slave trades. I don't need to remind you why we are here. Our promise to protect humanity is our main focus, and you will stay your course in this." His features turned somber. "I plan to avenge my mother's death. I will hunt and kill Odage and likely start a war with the Draki. I do not ask for your help, but if any of you wish to volunteer in the search for Odage then please step forward."

The entire room advanced in one synchronized step. Over thirty imposing vampires, including a few females encircled the king. Marcus never doubted everyone would want to be in on the hunt. They all respected Aidyn. Many had known him since he was a babe. At the age of five hundred years, he was the youngest male here, certainly the youngest to lead them. However, on this day, he was also the most lethal among them.

CHAPTER THREE

ODAGE WORKED his way along Bourbon Street, the putrid stench of evil heavy in his nostrils. The shifter held a fondness for New Orleans, a city that crawled with immortals and was the perfect place to find out where the next slave auction would be held. Meanwhile, he had other things on his to-do list as he sauntered into a local nightclub called Roxie's. The place was an upper class joint where humans and immortals liked to hang out. Of course, the humans had no idea who, or what for that matter, sat across the table from them. All immortals had the ability to take on human form and many actually preferred it. He stopped to survey his surroundings, searching for the perfect woman for his little project.

At the bar, he spied his prey. A petite female with long, golden hair. Her black tank top clung to her breasts, making her nipples pebble against the fabric. *Yes, I will enjoy torturing her.* Odage approached her, flashing a white smile. "Is this seat taken?"

"Um no, it's yours if you want it," the woman replied, smiling back.

"Can I buy you a drink?" he asked as he sat down.

"Perfect timing." She lifted her nearly empty glass and downed its contents.

He waved over the bartender. "Give the lovely lady here another glass of wine, and I will have a whiskey on the rocks." He turned back to the female beside him. "My name is Brad," he lied. "And you are?"

"Veronica."

The bartender came back and set their drinks on the bar. Veronica picked up her glass and held it up high. "To a fun-filled night."

"Yes. To a fun-filled night," he replied, touching his glass to hers. He downed his whiskey in one swig and slammed the glass on the bar. Alcohol didn't affect him as it did humans, but it sure as hell tasted good. The woman beside him was already tipsy. A few more and he would have no problems slipping her out of the bar.

She raised her brow. "Thirsty?"

"It has been a long, difficult day."

"I'm sorry to hear that," she cooed, rubbing his arm. "Maybe we should have another drink." She downed her glass of wine. "I know, how about a shot?" She tapped her finger on her chin. "Hmm. I think sex on the beach will do nicely."

It was now Odage's turn to raise a brow. "Sex on the beach? How about sex in a cave instead?" The thought of sand between his toes revolted him.

She twisted a strand of her hair through her fingers. "Well, I've never heard of that, what's in it?"

He laughed. "I was referring to the real thing, not a cocktail."

"Ooh, sounds kinky. I think I'd like to give it a try, but can we have the cocktail first?" She stuck out her pink lip and gave a little pout.

He flagged over the bartender and placed his order for four shots. One for him and three for her. He figured that should be about enough to push her over the edge. When the drinks arrived, he lifted his glass. "Bottoms up."

After she finished all three shots, she licked her lips. "Brad, you are one handsome man. I have never seen eyes as blue as yours." She gave a hiccup and a giggle.

"Why, Veronica, if I didn't know better, I would say you were trying to pick me up." Her scent confirmed her arousal.

She let out another drunken giggle. "Well, I am, silly. Unless, of course, you're not interested."

"Oh I am most interested." He caressed her cheek. "Shall we leave then?"

She stood and took his hand. "Let's get out of here."

Odage steered her through the crowded bar toward the door. When they stepped out into the warm, night air, he placed his arm around her shoulder and walked down Bourbon Street. It was Saturday night, and the crowds were thick. Leaning down, he began nuzzling her neck as he maneuvered her into a back alley. *Oh yes, she is getting hotter.* He was confident her panties were now soaked. The plan was to take her back to Romania, to his sanctum in the Carpathian Mountains. He had spent years building his elaborate home in the caverns. The caves were so far removed from civilization they would never be found. By the time anyone figured out what he had been up to, it would be too late.

He closed his eyes and flashed.

Veronica swayed. "Wow, I must have drunk more than I thought. I'm feeling a bit dizzy."

He gave a shrug of his shoulders. "It happens to humans when they travel this way."

"What? What are you talking about?" She gasped, and her jaw dropped. "Where the hell are we?" She spun around to stare behind her. "Wait, I thought we were just walking down the street." She rubbed her forehead. "I don't feel so well."

"You are a prisoner in my sanctum."

She took a step backward. "I don't understand. What do you mean prisoner?"

He caressed her cheek. "You will produce my first son, *sia itov,* my love."

She slapped his hand away. "Children? No fucking way. Look, I think we should forget this whole thing. I just want to go home."

It appeared the alcohol was losing its effect. He grabbed her by the neck, his fingers wrapped tight. "You have a choice. Either you will stay here and procreate with me, or I will kill you and eat your entrails."

She licked her lips, tears stained her cheeks. She tried to kick at him, but he pinned her against the wall. "Choose!" he growled.

She sobbed uncontrollably. "I...I want to live. Please don't hurt me."

He grabbed her hair and pulled, nearly jerking her off her feet. "Oh but I will enjoy hurting you. It's what I live for." He stormed down the corridor while she kicked and screamed, and his cock grew hard. As they passed a side table, she grabbed an expensive vase and hit him over the head. He stopped momentarily to backhand her across the face, knocking her to the stone floor. "Fucking bitch! Try that again, and I will forget that I intended to let you live." He pushed home his point by partially shifting into his dragon. "You know, dragons love raw meat."

She screamed then fainted. He bent down and picked her limp body off the floor. Tossing her over his shoulder, he continued to his destination. Once inside his bedchamber, he threw her to the bed, then proceeded to tie her wrists to the bedpost, ripped her tank top to shreds then moved down to her jeans. Once she was totally nude, he spread her legs and tied them to the corners of the bed. He stepped back and surveyed his work. Her lily-white skin made a delightful contrast against the black silk sheets. He eyed her pink slit and licked his lips.

"Wake up, my little pet." He placed his palm on her chest, forcing his energy into her. Her eyes flew open. Terror danced in her pupils, causing his cock to throb. He thrived on terror, was addicted to it like a drug addict. He recalled the terror in Queen Daria's eyes while he drained her and he shivered as a surge of power coursed through him.

"Did you know, Veronica, that I killed the strongest vampire in the world?" He removed his jeans, letting his enormous erection spring free. "I took her power and made it my own." He kneeled on the bed between her legs.

"P-please don't hurt me," she begged.

"Yes, my pet." He wrapped his hand around his large erection and stroked. "Beg me. You have no idea what that does to me. You should be honored, for I have chosen you to live in my world." Claws sprung from his fingertips as his cock inched closer to her. Not even the gods could thwart his plans now.

WHEN HE'D FINISHED with Veronica, he dragged her to one of the cells he had constructed on the lower level. The room held all the comforts a woman needed. Two sets of bunk beds and a bathroom. Once his minions were in place, they could care for her and any other females who were brought in.

Once she was placed in her cage, he slammed the door then headed to the wine cellar. His hands rubbed together while searching for the bottle of Merlot. He pulled the cork and poured two glasses, the heady scent tickled his nose. Fangs extended, and he bit into his wrist. He watched as the crimson liquid splattered into the wine and made ripples in the dark liquid. Taking a sip, the taste of oak coated his tongue. Dragon blood was toxic, but in small doses, it kept the victim in a drugged stupor. After three drops, his wound healed.

When he arrived back at the cell, he shoved the glass through the bars. "Drink."

"No." Defiance filled her voice.

He snarled and opened the cell door, letting it slam shut behind him. His large frame towered as he backed her into a corner. After what he had done, she still meant to defy him?

"You will do as I ask or suffer the consequences. Your stay here can be comfortable, or I can make every moment you're awake a hellish nightmare." He lowered his head until they were nose to nose. "Which. Will. It. Be?"

She closed her eyes and tried to flatten herself against the wall. "P-please let me go. I swear I'll never repeat what happened here."

A clawed hand snaked up to her throat and pressed her against the cold stone. "It seems you wish to do things the hard way?" he asked, grinding his erection into her pelvis.

She shivered and cast her eyes down in submission. "No, I'll drink it."

"Good girl," he cooed, releasing her then handed off the glass, watching while she sniffed then took a small sip. A look of surprise danced across her face. "Wine?"

"Yes, now drink it all, and I will leave you."

It appeared she needed no more encouragement. Bringing the glass to her lips, she downed its contents in one gulp and handed it back to him.

He snatched the crystal from her shaky hand then left the room. It was time for him to attend the demon auction.

MARCUS SENSED distress when he noticed Aidyn and Lucan in a conversation on the other side of the room. The king looked tense when Lucan walked away and waved Marcus over.

"I have a special assignment for you."

"Whatever, you name it."

"Lucan has reports of Odage in New Orleans."

He raised a brow. "Interesting."

"Indeed. A human woman departed with him and has not been seen since. Her family has reported her missing."

Even more disturbing. Unfortunately, his gut told him there was more to this than they could begin to imagine. "Do you suppose this has any link to the human slaves we've heard about?"

Aidyn balled his fists. "I wish I had the answers. I have an unpleasant feeling I can't shake. I feel like the devil himself is shad-owing behind me, waiting to strike."

"I know what you mean. I'll tell Garin and Seth to get ready. We can leave in the morning."

"I want you to go see Daniel first. He has all the information you need."

"You're not coming with us?" He fondled the dagger attached to his thigh. His fingers itched to throw it at something. Still edgy from his earlier visit with Gwen.

"No. I'm going to meet with Caleb. I want to see if he can offer any information."

He wondered how Caleb would react. Marcus liked the Draki, had fought alongside him in the Demonic war. "Be careful, he is loyal to Odage. Make sure you have someone with you."

Aidyn gave a wicked grin. "I will have Lucan with me."

He was pleased with the king's choice. Lucan, a commanding officer and warrior of the darkness, had the ability to bend shadows to his will. Scared the hell out of the rest of the warriors, including Marcus.

"I'm relieved to hear he will remain here with you."

"Marcus, you're like an old woman. Don't worry about me. I can take care of myself. What really troubles you anyway?" He motioned for Marcus to sit.

How to answer that? Lots of shit troubled him. Hell, he could write a book on the subject, but now, there was one thing on his mind. "May I speak freely?"

"You and I go back many centuries, and you have always been there for me when I needed you." Aidyn leaned forward and propped his elbows on his thighs. "I am and will forever remain your friend before I am your king. Never feel you have to ask permission to say what needs to be said." He clasped Marcus's shoulder. "I trust you with my life." He reclined back in his chair and waited.

"I understand the burden you carry is difficult. Please know that I'm here for you." Marcus glanced around the room." We are all here for you. There's not a warrior in this room who wouldn't gladly step in front of a blade and take a deathblow for you."

The king's brows rose to his hairline. "I know what's in their hearts, but why do you feel the need to tell me?"

"Because I know you." He leaned back in the chair, arms crossed over his broad chest. "You would shove us out of the way to save our asses and take the damn blade yourself." He gave the king a hard stare. "You can no longer do that, you are the last one left to lead us."

Aidyn set his shoulders. This conversation now a test of wills. "Perhaps I will get lucky and find a mate as you have. A woman to soothe my soul and warm my bed."

He pursed his lips. "Seems you've talked to my sister."

"Nope," Aidyn shook his head. "You forgot I know all." An evil grin curled across his lips.

"You're jacked up on power."

"I feel as if I have been plugged into an electrical socket, I will admit. This new power has me a bit...tense. I hope I don't fry someone by mistake." He lowered his voice to a whisper. "You've been around longer than me. Has this ever happened before? A human mate, I mean?"

He tried to think back as far as he could remember. "Nope. If it has, it was way before my time. As far as I know, there has never been a lack of females, not like we have now."

Aidyn scowled. "Indeed." He stood and slapped Marcus on the back. "Well, my friend, I have work to do. Make sure you stay in touch. And remember, a mate is a blessing, not a burden."

He wasn't inclined to agree with his king. Perhaps for Aidyn, a mate would be a blessing but not for him. He was too fucked up in the head, and his heart had long ago grown cold. There was neither room nor time for anyone else. Besides, why hadn't the gods blessed Aidyn? After all, he needed an heir. Marcus's dream of children died with Eliza.

CHAPTER FOUR

MARCUS FLASHED BACK HOME to collect a few things before heading to the human realm. He pulled down a duffel bag from the closet shelf and tossed in some jeans and T-shirts. Next was the Glock, a few daggers, and some throwing stars, which were carefully placed on top of the clothes.

"Now where did I put my amulet?" Every warrior carried the amulet of Khonsu, the Egyptian god of the moon. It allowed them to open a gateway from Vandeldor to the human realm but only when daylight burned here at home, which meant darkness on the other side. A sort of safety precaution the gods had built in to keep the guardians from accidentally showing up in broad daylight and creating a scene.

He snapped his fingers. "Dresser." That's where he'd placed it when changing for the coronation. He opened the drawer and pulled out the silver chain attached to a round, yellow sapphire.

"Khonsu, please guide me to the other side." The air in front of him stirred with the glow of thousands of diminutive white lights forming a circle. His thoughts focused, he envisioned the lake home then stepped through the gateway. Within seconds, he entered the living room of the Chosen one.

"Daniel," he bellowed. Walking to the massive stone fireplace he tossed the duffel bag near the hearth. Daniel was one of the select humans that knew about the guardians. The Chosen, as they were known, were picked by the gods centuries ago. The humans' ancestors passed the trade down through the generations. They were the link the warriors needed to the other side, often keeping intel on suspicious activity going on in their world. In exchange for their discreet loyalty, the guardians built them beautiful homes, bought them businesses, put their children through college as well as gave them a substantial paycheck.

Marcus flung open a window, allowing the warm lake breeze to flow through. Summer had always been his favorite time here, and this particular place was favored as well. The large log home was situated on Keuka Lake, in Upstate New York. The guardians had managed to buy up several acres, so this house sat in a cove with its nearest neighbor miles away.

"Daniel." *Where the hell is that boy?* He spun on his heel and headed toward the kitchen.

Daniel came flying around a corner and ran right into him, nearly knocking him off his feet. "Dude, long time, no see. How the hell are you?"

He pressed his lips together. "How many times have I told you not to call me dude?"

Daniel flipped him off. "Tell it to someone who gives a shit."

Marcus raised a brow. "Well, I'm glad to see I'm still number one." He loved Daniel like family, but one day he was going to throttle the boy. He fought the urge to smile. The boy reminded Marcus of himself at a young age. "Have Seth or Garin arrived yet?"

"Nope, haven't seen them. You here about the dragon?" Daniel asked, hopping on a kitchen stool.

"Yes."

"Man, Marcus, I'm sorry to hear about Queen Daria. She was a lovely woman. I suppose that makes Aidyn king now, huh?"

Marcus crossed the expansive kitchen and opened the refrigerator. Usual college fare: pizza and beer. Closing the door, he turned to face Daniel. "You should eat more nutritious food. That stuff will kill you."

Daniel's eyes rolled up into his head. "That's what I got you for, to keep me in excellent health. Besides, you drink blood," he gagged. "How good can that be?"

Marcus rubbed his hands up and down his chest as he flexed his muscles. "Looks like I'm in much better shape than your skinny ass." Taking a couple steps closer, he grabbed Daniel by the shirt and lifted him off the stool. "And, by the way, Aidyn is now our king, so when you see him, you will not call him dude or flip him off. Do I make myself clear?"

Daniel swallowed and looked down at his swinging feet. "Uh okay, noted. You can put me down now." Once back on the ground, he clapped his hands together. "So, I have something that might be of interest you."

"And that is?" Right then Garin and Seth arrived, tossing their bags on the floor as they entered the kitchen. "Ah, just in time. Daniel was about to fill me in on Odage."

Everyone moved to the oak table in front of the picture window that overlooked the lake. Morning sun filtered in and cast shadows across the wood surface. Daniel grabbed a stack of folders and laid one in front of each warrior then took a seat. Everyone flipped open their folder to reveal the picture of a golden-haired beauty.

"Her name is Veronica, and as you've already heard, she was seen with Odage, leaving Roxie's," Daniel stated.

Garin's jaw flexed as he ran a hand across the stubble on his head. "Her family reported her disappearance?"

"Yes, five days ago," Daniel answered.

Marcus lifted the photo and stared directly into the girl's sapphire eyes. "That would have been right after he killed the queen. I don't know what he's up to, but no doubt, she's in serious trouble." The situation didn't sit well with him. Not so much the fact the Draki Overlord had abducted a human. No, there was much more to this. He flipped to the next page, and something caught his eye. "The witness was human?"

Daniel nodded. "It seems none of the other immortals there that night are talking. Afraid to get involved?"

Garin pushed his chair back and moved toward the fridge. "No one in their right mind wants to piss off a dragon." He opened the door. "Pizza! Oh hell yeah." He pulled the box from the fridge. "Beer anyone?"

Everyone shouted a yes so, Garin grabbed four beers and kicked the door closed. Stacking the cans on the box, he walked back to the table. Opening the pizza box, he wrinkled his nose. "What? Where's the pepperoni?" He shot a glance at Daniel. "Dude, I need to teach you how to eat pizza."

Daniel glared across the table at Marcus who had previously reamed him a new ass. "I'd love for you to teach me how to eat pizza and call people dude."

Marcus cleared his throat. "Christ, can we get back to work?"

Seth, who had remained quiet since his arrival, finally spoke up. "I will seek the human and scan his memories to see if he has any more information."

"You sure you want to do that?" Marcus knew ever since the curse of Malsvir, Seth's gift had turned into hell on earth. While all the guardians could procure memories from those they fed on, Seth was unique. He could probe deeper than any other. Unfortunately, the curse now left him unable to purge those memories. Each time he took them, he grew closer to insanity.

"I will perform my job until the day you either cure me or kill me."

I hope to never have to kill you, my friend, he thought. "All right, we leave tonight for New Orleans. We'll meet at the Coffee Grind cafe at five. Until then, make sure you're at your peak." Meaning find a human and feed if necessary.

Garin pushed back his chair and flashed his fangs at Daniel. The boy threw his hands around his neck and pulled his shoulders to his ears. "No way, I'm not donating."

The warriors roared with laughter. "You're not my type anyway. I'm off to find a lusty woman," Garin said.

After Seth and Garin left, Marcus turned to Daniel. "When you have time, I want you to pull up all the unmarried daughters of the Chosen ones from the database." Daniel opened his mouth as if to say something then thought better of it. Instead, he simply walked away, returning several minutes later with the requested information.

Marcus took the thumb drive Daniel gave him and inserted it into his laptop. The mattress sagged beneath his weight as he sat down. *Shit, forgot to close the door.* With a flick of his wrist and a mental push, the door slammed shut. He was alone.

The first girl crossed his screen, a striking redhead who lived in California, but she was eighteen. He didn't think Zarek would join him with one so young. Certainly, he'd scare the poor girl to death. He scrolled to the next, a blonde in Michigan whose ancestors had been with the guardians since medieval times. She was older, twenty-two. He moved on, flipping through several more.

"Fuck, I feel like I'm surfing a damn dating site." He shoved the laptop across the bed, and his head dropped into his hands. *Fuck it! I don't have time to find her.* Odage was the number one priority. Then the slave traders who kept him busy trying to find their location and stop operations. Not to mention the feral demons who broke loose and tortured the humans.

Visions of silky legs wrapped around his waist. Hands fisting glossy locks while his tongue tasted her lips. He shook his head. "No, not going there. She'll just break my heart." Perhaps he needed to follow Garin and find a woman to satisfy his needs. A knock on the door interrupted his thoughts.

"It's open."

Garin pushed the door and entered the room. "Ready to leave?"

Marcus blinked. "Shit, guess I lost track of time. Yeah, I'm ready." He evaluated Garin with a critical eye. "You look...well fed."

"And well fucked too," Garin replied.

He shook his head, happy at least one of them got laid.

"What? I followed your orders. You should try it yourself sometime."

He laughed. "Maybe New Orleans will be my ticket to relaxation." Both men flashed from the room.

Marcus and Garin appeared in the alley behind the Coffee Grind cafe and proceeded through the back door. Sam, the owner, was at the counter and nodded as the men moved toward a table in the corner.

"I'll get these guys," Sam called out to the waitress while pouring two cups of coffee. He walked to the table and set the cups down on a red checkered cloth. "Just the two of ya?"

"No, Seth will meet us here," Marcus said.

Sam nodded and took a seat between the men. "I got the message from Daniel, that y'all were coming. Let me know if ya be needing anything while you're here."

"We're grateful for your service, Sam. How's business?" Sam's ancestors had been helping the vampires since the early eighteen hundreds and was now grooming his twelve-year-old son Nathan to take over the family business, so to speak. When Sam had asked to move to New Orleans, Marcus jumped at the opportunity to assist him. This man meant a great deal to him.

"Good. Ya picked a prime location for the shop."

"I'm happy to hear that. How are Dottie and Nathan?"

Sam grinned. "The wife has gone to visit her sister for a spell, and Nathan...well, he's becoming quite the computer whiz."

"I heard rumors about that. I'm anxious to learn what he's doing." Marcus touched Sam on the shoulder, sending energy through him for a quick scan. "How's your health?" Sam had been diagnosed with terminal cancer four years ago. Marcus killed the cancer and repaired the damage the vile disease had wrought. Many of the Chosen often ribbed him how they had the best medical plan any employer could offer. Marcus didn't mind as his top priority was to make sure they remained healthy. Not even a sniffle dared show up in his presence. But when their bodies began to wear from old age, he helped ease them into the next world without fear or pain. It was never easy losing friends, and he had lost plenty in his lifetime.

A tear glistened in Sam's eye. "Never better. My family and I owe ya a debt we can never repay." He chuckled. "Shit, the doctors are still dumbfounded, claiming a miracle. They're right, ya know, it being the work of God. You are God's true angels."

Garin leaned back in his chair and laughed. "There are those who would question Marcus being anything but the devil himself."

Marcus flashed a smile. "True. But I'm glad you're well. You will let me know if you need anything."

Sam nodded and stood. "Well, best be getting back. I'll bring over a pot and another cup for ya."

The men waited until Sam came back with coffee and an extra cup before discussing their plans.

"I'll go to the club where Veronica was last seen. You take Seth and find the witness so Seth can swipe his memories," Marcus said.

"You're in charge, but should we ask him to do this? I mean with the curse?" Garin asked.

Marcus ran his fingers through his hair. "I know he runs a risk every time he feeds, but he insisted on coming."

"Damn it, we're going to have to kill him one of these days, unless we find a cure for this curse."

"I know." Marcus sighed. "I'll do it. I'd never ask any of you to bear the burden." He fisted his hands, hating the fact he might have to kill one of his brethren.

Garin's brows creased. "I sense demons."

"Yeah, and not the friendly kind either. Fuck, you go look for the demons. I'll have Seth search for the witness." As if he didn't have enough on his plate. Now he had to worry about the demons and their illegal activities. "I'll see if I can contact Baal, maybe he's close."

"I'll smoke 'em out if I have to," Garin stated.

"No doubt, but try not to burn down the neighborhood." He understood how much Garin enjoyed fire. Hell, the vampire shot sparks from his fucking fingertips. "I'll wait here for Seth and give him his orders."

IT'D BEEN ages since Cassie and her sister had gone out for a night on the town. With her nursing career and Jill's messy divorce, life always seemed to get in the way. Tonight, they were sitting at a bar called Roxie's.

"Jill, I still can't believe you let that bastard take the Lexus." Cassie despised her ex brother-in-law. Jill had caught him sleeping with her best friend, and in her bed no less. To Cassie, that was grounds for a slow and painful castration.

Jill took a sip of beer. "Well, I hated that damn car anyway. Besides, I got the house and half his money. He can keep that bitch and her plastic boobs."

Cassie raised her glass. "Here's to her poking a fucking hole in them." They clinked their glasses in a fit of laughter.

"Seriously, what about you, Cass? When was the last time you were on a date?"

She lifted her shoulders. "I forget it's been so long." A sigh escaped. "It's hard to meet a nice guy." Seemed the only nice guy she could meet kept showing up in her dreams.

"What about all those doctors you work with?"

"Meh, they are all so fake. Kinda like Kelly's boobs." Another fit of laughter overtook the girls.

"Shit, I gotta pee." Jill stood. "Be right back."

"I'll be here." Cassie played with the straw in her drink and pondered her love life. *I wonder if I still remember how to have sex.*

Hopefully, it's like riding a bike. Bumps suddenly formed on her spine and her breathing increased. Had she not known better, she would swear she was having a panic attack. A sudden urge to look toward the door overcame her. She sucked in a breath. *Oh my God!*

The lighting wasn't the best, but the man who stood at the door looked like... No. Not possible. Certainly, her mind was playing tricks. Dark hair fell to his shoulders in disheveled waves, giving the appearance he just crawled out of bed. The tee he wore clung to a broad chest and biceps that would make most men cry with envy. When she managed to pull her gaze from his chest and move upward, she found him staring at her.

A hard swallow of the lump that formed in her throat was useless and when she realized he was heading her way, panic struck. She frantically averted her gaze, fearful to look at him again. Maybe he would simply vanish like he did nightly after he did sinful things to her body in her dreams.

"Hello." A masculine voice full of sin and sex prickled her skin.

She lifted her gaze, first to study the scruff on his jaw. The tips of her fingers ached to brush across it. Next, she focused on his mouth. Moist, fleshy lips that begged to be nibbled. Recollection of the wicked things his tongue did to her caused a shiver. When she finally made it to his eyes, she witnessed springtime storms. Dark gray with flecks of silver, that held a hint of danger. Swallowing, she wanted to pinch herself to awaken from this dream. Then again, she wasn't sure she wanted to wake up. There was no way in hell the man who brought her so much pleasure in her sleep stood here in front of her. She pulled on her mental rubber band. *Snap! Come on, girl. Reality check!* No doubt he had women lined up for the next decade. The man was built like a Greek god and she a mere peasant. What she wouldn't give to know his caress.

Oh but I already do.

Jolted from her thoughts, she realized he had spoken. *God, what a complete idiot I am.* "I'm sorry, what did you say?" *I was busy reminiscing about our nights together.*

He stared at her, his eyes shifting to a smoky gray. "I asked your name."

"Oh...Uh, it's Cassandra, but everyone calls me Cassie."

He tipped his head. "Nice to meet you, Cassie, my name is Marcus. May I buy you a drink?"

Holy hell, what do I say? "Thanks, but I'll have to pass." She realized Jill had stepped in beside her. *Thank goodness.* She jumped from her stool so fast it spun on two legs. "My sister and I need to be going. We have another engagement to attend." She gave Jill a pleading look. "It was nice meeting you, Marcus. Maybe we'll run into each other again." She turned and sped toward the door, not even giving him a chance to respond. Once outside, she dragged in a ragged breath before Jill smacked her on the arm. "What the hell is wrong with you? It was obvious that guy was interested."

"I know, but I don't want to get tangled up with someone like him."

Jill rolled her eyes. "Like what? Drop-dead gorgeous? My god, Cass, I have half a mind to throw myself at him."

Oh no, you don't. He's mine! She shook her head. "You know a guy that good-looking has no shortage of women."

"For crying out loud. You need to get laid, you know that?" Jill waggled her brows. "I bet he's one helluva fuck."

Cassie groaned. Her sister had no idea, but she wanted a man to love her. One who would be devoted to her. One who wouldn't leave her for her best friend. She grabbed her mental rubber band and snapped it again. *Right, one white picket fence coming up.* "I need an aspirin." She stormed down the sidewalk with Jill following behind her.

"Wait." Jill grabbed her arm and swung her back around. "Something more is going on here."

Cassie shook her head. "Nothing's going on."

Jill's brows drew together. "I can tell you're lying. Spill."

She let out a deep sigh and got ready to board the crazy train.

"I'm insane, but that man has been showing up in my dreams now for several weeks." She looked at the ground. "Erotic dreams."

"Where did you meet him?"

She lifted her gaze and looked back at her sister. "I've never seen him before in my life."

Jill's mouth shaped into a silent 'Oh'. "Maybe you saw him somewhere and don't remember."

Again, she shook her head. "How could any woman forget that?"

"You do have a point." Jill wrapped an arm around Cassie's shoulder, and they continued to walk down the sidewalk. A wicked grin curled on her lips. "Is he good in bed?"

She gave her sister a sideways glance. "You've no idea."

CHAPTER FIVE

MARCUS ENTERED Roxie's intending to do a little investigative work on Veronica. When he stepped inside, his eyes focused on the surroundings. The scent of demons wafted from the crowd, but nothing to worry about. In fact, the owner, Roxie, was a Kothar demon and she'd been running this establishment for the last ten years.

"Marcus, darling!" He recognized the feminine voice before the beautiful demon appeared by his side.

"Roxie, love." He pulled her into an embrace. Damn, she was still beautiful as ever and with a body men would kill to touch. In fact, many had. Roxie always held a fondness for Marcus, but he kept it strictly platonic.

"What brings you here, sweetheart?" She arched a blonde brow, her sapphire eyes glistened with danger. "You're not here to cause me trouble, are you?"

"No, love. I'm here to investigate the missing human."

"Oh yes, such a shame." She patted Marcus on the arm. "I hear Odage was seen with her, is this true?"

"That's what I hear. You know anything else?"

She shook her head. "No, afraid I'm not much help. I understand Aidyn is king now. My sympathies to you on the loss of your queen. Let me know if I can ease your pain." She winked.

He leaned down and kissed her cheek. "Thanks, darling, but you know we're only friends."

She pushed out her red lips. "You can't blame me for trying."

He smiled then moved into the crowd, intent on finding someone who had seen Veronica when his fangs lowered into his mouth. Spiced honey assaulted his senses. No, he thought. This couldn't be happening, not now. He prepared to turn and flee when he met her gaze.

His mate was here.

He rolled his fingers into tight fists as his cock began to press against his zipper. Taking several deep breaths, he tried to center himself. There was still a job to do, but he moved toward her. After taking a seat, he knew at once it was her. Her aura matched his. Sweat beaded on his brow, and his jeans became uncomfortable. Desire burned him and he needed to bind their souls. The battle with instinct that had him wanting to pull her from this place and take her to his bed was nearly unbearable. She would never understand his kind or his desires. To her, he would be nothing more than a monster.

The woman was breathtaking and he didn't doubt their bodies would be a perfect fit. The smoldering desire in her emerald-green eyes spoke of her own attraction to him. Yet, he sensed she thought herself unworthy. This upset him. He tried to speak to her and managed to get her name before she made her escape. He knew her scent and would be able to follow her to the ends of the earth. What the hell was Zarek thinking? A human with no idea his kind walked beside them. She would break his heart.

He stood to leave when a stunning blonde sat beside him, giving a wink. Her ample breasts barely encased in her black dress.

"Hey handsome, you here alone?" the female cooed.

He eyed her cleavage while his cock deflated. She was a tempting morsel, and he hadn't been laid in weeks. His mood turned sour.

Normally, he would have fed on her then fucked the hell out of her. But not tonight, he had no desire left. Instead, he dropped a twenty-dollar bill on the bar. "Sorry, honey, I have plans, but buy yourself a drink on me." He headed for the door, his mind a total mess. *Fuck you very much, Zarek.* His mate had ruined him, already.

When he stepped outside, he was ready to throttle someone. His thoughts kept going back to Cassie and wondered how she would feel beneath him. Would her flesh taste like spiced honey? He growled and shook the thoughts from his head then sauntered up to a nice-looking redhead who had given him the eye earlier. "Come walk with me." His voice smooth as velvet, he placed an arm around her shoulder. The woman smiled and snuggled in close to him not caring that he maneuvered her into the darkness, away from prying eyes. He covered her body with his in an embrace, giving the impression they were lovers. "You have nothing to fear. I intend you no harm," he purred in her ear. His voice mesmerized her.

He suckled her neck, bringing the smaller vein to the surface. Guardians never went for the jugular. It was messy, and humans bleed far too fast. Once he had the vein where he wanted, he secreted a numbing fluid from the tips of his fangs. The fluid ensured no pain when he punctured the skin. He bit, sliding fangs deep into her vein and drank. Warmth flowed down his throat, bringing power and strength back to his body. The burning in his belly disappeared, but a fire in his heart began. His mate was supposed to bring him life, not a stranger. Visions of him kissing every inch of Cassie's body clouded his mind. The woman in his arms gave a low moan of pleasure, snapping him back to reality. Her body trembled. He placed a hand over her mouth to stifle her cries as her orgasm took hold. Taking blood gave humans immense pleasure. It was a shame she would never remember it.

When her cries died down, he retracted his fangs then ran his tongue along the puncture wounds, his saliva instantly sealing it. Within seconds, there was no sign of what he'd done. He turned her back toward the crowd and whispered in her ear, "Thank you for your sacrifice. You will remember nothing of what happened." Then he walked away, now only half the man he was when he entered New Orleans.

ODAGE DRESSED IN DARK JEANS, a crisp, white button-down shirt and a black jacket. Booted feet touched the sidewalk, breaking the silence of the quiet street. The neighborhood fit his needs. It sat on the outskirts of New Orleans. The residents spent their evenings in front of the television, absorbed in a reality show, never bothering to consider the realism in their own front yards. A few of the home-less picked through the trash, looking for food and trinkets the self-absorbed humans grew tired of and tossed like yesterday's news.

He scanned and found a tall man rummaging through the garbage in front of a small brick home. He assessed his prey. Six-foot-five, medium build, around forty—he looked undernourished. Perfect.

Approaching the man, he spoke in a hushed tone. "Sir, may I buy you a warm meal and a cup of coffee?"

The man looked up, his blue eyes misted. "God bless you, kind sir. I'd be much obliged. I'd be happy to repay you, but I have no money." The man threw his shoulders back and straightened his spine. "I can work, though."

"I am sure we can arrange something, my good man." Odage wrapped an arm around his victim's shoulder and before the man could react, sank sharp teeth into muscle and bone. His fangs extended to pump poison into his whimpering victim. Partially shift-ing, he encased his prey in a black, leathery wing then waited for the poison to take effect.

The victim's heart pumped violently while a plea for help stuck in the man's throat. As soon as the chaos started, it ended. The body went limp, and Odage let him fall to the ground like a sack of garbage. He closed his eyes and shifted back to human form then scanned the area again for any approaching humans as it would take several minutes for death to come.

Odage observed with a callous grin as the body spasmed in a violent fit. Spittle spewed from the man's mouth, and his eyes rolled into the back of his head. With one last brutal shake, his victim gasped for breath then went silent. Odage glanced at his watch. Still time to attend the slave auction. Pulling a syringe from his pocket, he tapped it, making sure there were no bubbles. The green liquid inside cast an eerie glow before he plunged the needle into the man's heart then waited.

His nerves stretched so thin they might snap as he paced back and forth on the sidewalk. He grew tired of waiting. The transformation was taking longer than expected. The demon who sold him the vile had promised it contained the freshest blood. Had guaranteed it would bring back the dead, creating Odage's very own minion. He smiled, who knew the blood of a Kothar demon held so much power. No wonder they were prized in the slave market. Perhaps he should consider bidding on one himself.

He glanced at his watch again; ten minutes had passed. He was about to give up hope when the man gasped for air. In a blink, Odage came to stand over the body, hovering while the man opened his eyes. Excellent, the minion's eyes had changed from pale blue to black, indicating his soul now resided in the depths of hell.

"Rise," he commanded, taking a step back to survey his handiwork. The minion appeared younger and more solid. His muscle mass four times its former size.

The minion looked at Odage and responded. "How may I serve you, master?"

Odage spun around when he heard a voice behind him.

AFTER LEAVING the redhead a half hour before, Marcus's temper hadn't improved. So occupied with thoughts of Cassie that it slipped his mind why he'd been sent to New Orleans. *Fucking Christ, maybe I should go back to Roxie's.* He scrubbed his face, no point in going back. He might as well wait and see what the others discovered. One thing was certain, he'd better dampen his emotions before he scared the humans. How the hell had a slip of a woman already gotten under his skin?

Once inside the coffee shop, he spotted the other two warriors waiting. It was late, so they had the place to themselves. He pulled out a chair and poured a cup of coffee from the carafe on the table, not caring that he didn't like the stuff. He needed something to wash the unpleasant taste of the redhead from his mouth.

"So, did either of you have any luck tonight?" His voice sounded like gravel.

Seth gave him a leveled look. "Yes. I located the gentlemen who witnessed her leaving the club four nights ago."

"And?" Shit, he hadn't meant to sound so harsh.

"Odage. I saw a clear image of him leaving Roxie's the night the girl disappeared."

Marcus turned to Garin. "What about you?"

"The demons gave me the slip, but I did find out there's going to be a slave auction later tonight. Problem is, I have no idea where."

Marcus slammed his cup on the table, a crack split the side. "Damn it. We've got a dragon killing our queen and abducting human women, who knows why. Can't the fucking demons behave themselves for once?"

Garin shook his head. "What's wrong with this picture?"

Marcus glared at him. "What? Fucking spit it out!"

"Since when did the Draki become our enemy? They've never been known to pull a stunt like this. True, they're a moody bunch but never this," Garin replied.

"Shit, you've got a point." Marcus tapped his fingers on the table. "Okay. Seth, continue working on the missing girl. Find Odage's trail. Garin, find that fucking auction. Stay in touch, I'm going back to see

Aidyn and tell him what we have so far." He shot up, sending his chair skating across the floor.

"And pick that up," he yelled as he exited the door.

On the street, Garin came up beside him. "So, who pissed in your Cheerios?"

Marcus stopped in his tracks. "What the hell are you talking about?"

"Oh come on. You either need to kill something or fuck someone. If your foul mood slams me any harder, it'll knock me on my ass."

He raised a brow. "And here I thought I was doing a marvelous job of covering it up."

Garin snorted. "Pardon me, boss, but you're a fucking bomb waiting to explode. Now, tell Uncle Garin what gives, and I'll take you on in a sparring match when we get home."

It was the best idea he'd heard all day. At six-foot seven, Garin stood four inches taller and outweighed him by about fifty pounds. Like the rest of the warriors, he was a wall of solid muscle. Gods knew Marcus needed an outlet. Someone to take his aggressions out on, and Garin fit the bill. His friend held the gift of fire and had no problem cheating in a fight. Asshole liked to burn his opponent. No problem, maybe the pain would sting him back to his senses.

"You're on but don't be surprised when I rip your arms off."

Garin shrugged. "Go ahead, I'll grow new ones."

"Not before I kick your ass."

"Seriously, what's up with you?"

He debated whether or not to tell, but decided to go ahead. "I have found my mate."

Garin's jaw went slack. "Well that's good news, why so pissed off?"

"One, she's human. Two, I have no time or need for a mate," he forced the words from his lips.

Garin blinked. "Holy fuck, a human? Christ, how many years you gonna have with her, fifty? What are you going to do?"

The thought of losing another mate caused his vision to go red.

He grabbed Garin by the throat and lifted him off the ground. "Rip your fucking arms off!" He was about to take the warrior on when fear wrapped around him. He let loose of his grip on Garin.

"What the hell's wrong?"

"Fear, I feel fear!" He knew it wasn't his own. It came from someone else, but who?

"I'm not picking it up. For some reason, it's locked onto you."

Marcus dropped his jaw when he realized where it came from. "Cassie's in trouble."

Garin raised his brows. "Who?"

"You go back home. I'll catch up," he yelled. He needed to get to Cassie fast. Her fear racked his body. He was stunned, her emotions ran through him. How? They weren't even bonded yet. Where the hell was she? He closed his eyes and inhaled, his soul swam in spiced honey. *Take me to her.*

CASSIE SWALLOWED a scream as the scene unfolded in front of her.

When she'd arrived home from the club, she'd decided to go for a walk. Ever since laying eyes on Marcus, she couldn't get him off her mind. *How the hell does a man from my dreams show up in person? This is so stupid. I need to stop thinking about him. I'll never see him again anyway.* Muscle and sinew flexed in her mind and her nipples hardened at the thought of him touching her.

"God, I feel like such a slut!" she mumbled to herself as she walked faster. However, the thoughts wouldn't stop slamming into her brain. As she rounded the corner, she gasped at the sight of two men struggling with each other. One appeared to be—wait, biting the other guy's neck? Something was also wrapped around the man. It looked somewhat like a wing. Not knowing what to do, her mind in a panic, she hid behind a bush and watched between the leaves as the events unfolded. Fear wrapped its icy fingers around her and squeezed. *Shit*. Her cell phone sat on the nightstand at home. Her heart beat against her chest when the man dropped to the ground.

Oh god, he's dead.

She leaned in closer when she spotted a syringe being pulled out of the other man's pocket. It was filled with a green, glowing liquid and the man stabbed the unconscious person in the heart. *What's he doing? There has to be an explanation for all this. Maybe the guy is ill, and the other man is trying to help.* Here she was a nurse, hiding behind a damn bush.

What about the wing you saw and the person biting his neck? Oh shut the hell up, it was probably the shadows playing a trick on my eyes.

It was possible she'd misread the entire situation and freaked out over nothing. She contemplated offering help, but her body was frozen to its spot. After several minutes, she worked up her courage. Standing, she took a step toward them when the man on the ground stood. Hesitant, she strained to hear the conversation that took place between them, but they were too far away. She cleared her throat. They turned and looked at her. The fierce-looking one with the black hair stepped forward.

What to do now? "Do you need help? I-I'm a nurse." Maybe that would save her, yeah right.

"Shall I take care of her, master?" the other man asked.

Cassie took a step back and tripped, falling on her ass. The dark-haired man towered over her, the syringe still in his hand as he leaned down and inhaled.

"Human. We'll leave her." Then he turned and grabbed the other man by the arm. Both disappeared into thin air, gone like they never existed.

She began to sob. *Oh god, oh god, oh god. I'm losing my mind, a brain tumor, yes, that's it. I did not actually see two men just disappear.*

"Cassie?"

She screamed and turned to face the voice who called her name. "W-who's there?"

The hulking shadow stepped closer into the street light. She scooted backward. "Stay away. I-I have a gun."

"It's okay, don't you remember me?" The hulking shadow knelt in front of her. How could she forget the man who haunted her nights? It was Marcus.

She sobbed so hard her body shook.

"Christ, Cassie, are you hurt?" He reached out and touched her; she melted into him.

"N-no, I'm all right." Strange sensations ran through her body. Sensations that made her want to curl up in his arms. She'd met him earlier, only learned his first name, but she knew every inch of that glorious body.

"Do we need to call the police? Were you mugged? What happened?"

"No, nothing like that." Last thing she wanted was to involve the police. What the hell did she tell them anyway? At the moment, she was pretty positive she'd lost her sanity. After all, she'd seen a man with a wing disappear into thin air. A man who pleasured her nightly in her dreams came to her rescue. Yep, nuts. "Umm, can I ask a favor?"

"Sure, anything."

"I only live a block from here."

He held up his hand. "Say no more, I'd be happy to walk you home." He stood and helped her to her feet. His arm snaked around her shoulders and pulled her close, bringing comfort and strength. She had no idea what she was going to tell him about what she had seen.

CHAPTER SIX

MARCUS PULLED Cassie to his side as they walked home. It was easier with her close to scan for injuries. At least that was the excuse he told himself while his cock came to attention. This was a brutal wake-up call and she was dangerous to his wellbeing. When they reached her front door, she handed him her key. As he slipped it into the lock and gave a push, he sent out a pulse of energy, searching for danger. Once positive of her safety, he held out his hand. "It's fine."

She hesitated on the front step, wringing her hands. "Are you sure?"

"Yes, but I'll check the rest of the house if it will make you feel better."

She took his hand and stepped inside, pushing the door closed behind her. "I would feel better if you checked the other rooms. T-that is, if you don't mind."

He offered a smile. "Not at all, you stay here. I'll be right back. Then we talk."

She nodded, relief softening the lines on her face. He moved to the first room, which by coincidence happened to be her bedroom. His senses told him the house remained empty, but it made her feel better and he got to poke around. It would be a good way to learn more about her. His gaze moved across the queen-sized bed and made a mental note it definitely looked sturdy enough for two. He couldn't stop the image of her naked body sprawled out, welcoming him to lavish her.

Exiting, he stuck his head in the main bathroom before coming back to the living room. "All good," he announced as he moved to the kitchen. Noticing a kettle on the stove, he called out. "Would you like some tea?"

"I'd love some, thanks."

He grabbed the kettle, filled it with water then placed it on the burner. "Where do I find it?"

"Cabinet over the stove."

He opened the cabinet and chose chamomile. Next, he figured the mugs would be in the cupboard by the sink. Good guess. He fumbled with the tea package, his large fingers having a hard time opening the foil wrapper. Tea wasn't his forte; he always left that for his sister. While waiting for the water to boil, he reminded himself this was strictly business. After all, being a guardian meant he had to find out what happened to her, eliminate the threat then leave. Simple. The whistle from the kettle snapped him back to reality. He filled the cup then headed for the living room. "Here you are." Setting the cup on the table in front of her because he didn't think he could handle their fingers brushing across each other.

She forced a smile, her eyes wet with tears and his heart melted. How did she do that, and to a warrior of the gods, no less? He'd seen things no human could ever imagine. Lived eight hundred years, the last three hundred with a heart as cold as ice. He would not allow her to melt him now.

"Thanks for bringing me home."

"You're welcome. Want to tell me what happened?"

Pools of emeralds gazed at him. "No. Yes...maybe." Her eyes diverted to the cup of tea. "It's late, and I'm sure you have someone at home wondering where you are."

He frowned, this woman was a mystery and she still felt unworthy of his attention. Why? "There's no one waiting for me, and I have nowhere I need to be. Please, I'm concerned about you."

She let out a slow breath and then her body tensed as she related the horror of what she'd seen. He listened, wondered how she'd managed to witness something so foreign to her and not go into complete hysterics. He gave her credit, not many humans would remain so calm. She cradled herself. "I suppose you think I'm a crazy woman. Giant wings and people vanishing."

"I don't think you're crazy, Cassie."

Her thick lashes fluttered. "How can you not?"

Gods, those lips looked ready for kissing. He fought the urge to pull her into his arms and touch her softness once again. He wanted to soothe her, learn every inch of her body. Make her scream his name. "New Orleans is full of the unexplained." He waved a hand. "You know, demons, ghosts, vampires."

She laughed. "I believe in spirits. I'm a nurse, so I see death all the time, but I like to think my patients are going to a better place."

The gods gave him a healer? His people could use another healer. He shook the thought from his mind. *Remember why you're here.* Damn, he'd have to probe her mind, access her memories. He rose from his chair and moved in next to her. He sensed her heart rate speed up when he touched her hand and gazed into her emerald eyes. His energy coursed into her body.

"Listen to me, I need to access your memories." Her eyes grew droopy, but she fought his enthrallment. He pushed harder until her lids snapped closed.

He slipped into her mind and looked for the image he required. This cost him a vast amount of power, but it needed to be done. When finished, he would remove the memory of tonight and bring her peace. Finally, the image he wanted came into view and he played it back in his mind. *Holy Christ, it was Odage, and he's created a minion.* Marcus pulled back, deciding to leave the memory intact. He was unsure why he didn't remove it, perhaps he didn't have the heart to change her. Restless, knowing it was Odage she saw, he wondered if she was safe. There would be no taking chances, he'd call Baal and have Baal watch over her until he could come back. Aidyn needed to be apprised of what was going on. He also wanted to talk to his sister. Maybe she had some more information on this mate business. Not that he wanted to know, he was merely curious.

His reached for a lock of her hair, its silky texture caught on his callused finger. His lips pressed against her cheek; humans were so fragile. He still didn't understand why Zarek chose her. What a fool Marcus was to think she could ever love him. No, she'd run once she found out what he was, wouldn't she? Dare he even hope this beautiful woman would stick by him? He sighed and released her mind, moving back to his chair. She wouldn't remember his intrusion. Her eyes fluttered, and she stifled a yawn. He looked at the time and was surprised to see it was three a.m.

"I'd better let you get some sleep. It's late. Will you be okay?"

She smiled. Standing, she walked to him and gave him a hug. "Yes, I'll be fine. Thank you again for everything. You've been so kind to put up with me."

Her scent nearly drove him to his knees with desire. He fought to maintain control, knowing he'd have to force himself away from her or risk revealing what he was. After what she'd been through, it would push her over the edge.

"You're welcome. I enjoyed spending time with you. I'm only sorry the circumstances were not better." He reached into his pocket and pulled out a card. "Here's my cell number. Call me if you need anything. I mean anything at all. If I don't answer right away, please leave a message."

She reached out and took the card. "Dagotto Jets?"

"I own a private, charter service."

"Do you fly them or just own the planes?"

He laughed. "I usually don't pilot the clients, but I do love to fly when I have time. Maybe you'd like to go up sometime?"

Her face lit up. "Really? I'd like that."

He reached for the doorknob then turned back to face her. "I'll be out-of-town for a day or two, but when I return, I'd like to stop in and check on you. Maybe we can go out for dinner?"

Her cheeks went rosy. "That would be nice, yes."

He opened the door and stepped into the darkness. Once out of sight of the house, he pulled out his cell phone. Baal answered on the second ring.

"I need a favor. I have a female I need guarded against Odage. Don't let her out of your sight." He rattled off the address then stabbed the 'end call' button on his phone.

CASSIE CLOSED the door behind Marcus and leaned against it. The coolness seeped into her skin, helping dissipate the heat. Never in her life had a man affected her in such a way. When he'd pulled her close on the walk home, she was at peace. Something that evaded her for many years, ever since John left her on their wedding day.

Her mind raced back to that dreadful moment five years ago. She'd been clueless, mindlessly planning her wedding, never noticing the signs. John had become withdrawn, but she'd blamed it on wedding jitters. On the day that was to be the happiest of her life, she'd woken up to find a note from him. He'd left and gone back to California. Said he'd decided he'd wanted children of his own. She'd been crushed. Her infertility had never been an issue in their relationship. They'd always talked about adopting, so many children needed their love.

She had spiraled into depression. Stayed in bed for days, not eating. Had it not been for Jill, she might have never pulled out of it. She'd sworn off men until now. Marcus did something to her, stirred a passion she'd thought burned out long ago. *He'll break my heart, I can't live through that again.*

"Fool, you're not really living now." Cassie sighed. No, she wasn't. She'd been numb for too long. Perhaps it was time to live again. Exhausted, she headed for her room and fell into bed. Sleep overtook her as soon as her head hit the pillow.

MARCUS FLASHED BACK to New York. Here, he could open a gateway to Vandeldor without being seen. Rule four of the guardian's manual, don't draw attention to yourself. Fuck, if he had to count every time he'd broken a rule, well, he was sure he couldn't count that high.

Once there, he left Daniel with instructions. Contact all the Chosen worldwide and gather any information on missing humans and demons. Somewhere there had to be a connection between Odage and the slave trades. Next, he flashed into Gwen's living room. He'd talk to Aidyn after he saw his sister. "Gwen?"

She poked her head out from the kitchen. "Marcus. I felt a disturbance and figured it was you. Come, I'm making tea."

He strolled into the kitchen, giving his sister a hug and a kiss on the cheek. He took a seat and a grin formed on his face. "Seems you and someone else I know have similar taste," he said nodding to the tea kettle.

"Really? Who would that be?" she asked, placing two cups in front of him, pouring tea into each one.

"Cassie."

"Who is...?" She gasped. "Marcus, you found her?" She took a seat across from him.

"Yep, I found her in New Orleans, and now I have Baal watching her." He rubbed his forehead knowing he should have fed again before he came back home. The memories he'd pulled from Cassie had cost him more energy than he'd thought.

She frowned. "Why do you have Baal watching her? And what's wrong with you?"

He proceeded to fill her in on how he first met Cassie at a local club. He then told her about the fear he'd experienced before he'd found her shaking on a darkened street. He finished up with scanning her memories and what she had seen. "So that is why I have Baal watching over her. I needed to return home, and I'm terrified to leave her without protection. I'm also weaker than I thought."

She sipped her tea and held out her wrist. "Take what you need, brother."

"Thanks, sis." While vampire blood wasn't as potent as human, it would suffice in a pinch. The gods meant for the guardians to consume their sacrifice from the mortals so had made human blood superior. While food nourished them, blood gave them life and durability. Without it, they grew as weak as the humans they protected.

"Marcus, I'm so glad you have found her. The mating bond must be exceptionally strong for you to have felt her emotions so quickly."

He sealed the puncture. "Have you had any other visions?"

"Yes, you must call on Zarek. He will give you the information you seek."

Violence flickered in his expression. "Why the fuck didn't he give me that information when he decided to gift me with a mate?" He had to go into dragon territory to summon the god, and it pissed him off.

"Why are you so angry? You have been blessed."

He cringed. No one understood. "Because I don't want a damn mate!" His voice carried across the room.

Gwen remained calm, her grace ever-present. "Brother, you need to let go of Eliza. She would not want you to live like this. It's been three hundred years, move on."

He gave her a leveled look. She was right, and deep in his heart he knew it. "I need to go, thanks for everything." He stormed out the door and headed toward Aidyn's. Opening his mind, he found the mental link to his king. *Aidyn, I'm coming to see you. I have interesting news about Odage.*

Excellent, I also have some things I need to fill you in on.

I'll walk. I need time to think.

I will be here when you arrive.

He picked his way along the jagged rocks, following the lane higher up the cliff. Aidyn's home sat at the top of an outcrop looking over the Lejir Sea. He stopped for a moment and looked beyond the rocks. Peace encompassed him, and he found his mind wandering to Cassie. Would she appreciate the serenity of this place the way he did? He thought about his pending visit to Zarek, still unsure if he wanted to make Cassie his mate. He'd go. At least some questions might get answered. What would Marcus tell her? *Oh by the way, I'm a vampire. Let me flash you to another realm.* Yep, she'd fucking freak.

When he reached the top, he spotted Aidyn sitting, watching the sunset over the sea. He crossed the patio and took a seat next to his king.

"Seth has already filled me in on the details he uncovered about Odage," Aidyn said.

"Good. Have you spoken with Caleb?"

"Yes, it didn't go well. As a matter of fact, he will be joining us shortly, along with Garin and Seth."

"What happened?" Marcus asked.

Aidyn remained indifferent, sitting in his wicker chair, staring at the water. "He's pissed that I accused his leader of murder. Needless to say, we are treading on extremely thin ice here."

Marcus shifted in his seat. War with the Draki wouldn't be good. The dragons were the most powerful of the faction. "What's your stand on this?"

The king turned his head and pierced him with cold eyes. "I will kill Odage, as soon as I can find him." Changing the mood, he smiled and said, "Now tell me, who is this Cassie?"

Damn, he'd found out. Marcus again relayed the story about meeting her, but, more important, the memories he recovered from her that proved Odage was up to something. A disturbance in the air announced the arrival of Garin and Seth, followed by Caleb.

Aidyn rose from his seat. "Excellent, everyone's here. Let's go to my office."

The five men strolled into the house. Once everyone was in the room and seated at the large conference table, Aidyn spoke, "Caleb, Seth has come back with some information on Odage."

Caleb swung his head around, pinning his brown eyes on Seth. "Do you know where he is?"

"No. But I do know that he took a woman from New Orleans," Seth answered.

Caleb's eyes narrowed, and he leaned in toward Seth. Clearly, he meant to intimidate the vampire. "And you know this how?"

Seth moved closer, letting the dragon know he would not be terrorized. "There was a witness who saw her leave with Odage. I took the man's memories and saw him myself."

Caleb snorted. "So he found a whore to spend the night with. That doesn't make him guilty of kidnapping."

"There's more," Marcus said. "The woman I was with saw a man fitting Odage's description turn a homeless man into a minion."

Caleb threw his head back and laughed. "Odage doesn't have that kind of power. Your female is mistaken."

Aidyn stood, slamming his palms on the table and leaned toward Caleb, a sneer on his face. "Then where is he? You are either hiding him, or you don't have a fucking clue where the murdering bastard is."

Caleb shot up from his chair and moved in so close he was nose to nose with the vampire king. The warriors placed a hand on their weapons but didn't make a move. "I do not have to answer to you, *vampire*."

Aidyn hissed. His fangs elongated, and his muscles rippled with anger. "Your leader must answer to murder charges according to our laws."

Caleb pounded his fists on the table. "Fuck your laws, and fuck you! I will declare war if you do not cease this action against Odage."

Marcus stiffened as did Garin and Seth. Things were going to hell fast, and it looked like it was going to get nasty. All three warriors were ready to pounce at any moment should the threat against their king become real. Marcus linked with Garin and Seth. *Stay focused, men. Don't attack unless I give the order.*

Aidyn clenched his fists. "You are second in command, Caleb. You can only declare war if your ruler is missing. You have no idea where he is or... maybe you do, and you're in this together."

Shit, this might be the gem that breaks the dragon's back. Marcus stood. *My lord, please, step away from Caleb.*

Caleb's eyes glistened with anger. "You now accuse me of murdering your queen? The dragons withdraw their alignment with you, Aidyn. From this point forward, we are enemies." Caleb vanished.

Aidyn murmured under his breath. "So be it."

Marcus released the grip on his dagger and let out a breath. Caleb had once been a trusted friend and a fierce warrior, one who would not be easily taken. He understood defending his leader, hell, he'd do the same for Aidyn no matter what the king was accused of.

"Garin and Seth, go prepare the others for the possibility of war. Marcus, I will speak with you," Aidyn said.

Garin and Seth bowed. "Yes, my lord." Then vanished.

Once they left, Aidyn turned to Marcus, the mental push he received from his king meant he better not fuck up. "Let go of my sister, Marcus, and claim your mate." His voice gentled. "I fear she may need our protection."

CHAPTER SEVEN

HOT WATER ROLLED across his body, he wanted to burn the sting of Aidyn's last words off his skin. "Claim your mate." He reached for the soap and scrubbed, wondering if he could wash away his desires. It wasn't working. He imagined her hands running down his chest. *Soft, wet, naked curves pressing against him.*

"Fuck." He reached for the faucet and forced it to cold.

Once toweled off, he threw on a pair of jeans and a T-shirt, strapped a dagger to the outside of each thigh and tied his hair back. He scooped the amulet off the nightstand as he walked by and placed it around his neck then flashed to the mountains. Entering the Cave of the Gods, he scanned the area. No dragons. Hopefully, they were hunting, and he'd be gone before they got back. No telling how they would react if they discovered him in their territory. He'd like to think Caleb would turn the other cheek, but who knew if the Draki would still consider this cave a neutral zone.

It had been years since he last came here. He'd forgotten how majestic it looked. The walls swirled with iridescent colors and tiny veins of diamonds and rubies shimmered throughout. Steam rose from a pool in the center of the cave, sending droplets of water scattering on the rocks. At one time, the water was used to help birth their children. The mother would sit in the shallows and birth the child into its warmth. He stared at his reflection, there hadn't been any children born since the war. The thought of his mate's belly swollen with his child caused him to smile. Would this be the fresh start the guardians needed? He shook his head—not with the curse looming over them. A cure had to be found.

He moved to a large, flat rock along the edge of the pool and knelt on both knees. Removing the amulet from around his neck, he placed it on the rock in front of him. His fangs extended, and he bit into his wrist, blood splattered on the amulet. His sacrifice complete. Marcus chanted, speaking the traditional draconic language, a language humans had forgotten long ago. For centuries, it was the only language immortals used until English was born.

"Zarek, *ithquent di haurach*, god of fate. *Vi vrak di ithquent lasauic*, a child of god summons thee."

"What do you wish, my son?" a stern voice called from behind.

Marcus spun around on his knees and looked up at the god who towered over him. He never knew what to expect. This time Zarek wore a pair of faded jeans nestled low on his hips. His jet-black hair was pulled into a single braid— were those leaves and a stick poking out of his hair? *Oops.* He feared he might have interrupted the god's playtime. *Too fucking bad.* A god could choose to ignore a summons, except when summoned to this place. They were bound by their own laws to appear.

Zarek glared, his gaze burning a hole in Marcus. "Well?"

Marcus hid a smile. "Father, I have come seeking knowledge. You've blessed me with a mate, but she is human and I don't know what to do."

"Ah yes, Cassandra. She is a beautiful woman and will make a suitable mate," Zarek stated so matter-of-fact.

He bowed his head. "Thank you, Father, for giving me another chance."

"Eliza's death was not your doing. Some things are beyond your control."

Jaw clenched. "Why? Why did you not save her or any of the others?"

Zarek's nostrils flared, and he bared his teeth. "It is not for you to question what I do, Marcus."

"Yes, my lord." He lowered his eyes and awaited his fate. He expected the god to strike him down and wondered if his death would be swift and painless or if Zarek would torture him for days until he begged for mercy.

He would not beg.

"You think you could withstand my punishment and not beg for mercy?"

"Yes, my lord." This time his gaze met the god's swirling silver eyes, and he showed no fear. If he was struck down, then so be it.

Zarek's laugh echoed through the cave. "There is a reason you are the king's second-in-command. You are stubborn to the core, a true warrior of the gods. You live for the fight, Marcus, and you have no fear, well, except for one."

He raised a dark brow, waiting for Zarek to finish.

"You are afraid of one, small, human female."

Ok, so he did have one fear. "I don't fear her, I fear the curse and what it will bring upon her should I succumb." He tilted his head. "Why a human mate?" If the gods wanted to play matchmaker, there were other immortals who would have been more compatible.

Zarek crossed his arms over his chest. "Long ago, humans often mated with immortals. It was not uncommon for the Draki or even the demons to take a human mate."

"What happened?" He sat back on his heels since he was about to get a history lesson.

"Humans began to forsake their gods, wars started over whose god was better, blah, blah." Zarek waved his hand. "Basically, it was a pissing contest. In the end, the dragons and demons went into hiding, and humans forgot they existed. They became myths. It was then I decided to create my warriors, guardians to watch over our foolish children. We suspected that someday, the children of these mixed relations would come back for retribution."

"Retribution for what?"

Zarek rolled his eyes. "When the immortals went into hiding, their human parents sent the children with them. They didn't want to become outcasts in society for breeding with monsters."

That explained a lot. "I assume that is how both species became shifters? Human DNA?"

"Exactly," Zarek replied.

No wonder problems with many of the demon factions were on the rise. They were pissed, abandoned by their ancestors. He would have to remember to have Lucan check the ancestry of some of the missing humans. He'd be willing to bet there was a connection. Maybe these missing mortals were ancestors to the humans who bred with the demons. The children now sought revenge for being outcast.

"What about the curse?"

"Ah yes, the curse. Drayos was sneaky with that attack. You must find the cure and break the curse."

No fucking shit. Drayos placed the curse on every guardian. They had no idea, at the time, what it entailed. Not until it claimed its first victim when one of the warriors started acting crazed and actually killed the human he fed on, Marcus used his healing power to look inside the vampire for any abnormalities. What he found horrified them all, the man's entire soul turned dark. No light left, only evil. Marcus tried everything to heal his friend but to no avail. Instead, Marcus removed his head. When he checked the rest of the males, he found the same shadow lurking inside them, though it varied in size. No one understood what triggered its growth as it was different for every individual. Ticking time bombs. All of them, and the sad truth was, if left unchecked, they would decimate the human race. Perhaps that had been Drayos' plan all along. Revenge on humanity.

"Rise, my son," Zarek commanded.

Marcus obeyed and rose to his feet, but the god still towered over him. Marcus watched Zarek bring his wrist to his mouth and sink his fangs deep then thrust his arm toward Marcus. "Drink and you shall receive the knowledge you desire."

Once again, he obeyed, took several pulls of the warm life force, noting the taste of raw power. Images filled his head so fast he fell to his knees.

Zarek reached down and touched Marcus on the head. "You have what you seek, my son. Your cure lies inside. You hold the key you seek to unlock your curse." Zarek vanished.

"What? Hey, come back!" He scrubbed his face, fucking riddles. He had what he needed to convert a mate, but now he had a headache named Zarek.

Aidyn, I have what I need and am coming back to see you. Maybe the king would be able to answer the riddle.

Excellent, I look forward to finding out what you have learned.

He gathered his amulet from the rocks and flashed straight for Aidyn's office. When he arrived, the king looked up from his paperwork. "Marcus, sit." He motioned toward a large leather chair directly across from his desk. "Tell me, were you successful?"

He nodded and began to relay the images that were burned in his memory. This information was vital to every single guardian because it told of the binding ritual and how a human could become immortal.

"The female must endure that?" Aidyn asked, his back going rigid. "Certainly, they could be placed in stasis to ease the pain. I mean it's a complete change in their anatomy to be able to process blood as we do."

"Perhaps that would work, something to keep in mind. There's more." Hesitation rang in Marcus's voice. This was news even he didn't want to deliver.

"Something tells me this isn't good. What is it?" Aidyn asked, leaning forward.

"Zarek showed me more. You must see for yourself."

Aidyn stood, his palms flat on his desk as he leaned closer to Marcus. "Are you feeling strong, Marcus?"

"Yes." He'd been given an extra boost from Zarek, after all, so he could afford to lose a bit of blood. He began to stand and offer his wrist when Aidyn placed a hand on his shoulder.

"No, remain seated. I don't need your blood."

"What?" His brow creased. Guardians took memories from humans by entering their mind, but with other immortals, they needed their blood to pull memories or visions.

Aidyn placed his fingertips at Marcus's temples then closed his eyes. Energy pulsed through his body in tidal waves.

"Son of a bitch!" Aidyn moved back to his seat. "We must kill Odage now for certain. He intends to release hell's most violent demons into the human realm."

The king leaned back in his seat and laced his fingers together then dropped them below his unshaven chin. "I need to think."

"Do you know the history between the humans and the dragons?" Marcus asked.

"Of course, they once mated. It's how they became shifters."

"How did you know? I was never given that history lesson."

Aidyn arched a brow. "I'm your leader. I know many things."

ODAGE SAT on his throne and caressed the smooth, black marble of the dragon's head. He surveyed his surroundings, pleased with the finishing touches placed on his sanctum. Soon it would be filled with humans carrying his spawn.

The auction had proven fruitful with the purchase of two Kothar slaves, a male and a female. The woman he sent off to care for Veronica, and the male was now stationed with his minion Roman. Everything was coming together as planned, time now to focus on building his army and finding the amulet.

"Odage," the omnipotent voice echoed across the room.

His body stiffened and palms began to sweat. "Yes, my lord?" Somehow, he managed to keep the fear from his voice.

"I have a job for you. The vampire Marcus has been gifted a human mate. You will find her then take her from him."

Odage scanned the empty room. He recognized that the voice came from the pits of hell, but he still wanted reassurance that his master had indeed not manifested in the flesh. "What will you have me do with her, my lord?"

The voice let out a wicked laugh. "Consider her a gift from me. Do with her as you please."

"Thank you, my lord. I shall enjoy this gift." He licked his lips. What sweet victory stealing the healer's mate would bring him. The thought of having her in his bed caused him to grow stiff.

"I only ask for a few drops of her blood, that is all. Now, what progress have you made on the amulet?" the voice demanded.

His master spoke of the amulet of Tobor. Odage knew it well. He'd discovered one half of the amulet while searching in the Carpathian Mountains. The glistening object caught his attention, and being a dragon, he quickly scooped it from its hiding place. Its design intrigued him. An arrow cast in gold with an enormous fire ruby in the center. When he'd wrapped his palm around it, the power had vibrated through his entire body.

"I have a plan, my lord."

"Good, see that you do not fail." Invisible, icy fingers curled around Odage's throat, restricting his airway. "Or else your punishment shall be severe."

He tried to speak. When the biting grip left his neck, he dropped to the floor, gasping for air. It took several minutes for him to regain his composure before he stood again. He needed a plan to find the vampire and take his female.

"Roman!"

Roman quickly entered the throne room, dropping to one knee. "Yes, my liege, how may I serve you?"

He gave a look of impatience then waved his hand for the servant to rise. "We will be leaving shortly. Prepare for a trip to New Orleans. There's a certain female I must pay a visit to."

"Yes, my liege."

CHAPTER EIGHT

THE AROMA of Columbian coffee and chocolate wafted to her nostrils making her wish the coffee pot would hurry up. The doorbell rang and she glanced at her grandmother's pendulum clock on the way to the door, eight thirty a.m. When Cassie looked through the peephole, she freaked. *Marcus. Oh shit, I'm a mess.*

She'd jumped out of bed earlier and thrown on a pair of gray yoga pants and a pink tank top. Her hair was piled on top of her head and her cheeks were flushed. Her erotic dream had gone from weekly to every night since he'd brought her home almost a week ago.

She opened the door and swallowed her fear.

"Marcus, nice to see you. Come in."

"I'm sorry, Cassie. I know it's early, but I just got back into town and wanted to make sure you were all right." He walked through the door.

"That's sweet of you. Yes, I'm fine, much better than the other night." She tried to ignore how her body reacted to his presence, but damn, she wanted to touch that broad chest and make his muscle's dance beneath her fingertips. Her gaze traveled down the black tee that molded around his hardened muscles and to the faded jeans that sat snug on his hips. She stopped at the belt line, not daring to look farther. The way he touched her was still fresh in her memory. How was it, the man who brought her such ecstasy in her dreams was standing in front of her?

"I'm glad to hear that. I brought you some beignets, still warm even." He handed her a white box.

She let out a squeal of pleasure. "Beignets are my favorite! Come have some coffee and share these with me."

"I'll stick with the coffee. I'm not much of a sweets eater."

She turned and shot him a raised brow. "Really? You have no idea what you're missing then."

He laughed. "I'll have to take your word for it."

She placed the box on the table and moved to grab another mug. "Cream?" Then filled the mug with coffee.

"No, thanks, black is fine."

She hid a smile. No, he wouldn't be the "cream" type. If a wager were made, she'd say he was a beer drinker followed by a tequila chaser. She placed the mug in front of him, and he reached for it, their fingers touching. Heat jolted through her and plunged straight to her sex, making it difficult to sit opposite him. While trying to steady her breathing, she placed her hands in her lap so he couldn't see them shaking.

"So how was your trip?" She struggled to steer her mind in another direction to keep from blushing.

He sipped his coffee. "Good, very informative." He took another sip then placed his mug on the table. "Cassie, go to dinner with me. Please."

She stared at him, unable to believe what he'd just asked her. He'd tried to warn her before he left the other night, but she didn't think he'd actually follow through. Hell, she never expected him to show up this morning, but here he sat at her kitchen table as delicious as ever and it left her feeling like a school girl.

"I'd like that."

"Great, six work for you?"

"Yes." *Crap, what am I going to wear?* Her mind was already doing a mental sort through of her closet, trying to decide on the best outfit. Maybe Jill could come over and help her pick something out.

"Great, I'm looking forward to it." He rose from his chair. "I have some things I need to take care of. See you tonight then."

She walked with him to the door, her nerves still rattled. He turned his silver gaze upon her. "Okay, I'll see you later." She leaned toward him, her hands planted on his chest and kissed his cheek. Her lips lingering for a moment before she stepped back. "Thanks again for everything."

After he left, she leaned against the door, her heart racing. She hadn't meant to kiss him, but an invisible magnet pulled her toward him. When her hands touched his chest, ropes of muscles moved beneath her palms. She'd wanted more, her body burning from the inside out.

"Christ, that man will be my undoing." She glanced at the clock, *shit, only nine hours to get ready. I'd better get started.*

MARCUS STOOD on the other side of the door. "What the fuck just happened?" He'd practically begged her to go to dinner with him. Apparently, his determination melted the minute he walked through the door. When her hands touched his chest and those velvety lips on his face... Shit. He had to restrain himself to keep from pulling her close. His mouth watered with anticipating the taste of her and he knew he would consume her. The scent of her arousal added to his own. Never in his existence had he wanted a woman so desperately, not even Eliza.

He took in a breath and released it, trying to find calm. There was no more fight left in him. His inner voice said he would have her, she was his, and he always took what belonged to him. Sensing no one around, he flashed to the Coffee Grind where he slipped in the back door and headed straight for the basement. Sam kept a special room down there where the guardians could meet in private. Aidyn, Garin, Seth, and Sam were already huddled around the oak conference table. Several large monitors covered the wall with a couple of keyboards sitting on a long desk in front of them. At the helm sat Sam's son Nathan. Marcus walked over and touched the boy on the back.

"How's it going?"

Nathan threw him a big smile. "Everything is great, Mr. Dagotto, sir."

Marcus couldn't help let a chuckle slip. "Remind me to introduce you to Daniel sometime. Perhaps you can rub some of your manners off on him."

"I'd like that, sir."

"So tell me, what is all this?" he asked as he waved his hand in front of the large screens.

Nathan's face lit with excitement as he started to chatter endlessly. It seemed he was quite the geek when it came to technology. He'd been helping out by writing a program that would infect any computer that tried to hack into their system. Marcus was impressed, the boy showed a lot of talent for such a young age.

"This is excellent work, Nathan. Something tells me that we're going to be sending you to college at a very young age."

"Thank you, sir."

Lucan entered the room, so now they could get down to business. One by one, the five monitors lit up with faces of guardians stationed in other areas of the world. Marcus took a seat as Aidyn began to speak.

"I have some disturbing news. It seems Odage is plotting the demise of the human race."

Rumblings echoed throughout the conference room. "My lord," Lucan spoke up. "How is he planning this? I mean how could he possibly?"

Aidyn leaned against the table. "We have to assume he has help, but from where, I have no idea. We do know he's been seen making a minion."

More rumblings and cursing followed. A voice called out from one of the monitors, "My lord, if I may be so bold. How did we acquire this information?"

Marcus faced the warrior on the screen. "I was given this information from Zarek." The room grew so quiet you could hear a mouse pissing on cotton. He knew their thoughts mirrored his own. Some serious shit was coming down if a god handed out this kind of information.

"Fuck." Garin tossed the pen he'd been twirling between his fingers.

"There's more." Aidyn looked at Marcus who nodded in approval. "I believe the gods are trying to help us in a rather unorthodox way." Aidyn paused. "They have given Marcus a mate, and she's human."

"Interesting."

Everyone turned to look at Seth who was usually so quiet. He cocked a brow. "Will she become one of us?"

"I've acquired the knowledge. I'm just not sure I'm ready for a mate," he lied. Of course, there was no doubt he would claim her. Her essence was already ingrained into his very soul. She was part of the air he breathed. He only hoped he didn't fail her.

"Are you fucking nuts? I'll take her if you decide you don't want her," a voice from the screen said.

Clenching his fists, he growled and was disappointed the guardian wasn't in the room as he would have enjoyed tearing the bastard's head off.

Aidyn looked back at the wall of monitors. "Report anything unusual. In the meantime, I expect Odage's head on my desk. You all know what needs to be done." He turned away. "Lucan, I have a special assignment for you. Wait for me upstairs while I speak with Marcus."

"As you wish, my lord."

Once Lucan and the others were gone, Aidyn cast his gaze on Marcus. "Well?"

"Against my better judgment, I am taking her on a date tonight."

Aidyn snorted. "You fret like an old woman. Many among us would gladly switch places with you."

His gaze narrowed. "So I've heard."

CASSIE STOOD in front of the full-length mirror and twisted from side to side. She had emptied her closet and found nada, then shopped with Jill. Finally, they settled on a simple black halter dress, liking how the material clung to her shape. She slipped on a pair of strappy, high-heeled, black sandals and gold hoop earrings. *I'm as ready as I will ever be.*

A low rumble caught her attention, and she ran to the window, letting out a gasp. In the driveway sat a Shelby GT 500. Candy-apple red with silver metal flake that shimmered in the sun. She swore her heart skipped a few beats when Marcus exited the car. As she opened the door, an ocean breeze wafted past. God, she loved his scent. His hair was tied back, giving a better view of a strong jaw covered in dark scruff. The blue shirt only made his gray eyes snap like a summer storm. Everything about him spoke of dangerous bad boy. So, why did she want him so bad?

"These are for you." He handed her a bouquet of roses. They were the purest white she had ever seen, with dark red edges, reminding her of crushed velvet.

"I've never seen anything like them. They are beautiful, thank you."

Marcus grasped her hand, placing a kiss on her knuckles. "Not as beautiful as you."

Her cheeks grew hot. "Thank you." She couldn't remember the last time she felt so special. In many ways, he reminded her of an old-world gentleman, yet a dark, dangerous air surrounded him.

Like he hid something. "Let me put these in some water then we can go."

"Take your time, love." He followed her to the kitchen.

"So, nice car you have. What year?" Men loved their cars, and it seemed like a good topic of discussion at the moment.

"You like? Sixty-seven. She is one of many cars I own."

"It's beautiful. How many cars do you own?"

He laughed. "I am into cars like women are into shoes, addicted."

She laughed. His sense of humor put her at ease. Cassie looked forward to getting to know him better. She just hoped he didn't turn out to be a loser. Carrying the vase full of roses from the kitchen, she placed them on the coffee table. The aroma filled the air with sweet perfume. "Where did you find these?"

"I'm afraid that's a secret."

"I understand, some kind of new hybrid?"

He flashed his white teeth. "Something like that."

"Okay, I'm ready if you are."

THE DRIVE to the restaurant proved quiet and uneventful. Marcus had chosen a seafood place on the edge of town, and with traffic being light, it had only taken twenty minutes to get there. He slipped the car into a spot close to the entrance then switched off the engine. Moving to the passenger's side, he opened the door so Cassie could exit.

"Thank you."

"You're welcome." He placed his hand at the small of her back, noting the sensation that sizzled through his fingers. He also couldn't help appreciate how she filled out her dress. The black fabric clung to her breasts, and the cool air caused her nipples to pebble. He licked his lips, aching to taste her and it didn't help that the long column of her neck was exposed since she'd piled her hair up. It was all he could do to keep his aching fangs from making an unwelcome appearance.

If he managed to get through this night without fucking up, it would truly be one of Zarek's miracles.

When they walked through the door, they were greeted by a friendly smile. "Mr. Dagotto, we have your usual table ready. Right this way."

They followed the host to the back of the restaurant and Marcus noted every head that turned to watch Cassie walk past. He glared and let his power whip out at one in particular who stared at her well-rounded ass. The man had a look of surprise on his face after Marcus slapped him with a mild energy pulse. Another rule broken, well, sort of. Never do intentional harm to a human unless they intend harm to others.

Gray area. Besides, the man's wife is sitting right there. His behavior harmed her. Not that his excuse would hold up before Aidyn or Zarek, but he didn't give a rat's ass.

When they reached the table, Marcus slid out a chair for Cassie then took the seat across from her.

"What a view. The sunset is spectacular."

He smiled when he detected a twinkle in her green eyes. He'd hoped she would like this spot. It was his favorite, an intimate table in the corner with a view of the water. The sky was swathed in pastels as if the gods themselves had splashed paint across its canvas. He couldn't remember ever seeing a more beautiful sight, other than the woman who sat across from him. He sent up a mental thank you and apology to Zarek.

"Champagne?" He pulled a bottle from the bucket sitting on his left.

"Yes, please."

He poured two glasses, handed her one and raised his own. "A toast. May the guardians watch over those you love." Their glasses clinked.

"That was beautiful. I take it you believe in guardian angels?" she asked.

He unfolded his napkin and placed it in his lap. "I have it on good authority that they do exist." He looked around the room then leaned forward. "Who knows, there could be one here now." He gave her a wink.

She laughed. "I like the way you think, it's refreshing."

He decided the sound of her laughter, the way her eyes shone and her cheeks turned a rosy pink was exactly what his heart needed. What he'd been missing for so many years. A layer of ice melted in his soul to be replaced by her fire.

"THAT WAS one of the best dinners I've had in...well, forever," Cassie laughed.

"I'm glad you enjoyed it. Now for some dancing."

She couldn't remember the last time she'd had so much fun, and the evening was still young. They'd decided after a dinner of lobster to head over to Roxie's for a few drinks. Cassie glanced over at Marcus as he maneuvered through traffic and wondered when the other shoe would drop. She'd never met anyone so handsome, or considerate, or who made her laugh as much as he did. It almost seemed too perfect. Had her guardian finally thought she deserved happiness? Her mind raced back to John. It had been five years since her wedding day, the day her heart had been left in tatters. Five years since a man had touched her or entered her body. She shivered.

"Are you cold?"

"No." Anything but cold, she was burning alive and blamed the man in the driver's seat and could hardly believe she was considering sleeping with him.

He managed to find a parking space close by so they didn't have far to walk. When she stepped out of the car, he offered his arm. When she wrapped her fingers around his bicep, she swallowed a groan. The muscle like concrete, hard and unforgiving. When he flashed her a wicked grin, her panties burst into flames.

Entering the club, they made their way to the bar and found a couple of empty stools. Memories flooded her mind as she remembered the night they'd first met. Never once did she anticipate coming back here with him.

"What would you like to drink?"

"Beer would be great, thanks," Cassie said.

Marcus waved the bartender over and ordered two beers.

"So, I had to talk about myself at dinner, now it's your turn. Do you have any family?"

"Like you, my parents are dead. There is only my younger sister Gwen and myself," Marcus replied.

"I'm sorry to hear that. It's hard losing your parents. Are you and your sister close?"

"Yes, we are."

The band started the next song, one of her favorites. Al Green's 'Let's Stay Together'. She looked up to see Marcus standing next to her, holding out his hand.

"Would you care to dance?"

"I'd love to." Could this evening get any better? She slipped her hand into his as they walked to the dance floor and he slid his hand to her waist, pulling her close. She gasped when their bodies made contact and swore electricity shot between them. There was something about this man who eased her worries and made her feel like nothing could harm her. She looked into his eyes, where a darkness lurked in their depths. What was it? *I'm probably going to find out he has a wife.*

No wife, my love, only you.

"Did you say something?" She looked up into his eyes, totally startled.

"No."

"Must have been the music." Or, she really was losing her ever-loving mind.

CHAPTER NINE

ODAGE MOVED from the bed where he left the female asleep. He had business to discuss with Sidara, so quietly slipped on jeans and a shirt then left the room. On his way out, he beckoned one of his minions. "Make sure the female is gone before I get back. I don't care what you do with her." She was not worthy enough to carry his spawn, so he would not be taking her back to Romania. No doubt his minions would have fun with her before they killed her. Should he walk or flash directly to the mansion where Sidara resided? Since he certainly wasn't in the mood to deal with the drunken crowds of Bourbon Street, he flashed.

The grounds moaned with black magic when he stepped across them. No one—immortal or, human—dared come close to the old mansion. The town's people believed the house haunted and they were partially correct. He walked to the front door, not bothering to knock before slipping inside. The old house was still lit by candles and kerosene lanterns, lending to its mysterious effect. Heavy tapestries covered the walls, and thick Persian carpets adorned the floors.

"Sidara?"

The voodoo priestess stepped through a doorway at the top of the ornate staircase. "Odage, to what do I owe the pleasure of your company?" she asked, gliding down the stairs. When she reached the bottom, she held out her hand. Odage grasped it and placed a kiss on her knuckles.

"You are lovely as ever, my dear." Her raven tresses hung in thick curls to her waist, and her cocoa skin was enhanced by the red dress she wore.

A wicked laugh passed her ruby lips. "And you are still the smooth talker, I see." She sashayed toward the sitting room. "Come, have a drink with me," she commanded while pouring brandy into a snifter.

He followed in a blinding heat. "I would love a drink."

Sidara poured another snifter and handed him the glass. "Now, what can I do for the handsome dragon? Hmm?" She traced a red nail down the plunging neckline of her gown.

Odage licked his lips, the thought of tasting her fruit made his head spin. Business first, then pleasure. "I need a spell, one that will hide my presence from the vampires."

"Really? Sounds like the dragon is up to some naughty business. I have something that will help you." She glided to an old, wooden cupboard, spoke softly under her breath then opened the door. Reaching in, she retrieved a black, silk pouch. "Yes, this will do. Follow me." She strolled back toward the kitchen where she proceeded to empty the bag's contents into a pot of boiling water. Odage wrinkled his nose when a foul stench filled the air.

"What is that?"

Sidara threw him a wicked smile. "You don't really want to know what's in it before you drink it, do you?"

"Drink that?" He was momentarily offended that she expected him to drink something that smelled so vile, but then he quickly remembered he needed Sidara on his side. Piss her off and who knew what she'd do to him. "It will keep me hidden?"

Sidara poured the boiling contents through a sieve then into a mug. "Yes, for twenty-four hours, you will be hidden. You could walk into the king's home, and he would never track you. This along with your ability to cloak should give you complete invisibility. Now drink."

He grabbed the offending cup and downed its contents in one gulp. The taste far worse than the aroma had him taking a deep breath to keep from retching. She had been right. He held no desire to know what the drink consisted of.

"How long before it takes effect?"

"Maybe an hour. Is there anything else I can do for you while you're here?"

Odage considered for a moment. "Yes, now that you mention it. I need to find a particular amulet. Can you locate it for me if I show you the other half?"

Sidara pushed her chin in the air. "I'm afraid you need a memory ghoul for that task. Oroumea might be able to help you, for a price."

Ah yes, why had he not thought of Oroumea? "Thank you, how much do I owe you?" He reached into his pocket and pulled out a shiny diamond, at least five karats in weight. "This enough?"

Sidara eyed the piece he held, traipsing closer. She reached out and snatched it from his grasp. "I always love doing business with you, Odage." Then in one swift movement, her lips touched his, her body pressed against him. There would be time to seek Oroumea later, right now he might as well enjoy the woman unzipping his pants.

"MARCUS, I had a terrific time tonight. I can't remember the last time I laughed so much," she said as they exited the club.

He put his arm around her shoulder and pulled her close. "I'm happy to hear that. I must admit I haven't had this much fun myself in...a very long time." He planted a kiss on the top of her head. Spiced honey caressed his senses and went straight to his groin. *Christ, I wish*

I could tell you all about us and the bond we share. Somehow, he had to get her home and then walk away. She wasn't ready for him. Not yet. Her body grew tense, and she turned her head to look behind them. He flared out his senses but picked up nothing unusual. "What's wrong, love?"

"I feel like we're being watched." She snuggled into his chest. "I'm sure it's my overactive imagination."

He squeezed her tighter as if to reassure her safety, then reached for his link to the king. *Aidyn!*

Yes?

I sense nothing, but Cassie feels like we are being watched.

Then we should trust her instinct. Lucan and I are right behind you. We'll check it out.

Thank you.

Marcus ushered her down the street and toward the car while remaining alert. *Aidyn, I sense two minions, but nothing more.*

No, there is someone else. Lucan is going after the minions and I will continue to follow you. I can't find Odage, but I know he's here.

Thank you, I feel better knowing you are watching over my mate.

Aidyn's chuckle reached Marcus. *So now you refer to her as your mate? The date must be going well. She is a beautiful woman, Marcus. Count yourself a lucky man.*

Perhaps you are right.

I'm always right. Garin has joined me. He will follow you, and I will go help Lucan. Hopefully, I will get some answers from the minions before he kills them.

Marcus got Cassie back to her house in record time where he planted her on the couch with a glass of Chardonnay. It was all he could do not to pace the floor, but he knew Aidyn and the others were watching. He'd forced himself to relax and sat next to Cassie with his own glass of wine.

"Thanks again for a great evening."

"I'm glad you had a good time. Does this mean you'll go out with me again?"

She grinned. "Absolutely."

He stood. "I had probably better get going, it's late, and I'm sure you're tired." Yet he hesitated to make a move for the door.

CASSIE GLANCED AT THE CLOCK, it was one a.m. But the last thing she wanted to do was sleep. Setting her glass down, she moved off the couch. "I'm not tired." She reached for his hand and her courage. Marcus didn't appear to want to leave, so she took a gamble. "Kiss me."

He pulled her close and ran his fingers down her cheek. Leaned closer and brushed his lips against hers. Gently, he nibbled her bottom lip, coaxing her mouth open with his tongue. She moaned, parted her lips, allowing him to take full advantage. He pressed his way deeper into her mouth, held the kiss before he broke away.

Opening her eyes, she let out a sigh. "You're a good kisser, Marcus." She leaned into him and pressed her body against his. With her arms around his neck, she pulled him to her, and their lips came together once more. Her tongue did a deliberate slow dance across his, making him moan. Her core turned to lava, the heat almost too much to bear.

He pulled away and took a step back. "Cassie. I could stand here and kiss you all night, but I'd better go before I make an ass of myself and you end up hating me."

Once again, she reached for his hand, understanding what he meant. "Why do you think I would end up hating you?" She worried it might be the other way around. Would he think her a wanton woman? She tried to cap her desire, but the need to live what happened in her dreams overruled common sense.

"I will not lie. I believe in the truth, always. I want you. I want to lay you on the bed and make passionate love to you until neither of us can move."

"Then what's stopping you?" she whispered.

"Love, did I hear you correctly?" His jaw dropped slightly.

Her gaze moved to his stormy eyes. "I will admit, I'm not the type who sleeps with a man on the first date." She looked down at his chest. "Hell, not even the second or third." Moved back up to meet his. "I can't say what it is, this connection I feel. I just know I need you."

He pulled her close, his mouth crushing hers. Their tongues glided across each other in a play for dominance. Her nipples hardened and strained against the fabric of her dress. With only the thin layer of material between them, there was no missing his erection. She pulled away and gasped for air then led him to the darkened bedroom. Her courage wavered for a moment. She'd come this far, there would be no stopping now. She didn't want to stop.

"Marcus, I don't know how to explain it. I trust you, and to be honest, your touch sets me on fire. I need you, but if this isn't what you want, then I'll understand." She held her breath and waited for his response.

He closed the distance and cupped her cheek. "There's no way in hell I'm leaving now, unless of course, you toss me on the street."

She reached for his shirt, her fingers trembling as she loosened the first button. He grabbed her wrists. "If at any time you want to stop, tell me."

"I won't stop." She continued to fumble with the buttons until they were completely undone. Pushed the shirt over his broad shoulders and down thick biceps, lingering to allow herself the pleasure of hard muscle beneath her fingertips. When the moonlight danced across his chest, she inhaled. The man was remarkable, better than her dreams because he stood in front of her for real this time.

He removed the clip that bound her hair and loosened her curls until they spilled around her shoulders. The desire that burned in his eyes made her dress feel like a second skin. Tracing a line along the column of her neck, the tips of his fingers caused her to shiver. She hardly noticed when he reached behind her neck and untied the halter, until the dress fell to her waist. Normally she might have felt exposed, but all of the nightly dreams made everything familiar. They were like old lovers.

When he bent and pulled her nipple into his mouth, she arched her back and moaned. Every nerve in her body fired and she could hardly breathe. Would her heart be able to take the thunderous pounding from her arousal? All she wanted to do was get him naked.

"You have too many clothes on," she whispered, reaching for the button on his pants.

He released her and she nearly cried out from the ache he left behind. "I could say the same for you, love." He kicked off his boots while she finished shoving her dress to the floor. Grabbing the waistband of his pants, she yanked them down and he stepped free. There was no missing his erection as she was eye level with all its glory.

She licked her lips, desperate to savor him. He was much bigger than she had experienced in the past, but that only heightened her arousal. Dropping to her knees, she ran her tongue over the tip of his shaft. He tasted of salt and seduction. He slid his fingers into her hair and fisted.

She moaned around him. Sucked him in, taking as much as she could and became drunk by the pleasure she gave him.

He threw his head back. "Damn, that feels so good. Don't stop."

As if she could. No, she was a woman possessed, determined to take him over the edge. At this moment, she wanted nothing more than to return the pleasures he had given her every night for the past several months.

CHAPTER TEN

SWEAT BEADED ON HIS FOREHEAD. Close, so very close. He never expected this. Had dreamed about it, but never imagined it would happen like this. He wanted to beg her to stop, but the words caught in his throat when he yelled out her name. Damn. He was falling, his body burning in a black hole of desire and he thought his release would never end. When he finally snapped back to reality, he still wasn't sated. He wanted all of her.

She pulled back and he scooped her up, laying her on the bed. "Cassie, you're the most beautiful woman I've ever seen," he whispered in her ear. He lapped the valley between her breasts then licked his way to her pink bud, wrapping his lips around it. He teased until she cried out. Cupped her other breast and rolled her nipple between his thumb and finger.

She arched her back and cried out.

He licked his way down her taut belly. Her body was more than he could have ever believed. His desire to please her, to give her more than she had just given him drove him to near madness. He had never felt this way about any woman. Ever. His desire might be his undoing, but he was unable to stop. To hell with the consequences, he'd deal with those later.

When his tongue found her soft folds, he licked. Drank in her taste as he inserted two fingers and began to thrust them in and out. Slow at first, then he quickened the pace. Her breaths came in frantic gasps. She was teetering on the edge and he was about to bring the female who had been chosen for him to orgasm. Never would she know the touch of another man.

He would kill any who dared.

"Don't stop."

Her core tightened around him, sucking his fingers in deeper. She burned like an inferno, and his fangs lengthened. Scraping along her nub, he was unable to hold them back any longer.

"Marcus," she screamed. Her body bucked while he continued to swirl his tongue between her folds. He pumped his fingers and nibbled her clit, determined to bring her over the edge again. His free hand reached up and rolled her nipple between his fingers, and she blessed him again with her screams of pleasure.

"Marcus, please," she begged. "I need you inside me." Her breasts heaved up and down with each frantic breath.

He groaned. That was precisely where he wanted to be as well. "Don't worry, love, I'm not finished bringing you pleasure." Moving to his knees, he poised himself over her for a moment before he came to his senses. She didn't know he was immortal, therefore immune to human disease. He slipped off the bed and rolled on a condom with incredible speed, then was back, rubbing the tip of his shaft along her slickness. He thrust until he was seated deep inside. Quivered in pleasure for a moment while he enjoyed her soft wetness wrapped around him. He was where he belonged. He and his mate were joined in carnal desire.

She bucked wildly beneath him. Her heat engulfed him, sent fire through his body. She was both heaven and hell, and the beast who hid deep inside him emerged, pinning her arms above her head. His pace quickened. The need to drink from his mate overwhelmed him, but he fought it. He sensed her closing in on another orgasm, so he stopped with only the tip of his cock still inside her. The animal in him wanted...no, needed her to beg him. He ran his tongue along her neck, causing her body to quiver.

"Marcus, don't stop."

HE STOPPED, oh why the hell did he stop? She shifted, but he had pinned her down. Damn but he pushed the right buttons. Three orgasms already and still she wanted more. *Greedy bitch. Yes!*

"Marcus."

Damn it, he licked her neck. Her thoughts moved back to her dreams of when he bit her. God, she wanted him to bite her now. She almost wished he had fangs. *I'm mental.* Her mind wouldn't stop torturing her.

"Marcus, please. I need you." She wasn't beyond begging at this point. It must have worked because he thrust into her, filled her, stretched her and took her to unimaginable heights. He was a perfect fit. She moved her hips, and he started to thrust. His pace hard and fast. God, she couldn't get enough. *More, more, more!* He moved his mouth from her neck to her nipple. Her body burned like she'd been dipped in melted wax. She was on the edge, ready to leap to the other side.

"Come for me, my love," he whispered.

Body and mind were flung into a bright light. Pleasure gripped her and squeezed until tears rolled down her cheeks. It was never-ending, wave after wave of mind-numbing ecstasy. She walked a fine line between pleasure and pain.

"Cassie!" His face twisted with pleasure, and she swore to the heavens he did have fangs.

They both lay panting, their bodies slick with sweat when he pulled her into his arms and kissed her. Warm and tender, unlike a few minutes ago when he had been animalistic. She decided she liked both sides of this man. They faced each other, on their sides, still connected. He caressed her cheek.

"Are you all right, love? I didn't hurt you, did I?"

She broke into a smile. "No, as a matter of fact, I have never been better." She moved a wisp of hair from his eyes and felt a sudden pang. Without a doubt, she could fall in love with this man. It seemed silly to her. She hardly knew him, yet there was a connection. A sense that she already knew him. *Stop or you'll get hurt. End it before he breaks your heart.*

"You seem sad. Did I do something wrong?"

"No, everything is perfect." She curled into him and closed her eyes, letting the darkness overtake her.

Cassie woke to strong arms wrapped around her. A smile crossed her lips at the slow, methodical breathing behind her. Muscles ached in all the right places, and her mind reeled from the explosive orgasms of the night before. Christ, the dreams in no way compared to the real thing. It was so much more. She pulled out her emotions and examined them, but was still left perplexed. Fear drove her to end this, but need said what if? What if unfounded fears ruined a chance at happiness? Take it one day at a time. Live in the moment, mother always said. *I miss you, Mom.* Mother would have understood her apprehension.

She rolled over and gazed at the handsome man who slept beside her. Desire stirred. In the light of the morning, the black ink on his left bicep came into view. A symbol, with a pair of wings spread out behind it. She tilted her head and reached to caress the mark.

"Good morning, sunshine," he whispered.

Flinching, she pulled away. "I'm sorry. I didn't mean to wake you."

He grabbed her hand and brought it to his lips, planting a soft kiss on her knuckles. "Never fear touching me, I belong to you."

Not sure what the words meant, she went back to caressing his tattoo. "What does your tattoo mean?"

His steely gaze never left hers. "It's an Ankh, the Egyptian symbol meaning life or living."

"Of course. I recognize it now." She squinted. "What do the wings mean?"

"They represent the guardian angel."

"A living guardian angel. Right?"

"Right." Spoken against her lips.

A moan escaped. "Care to join me in the shower?"

"I'll race you," he replied.

He threw back the covers to reveal a fully erect cock. She licked her lips and jumped from the bed, racing to the attached bathroom. Cassie was grateful there was a large, walk-in shower that would allow for extra-curricular activities. He slid in behind her and reached for the knob, turning on the dual heads.

The glass door was slid shut, and steam rose to the ceiling. She stood under the water and let it roll over sore muscles. His kissed her neck.

She moaned.

He reached for the soap, lathered his hands and ran the suds over her sensitive breasts.

"Marcus." She reached for him. Her thumb rubbed over the tip of his cock, causing it to jump.

He leaned in, his tongue forcing her lips apart and pressed her against the wall. She teased him with slow strokes while her body ached to take him in. His tongue flicked across her nipple, causing her to arch her back.

"God, Marcus, I want you. I need you to fuck me senseless." *Christ, tell me those words did not just come out of my mouth.* She didn't recognize the woman she'd become in the last twenty-four hours. Not even John had brought out the naughty inside her.

He nipped her earlobe. "I never disobey." Turned her, grabbed her arms and placed her palms on the shower wall. "Don't move." His voice a command not to be questioned. His knee came between her legs, spreading them apart. Long fingers slid through her slick folds and sent fire to her clit before he entered from behind.

She gasped. He filled her, stretching her to the limits. He pulled back, only the tip of his cock still seated inside. She tried to push against him, but he held firm, preventing her pleasure.

"More," she begged.

He thrust deep, hands clasped over hers, pinning them to the wall while he licked a heated trail up her spine. "Are you enjoying yourself, love?"

"God, yes. So good."

"Yes, you feel so good. I don't think I'll ever get enough of you."

Slow movements drove her insane. *God, he's going to kill me slowly.* "Harder," she panted.

One hand kept hers pinned against the wall while the other moved down to her clit where he made lazy circles. His cock slid in and out, faster, harder until he slammed into her. Pressure built first at her toes then worked its way up her legs until it reached her core. Heat flooded her and she threw her head back. Cried out as wave after wave of pleasure pounded her body.

He turned her around, grabbed behind her knees as he lifted her off the floor. She wrapped her legs around his waist which only gave him better access. Pressing her back into the wall, he continued his thrusts. She dug her nails into his shoulders while she kissed him. Their tongues matched the ferocity of their sex.

"Damn, love. I'm going to lose it," he whispered against her lips.

The explosion happened. His cock swelled and filled her with his hot release. She climbed to the heavens and crashed down with him. They cried each other's name as he gripped her tight. After the waves subsided, he set her feet on the floor, her knees nearly buckling.

He cupped her face and placed a gentle kiss. "Sweetheart. I don't think...hell, I can't think."

"Me neither. Maybe we'd better get cleaned up." They untangled themselves and that was when it hit her. "Oh my god! We didn't use a condom."

"Damn. I'm so sorry. I promise I'm safe and as far as you getting preg—"

She held up her hand to stop him. "Don't worry about that. As long as you swear then I trust you." She went back to showering and they finished up in silence. Cassie dressed in a pair of jeans and a tank top then ran a comb through her hair before heading to the kitchen. "I'll start coffee," she called behind her.

What the hell am I thinking? He looks at me and sends shivers up my spine and torches my panties. Her mind was uneasy as she placed the carafe on the burner and pressed start. Marcus came up behind and wrapped his arms around her waist. Planting a kiss on the top of her head. "You seem troubled, what bothers you? Is it the condom?"

Dare she say the words that haunted her mind? Best to be honest, after all, he had been last night. She turned to face him. "No, it's not the condom it's just I don't want you to think poorly of me." She stared at the floor. "I mean...I'm not normally like this."

"So passionate?"

"Such a floozy."

He gripped her chin. "Never say that again. You are a passionate woman who knows what she wants." He brushed his lips across hers. "Never be ashamed of that."

She offered a smile. "Thank you."

The coffeemaker beeped. "Coffee?"

"Sure."

"If I remember, you like it black." She reached for a mug.

"Good memory."

Cassie poured two mugs, handed him his, then put cream and sugar in hers. "Are you hungry? I can make breakfast."

"No. I'm not much of a breakfast eater." He took a seat at the table. "What's on your agenda today?"

"Jill and I are meeting for an early dinner." Her eyes widened. "I know, why don't you come and bring your sister?"

"Are you sure?"

"Yeah, it'll be fun."

He sipped his coffee. "I'll check with her, I'm sure she'd love it." He stood and rinsed his cup in the sink. "I should go. I have a few things to take care of." He kissed her. "I'll call you later and get the details for dinner."

"Sounds good."

CHAPTER ELEVEN

THE MINUTE MARCUS stepped out the front door, Lucan summoned him.

Marcus, put your dick back in your pants and get your ass home. The king is calling a meeting.

Tell Aidyn I will be there shortly. Oh and Lucan?

What?

Fuck you!

He heard the guardian snort. *Haven't you had enough already?*

He shook his head and climbed into the car. *You and I will talk later.*

I look forward to it.

He shoved on a pair of sunglasses and backed out of the driveway. Heading to the storage where he kept all of his toys safely tucked away. After half an hour, he had the car parked and was on his way back to Vandeldor. Aidyn, Garin, Seth and Lucan were already seated at the table in Aidyn's office when Marcus entered.

"Good, now we can get started," Aidyn said and looked at Marcus. "Your mate was correct. Someone was watching you last night."

Marcus leaned forward in the chair, tension hardened every muscle. "You mean other than the minions?"

"Yes. Neither Lucan nor I could sense who, but..." Aidyn rubbed the back of his neck. "Odage was there, I just know it, but I couldn't find him. The bastard was hiding somehow."

"We followed the minions, they had two women with them. No doubt they were taking them back to Odage," Lucan said.

"The women are safe?" Marcus asked.

Lucan nodded. "Tucked into their beds when I left them."

Aidyn pushed back his chair as he stood. "Your orders haven't changed. Return to the human realm and find that fucking dragon. I know I don't need to tell you that this could get ugly. I'm meeting with the demons from our faction tomorrow to see whether or not they will assist us."

Everyone nodded and left the room with the exception of Marcus. "Do you think the demons will side with us?"

Aidyn poured himself a whiskey. "Oh they will side with us. The question is, will they help us." He tossed back his drink then slammed the glass on the table. "I don't like this whole situation. I smell trouble, but I can't place it. Keep alert and remember not everything is as it appears. Above all, protect your mate. If you can get her into hiding, all the better."

Marcus scrubbed his face. "How the hell am I supposed to do that?"

"I wish I had an answer for you."

"Fuck!" He poured himself a whiskey and swallowed it in one swig.

PALE AZURE LIGHTS shimmered in the darkness of the New Orleans cemetery as three figures appeared. Fog rolled low across the ground, giving a foreboding feel. Odage glanced around to get his bearings before they proceeded farther.

"Roman, this way." Motioning, he moved past a statue of the Virgin Mary. An unadorned concrete crypt covered in vines lay ahead. Roman grabbed the girl he had procured earlier and dragged her.

Odage stopped in front of the crypt and began to chant. *Lleisgar vur confn forth Oroumea. Si sweekmon wer irthir di dout memories,* rise and come forth Oroumea. I seek the knowledge of your memories. He waited, wondering if he was in the right place, when a black mist rolled from under the crypt door and began a swirling dance around his feet. Gradually, it wrapped around his legs like a black serpent only to stop when it reached his chest. The mist squeezed, his lungs constricted then a velveteen voice caressed him.

"Who dares to wake me?"

"I do, Oroumea. I seek your services." He'd certainly not expected to be nearly choked to death.

"Do you have payment?" the mist whispered.

"Yes. Roman, bring forth the girl."

The mist released him and swirled to the girl. It encompassed her entire body for several seconds before it moved away and began its slow seductive dance toward the sky. In its place, the silhouette of a woman stood in the night. Oroumea wore a long, fitted black gown and her raven hair made a contrasting display against her pale skin. Her eyes glowed an eerie green, indicating her hunger. She glided across the ground and stopped in front of Odage. Long fingers reached out and ran a red fingernail along his cheek, cutting until blood appeared. She brought the blood-covered nail to her lips and tasted. He fought to keep his anger in check. This woman might be the only link to his destiny.

"I accept your payment, dragon. What is it you seek?"

"I want the location to the other half of the amulet of Tobor," he replied.

She closed her eyes for several moments, silence filled the night. "I do not have the knowledge you seek, but I will find it. The price will be high."

"I am willing to pay any price."

"Any price, dragon?"

"Yes, I must have the amulet."

The ghoul cast a wicked grin. "Make me your queen. You cannot hope to succeed at your little plan alone."

He quirked a brow. "How do you know of my plan?"

Malice played across her face. "No one enters my home and seeks services without my reading their minds first."

He pondered for a moment. The woman was definitely evil enough to be his queen, but it was a high price to pay. He could continue his search alone but didn't have that kind of time. She would prove useful. It might even be fun having someone to share his thoughts with.

"Agreed." He turned to the redhead and tilted her chin upward. "You will stay here with the lovely Oroumea. I'm afraid my new bride is hungry and needs to feast on your brain." He walked away. Bloodcurdling screams echoed in his ears.

MARCUS LEFT Aidyn's and walked back to his own cottage, tucked deep in the forest. Once inside, he sat on the couch, head in his hands. Last night had been incredible. His body responded in ways he never imagined. With no choices left, Cassie would be told what he was. She needed protection from any danger that Odage, or the rest of the dragons posed. His mind wandered to Eliza. The woman who had once been destined to be his mate. Her vacant eyes still filled his vision. The sensation of his blade as it slid through her neck and severed her head still stung his hands. *I'm so sorry, my love. I failed you.*

Determined this would be the last time he'd think of her, he accepted the time had come to put Eliza to rest. Never had he intended to mate with Cassie, but the choice was no longer his. The mating process started when he'd entered her body. He had sensed she'd felt it as well, her emotions flared while struggling with the changes within. Only one thing left to do. Prove he was worthy of her love.

Shoulders back, he stood straight, resolve set in. He swore on his life he wouldn't fail her. Tonight, he'd tell her the truth and pray to his gods she understood.

His mind reached out for his sister.

Gwen?

Yes, brother?

I'm meeting Cassie and her sister later tonight. I told her I'd bring you along. Care to join us? He smiled, knowing full well she was currently jumping up and down with excitement.

You really need to ask? Of course, I want to go. Oh Marcus, I'm dying to meet her.

I will pick you up at five.

Thank you, I'll be ready.

CASSIE AND JILL sipped margaritas as they sat outside the restaurant, watching tourists walk by. She told Jill about Marcus, and as suspected, her sister had been thrilled she was finally dating.

"So, when is your handsome prince going to arrive?" Jill asked.

"Here he comes." Cassie spotted him up the sidewalk with a beautiful woman by his side. Had she not known it was his sister, jealousy would have reared its ugly head. Slightly shorter than Marcus, with chestnut hair to her mid-back, she was stunning. Her golden skin was set off by the coral tank top and jeans she wore. When they approached, Marcus leaned down and kissed Cassie on the lips, sending a slow burn to her core.

"Cassie, I'd like to introduce you to my sister, Gwen."

Cassie stood and extended her hand. "I'm thrilled to meet you, Gwen." Pointing to the other side of the table, she introduced Jill. "This is my sister, Jill."

The waitress approached. "Can I get you guys something to drink?" Cassie observed how the girl gave Marcus a dreamy-eyed look. Jealousy boiled in her blood. *What the hell is wrong with me?* As if sensing her dilemma, he reached over and took her hand, placing his lips on her knuckles.

"I would love one of those margaritas," Gwen replied.

"I'll have a whiskey on the rocks," Marcus added. "You ladies ready for another?"

Both Cassie and Jill nodded, and the waitress walked off to get their drinks.

Gwen leaned forward in her seat. "So, Cassie, Marcus tells me you're a nurse?"

"Yes. I work at the local children's hospital."

"It must be very fulfilling, helping children."

"I love my job, though it can be heartbreaking at times. Losing a patient's never easy."

Gwen's features softened. "No, I don't imagine it is. Especially those that are so young and innocent." Turning to Jill. "And what do you do?"

Jill laughed. "Runs in the family. I'm also a nurse. I care for hospice patients."

"You do a great service, helping those so ill," Gwen replied. "You both do a great service helping others."

The waitress stepped up with a tray of drinks and set napkins and glasses in front of them. "That'll be twenty bucks."

Marcus handed her thirty and told her to keep the change. The waitress's eyes grew wide. "Thanks."

Over the course of the next few hours, they decided to order several appetizers rather than dinner. Cassie liked how Marcus doted on his sister, his love very much evident. Jill had been right. Cassie's original judgment had been based on his looks, and so far she had been dead wrong. Three hours later, Jill gave a stretch and stood up. "It's been fun and all, but I need to head for home. You guys continue without me."

Marcus looked at Jill. "You have a ride home?"

"No, I can walk. I don't live that far."

"Jill, why don't we walk you? It's getting dark, and the streets can be dangerous," Marcus said.

"Really, I'll be fine."

This time, Cassie spoke up. "Jill, I'd feel better if you let us walk with you. Besides, I could stand to stretch my legs."

Jill sighed. "Fine, if you insist. I'm not going to stand here and argue with you."

Everyone got up and headed for the sidewalk, mingling with the crowd as Jill led them down the street. Cassie was relieved Marcus had offered to walk Jill home. Her sister liked to take the shortcut across the abandoned area of town, and that scared the hell out of her. All kinds of riffraff hung out during the daylight. She could only imagine what happened when the sun set.

As they made their way across town, Jill steered them toward the shortcut. "Jill, are you sure it's safe to go this way?" Cassie asked.

Jill scoffed. "I do it all the time. Yeah, there are a few homeless, but they won't bother anyone. Besides, it's not even dark yet."

Cassie's tension grew and rolled in her stomach. She didn't like this, not one bit, and gave Marcus a pleading glance. As they approached the halfway mark, two enormous men jumped from the shadows.

Cassie screamed.

The men's muscular bodies towered over Marcus's large frame. Their faces twisted into a sneer.

"Looky what we've found, a nice evening snack," one of them growled, licking his lips.

Marcus shoved her and Jill behind him. "No matter what happens, Cassie, stay between Gwen and I."

Cassie grabbed her sister and pulled Jill close. Not understanding what was happening, there was no time to ask questions. In the blink of an eye, the two men produced swords. *Holy shit!* A second later, both Marcus and Gwen held similar swords. *Where did they get those?*

"We've come for your mate, vampire," one of the men snarled.

"Like hell," Marcus growled. His neck corded and nostrils flared. She feared he'd kill the devil himself should he step into the fray.

The two men circled. Cassie and Jill stood in the middle while Marcus and Gwen faced the threat head-on. The first man rushed Gwen. Their swords clashed, and sparks flew. Cassie looked behind her to see Marcus in a similar battle. Her focus wavered, her attention divided between the two, trying to take in what was happening. Her mind unable to comprehend the situation.

She heard Gwen yell, "Damn you. That was my favorite shirt, now I'm pissed."

A red stain grew on the front of Gwen's chest. "Oh God, Gwen's hurt."

"Don't worry, Cassie. I'll be fine," Gwen yelled back.

Everything moved in slow motion. Gwen pulled her sword up then swung down, the sickening sound of a blade slicing through flesh and bone echoed in the air. A head hit the ground with a loud thump. Cassie's stomach lurched and would have lost its contents except Jill cried out, bringing her back to reality. She whipped around in the direction of her sister and screamed. A third man appeared and had his mouth latched onto Jill's throat. His eyes glowed green. Blood and saliva ran down Jill's neck.

"Jill!" Cassie shouted, running toward her sister only to have Gwen grab her. She fought, but the other woman was too strong. "You must trust Marcus," Gwen whispered in her ear.

Marcus appeared behind the man, his blade sliced through the top of the man's head, nearly splitting it in two. He screeched and dropped Jill, turning to face Marcus. Cassie didn't wait, she pulled free of Gwen's grip and sprang forward, dropped to the ground where her sister lay. She ripped off her shirt and pressed it against her sister's neck. Whatever that thing was, it tore a hole the size of her fist in Jill's neck.

Sobs racked her body. "Jill, please don't die. I can't lose you. We need an ambulance! Hold on, you have to stay with me." Jill's blue eyes paled then glazed over; she was dying. "No, this isn't happening."

"Sweetheart, I can help her, but you need to step back."

Cassie looked at him, tears streamed down her cheeks. "She'll never make it to the hospital. I'm gonna lose her."

"No, sweetheart, but you need to move back. Hurry."

Gwen's arms wrapped around Cassie and pulled. "Now is the time to believe in miracles, little sister."

Her gaze was riveted on Marcus and Jill. He placed his palms over the gushing wound and his lungs expanded then exhaled as he closed his eyes. White light encased his hands and radiated around the wound. It continued down Jill's body until she was totally bathed in it. A prickling sensation rolled out and touched Cassie's skin. The light changed. Diminutive pinpoints of blue danced all around her sister, sparkling like a million tiny stars, and then they vanished.

She was hallucinating. It was the only explanation. The wound on Jill's neck completely healed. Moving closer, she took her sister's wrist and felt for a pulse. *Thump thump.* A perfect heartbeat. Breaths were slow and rhythmic like that of sleep. Marcus caressed the tears from Cassie's cheek.

Her gaze met his. "I don't know how you did it, but thank you."

Voices shouted from behind, she turned to witness two large men approaching. "More are coming." Frantic hands tugged on his shirt.

"It's okay, they're on our side."

"Is anyone hurt?" one male asked.

"No, my lord, Marcus was able to heal this one. She is sleeping now," Gwen replied.

One man knelt down, soft brown eyes looked into her soul. "Are you all right, Cassandra?"

Her tongue twisted into a knot, making it difficult to speak. "I... I'm fine, I think."

He offered a warm smile then stood. "Marcus, take the women back to Vandeldor. I'm sure Cassandra has many questions for you."

Marcus scooped up Jill and stood. "Yes, my lord."

So many questions flowed through her mind. What happened? Who are these people? Why do they call this one 'my lord'? But most important, what the hell is Marcus? Clearly not human.

"Cassie, take Gwen's hand. Everything will be fine. I'll explain once we get you to safety," Marcus said.

She shoved a shaky hand out and took Gwen's. With no idea where she was going, she knew Marcus and Gwen had saved her from whatever those monsters were, and Jill was still alive. She would trust him to explain everything as promised, later.

CHAPTER TWELVE

I MIGHT HAVE LOST HER. His muscles went rigid at the thought when he flashed them back to his home. Marcus had planned to tell her everything. There was no skirting around the issue any longer. However, he never intended her introduction to his world to be like this, but had envisioned showing her the beauty of his home and his pride in his warriors. Her only exposure—the icy, blackness of evil. As he carried Jill to his guest bedroom, he couldn't help but be delighted by his mate. She wasn't hysterical as many females might be, but she was afraid. Her emotions stirred in him like his own. His connection to her grew stronger with each passing moment.

"Is she really going to be all right?"

He reached around and pulled her close. "Yes, she will sleep for a while. A lot of blood was lost, but she'll be fine. Come, let her rest, we need to talk."

Her eyes moved up and met his. The sparkle gone, replaced with pain. "Yes, I guess we do."

He led her to the living room and sat her on the couch. Gwen came in with a hot cup of chamomile tea. "Drink this. You'll feel better." She placed the cup on the table in front of Cassie.

Cassie rubbed her head. "Thank you, I'm feeling a little lightheaded."

"That happens when humans flash." She knelt on the floor. "Everything will be fine. Marcus will explain, but should you need me, you only have to ask."

"Here, put this on." He handed her one of his T-shirts.

Her eyes filled with gratitude as she placed the shirt over her head and slid it past her breasts. "Thank you."

He waited until Gwen closed the door behind her then reached out to take Cassie's hand. She pulled away, and his heart dropped. "Let me start from the beginning."

At first, she refused to look at him. "What are you, Marcus?" Finally, she raised her gaze to meet his. "You're not human, that much I know. And what were those things... Those monsters who attacked us? They weren't human either."

He finally sat next to her but far enough away to give her some space. "It's a long story."

"Somehow, I don't think I'm going anywhere."

"My people were created by a god named Zarek. He is the king of all gods, the one who gave me the ability to heal others." He paused, waiting to see her reaction. Her emotions remained masked on the outside, but inside, he sensed her turmoil.

"That's how you saved my sister, you healed her somehow?"

"Yes. We were created as the guardians of the human race. As you saw tonight, there are evil beings who would harm you. It's our job to protect. The ones who attacked us are called minions. They were created from humans by another immortal."

Her eyes lit up. "Is that what I saw the other night? Was that man creating a minion?"

"Yes. That was Odage. We're not sure what he's up to." He hesitated for a moment. "Something is very wrong with him, and his people are on the verge of war with us."

"His people? You mean he is not the same as you?"

"No. His people are weredragons."

A nervous laugh. "What the hell is a weredragon?"

"A man or woman who can shift into a dragon."

She pushed herself back farther into the couch and brought her knees to her chest. "You mean like a werewolf?"

"Exactly, and yes, they exist as well."

She took a sip of tea. "Got anything stronger?"

He laughed. "How about a glass of wine?"

"Seriously? I was thinking more along the lines of a shot of Tequila, or several."

He headed to the bar on the other side of the room. Grabbed the bottle from the glass hutch and poured a shot. "Got it, one shot of liquid courage coming up."

She followed, taking a seat on a stool in front of the bar. "Oh you have no idea." When he placed the glass in front of her, she swiped the liquor off the bar and tossed it down her throat. Her color returned. "Can I ask you a question?"

His gaze softened. "You can ask me anything."

"You said before you believed in the truth, is that what I will get from you? The truth?"

"Always, I cannot lie. It's not in my nature to do so."

"Are you my guardian angel?"

"I'm not quite sure how to answer. In a way, yes."

She rubbed her temple. "Shit. I slept with my guardian angel. I'm going straight to Hell for this one."

"You're not going to Hell and never say that!" He hadn't meant to snap.

"Wow, I take it that's a real place too."

"Very real and no where you want to go."

"I'm so confused, but whatever, we can come back to that later." Green eyes scorched his soul. "Do you by chance have fangs?"

"Yes, why do you ask?"

A delicate finger pointed at the glass indicating a refill. He obliged then placed the bottle on the bar.

"I've had dreams of you biting me."

He smiled. *If you only knew, my love.*

"What did you say?"

Damn, she picked up his mental thoughts. He rested his elbows on the bar and leaned closer to her. "Did you enjoy it?"

Her face grew ten shades of pink. "I...uh."

"Only the truth, we vow it right now to never hold anything back from each other."

She grabbed the bottle and poured another shot, tossing it back with ease. "Only the truth." Her eyes dropped to her lap. "Yes, I enjoyed it very much."

He moved to the other side of the bar. "Can I touch you, Cassie?"

She hesitated before answering. "Yes."

He brushed his thumb across her cheek. "There's more to the story." He slid onto the stool next to her. "Many of my people were lost to a war with a demon more than three hundred years ago. Very few females survived, many of the men have been unable to mate." He saw a look of fear cross her face. "Let me finish, sweetheart. Yes, as you are aware, we can have relations with humans, but it's different. When we find our true mate, it's a bonding of the heart, mind, body and soul. It's so much more than a human relationship can ever be."

This time she took a sip of Tequila. "So what you're telling me is I'm just a fuck until your mate comes along?"

He grabbed both her hands and pulled them to his chest. "Never. What I'm trying to say is the gods chose us to be together. *You* are my mate, Cassie."

WAIT, *he just said I was his mate?* She jumped off the stool and paced the room. Was that why he'd been showing up in her dreams? She had to be missing something, some hidden meaning.

"Shit. First, I find out I've been sleeping with my guardian angel. Next, I bear witness to the real boogieman, and now you tell me, we have been chosen to be together?" She did a face-palm to her forehead. "How could I forget, you have fangs. Which leads me to my next question. I suppose you drink blood? I mean, otherwise, why would you have fangs?"

"Yes."

She stopped mid-stride. "But I saw you eat food."

"I do eat food, but blood gives me strength."

"Holy fuck. I feel like I stepped into a damn novel. Please tell me you don't sparkle."

A dark brow shot up. "Please! Only if you dip me in glue and roll me in glitter."

The image of his broad, well-defined chest covered in gleaming tinsel nearly sent her into a fit of laughter. No, he looked much better with a naked chest. A shiver crawled up her spine. Much better indeed.

His lips curled into a sly grin. "I'm pleased you like me better naked." He waggled his brows. "Just say when, love."

She gasped. "You're in my head. Get out. Get out of there this instant." She placed her palms over her scalp as if it would help. "I should have known you could read my mind."

"I'm not reading your mind but hearing your thoughts. Just as you have begun to hear mine, our bond is growing stronger."

Could this day get any weirder? "How can I be your mate? I mean, doesn't your mate have to be like you? How long do you live anyway?"

"We can realistically live forever, there are a few ways to kill us, and as I said, many were lost in the war." He scrubbed his face. "I don't really know why we were chosen to be together, but I know you feel our connection."

"Yes, I will admit my attraction to you has been mind-boggling to say the least." She noticed he looked at the floor. He was hiding something, she was sure of it. "What are you not telling me?"

"You are to become one of us."

"Oh hell no!" Wait, she still wasn't sure what he was. A vampire angel? She rubbed her neck, the thought of him taking her blood sent moisture to her core. *I must be fucked in the head.* "I'd remember if you had taken my blood, wouldn't I?"

His tall frame leaned against the bar. "You are untouched. I would recognize if any other had ever tasted you." He leveled his eyes. "The pleasure my bite brings you will be unforgettable."

Arrogant bastard, but somehow, she knew he was right. She walked over and grabbed the rest of the shot and drank it down. "I don't get it. You say you're a guardian, but yet you take our blood and without our consent." It was her turn to cross her arms over her chest. Chin tipped up. She had him on this one, she was positive.

He snorted. "Did you not pay attention in school, woman? The gods have always required a blood sacrifice."

She exhaled sharply. Well damn, he had her there. "Okay. Look, I have a million more questions, but I'm tired, and I need time alone...to think. Can you take Jill and I back to my house, please?"

"I'm sorry, but it's not safe there. Those minions came for you, they meant to take you from me."

She shuddered as she remembered the men and what they had done to her sister. Suddenly too much for her, she burst into tears. She never heard him approach but found strong arms encircling her. Bringing the comfort she so desperately needed.

He stroked her hair and kissed the top of her head. "Please, baby, I know it's been a lot, but my heart breaks to see you cry."

She looked up at him. So much worry covered his face. "What do we do now?"

"We'll work this out." His mouth sought hers. Gentle at first then more desperate. Yes, this is what she needed. This strong man, no matter what he was, would make her forget.

Pulling away, she panted. "Marcus, it seems crazy, but I need you to make love to me."

He scooped her up and headed for the bedroom. "I'll give you anything you wish." He laid her on the bed, then with careful hands pushed the oversized T-shirt he'd given her up past her stomach. She sat up and lifted her arms so he could pull the shirt over her head. Next, he unsnapped her pants, and she lifted her hips. The jeans landed on the floor next to the shirt. All that was left was her red lace bra and panties. Her fingers fumbled for his jeans. He stepped back.

"Allow me."

She watched while he grabbed the bottom of his navy shirt and pulled it over his head. She licked her lips, never had she seen such well chiseled abs. Anatomy studies would have been more fun with a specimen like him. He unzipped his jeans then inserted his thumbs into the waistband and pushed down, freeing his erection. She was suddenly thankful he didn't wear underwear. He slid in next to her, his warmth flowing over her as he unhooked her bra from the front and let it fall to the sides of her breasts. He bent closer until all she could feel was hot breath, causing her nipples to harden.

Her breaths increased, and she arched toward him, but he made her wait. Finally, his tongue flicked out, touching her nipple. A plea escaped her throat. "Please."

His tongue swirled around her pink bud then sucked it into his mouth. Fingers swept between her folds.

"You're so wet for me."

"Marcus, I need you inside me. Now."

He grabbed her panties and ripped them free then pulled her legs apart and pressed the tip of his cock against her entrance.

Her breath stopped. "What are you waiting for?"

"You should know, we have no need for a condom."

"At this point I don't even care."

He inched in while he pinned her hips to the bed, preventing her from thrusting upward. Inch by agonizing inch, he slid into her until at last she was filled. She moved under him and let out a moan. "So good."

"Sweetheart, you know what I am. I can no longer conceal my true identity."

Their gazes met. His eyes molten silver, fangs extended. She reached up and traced his lips. How was it possible he could be even more handsome in this state of arousal?

"Please tell me I don't frighten you. I would never hurt you."

He sucked her finger into his mouth as his cock slid in and out of her. "I'm not afraid." Never afraid of him. In this moment, she never felt safer.

She greeted his every thrust. She teetered on the edge as he whispered in her ear. "Trust me, and I will bring you pleasure beyond belief."

"Yes." God, she was close. What more could he do to her? As if to answer her question, his lips wrapped around her pink bud, a quick, sharp prick and a fang slid into her nipple. Her eyes rolled back as the most intense orgasm gripped her body and pulled her under. Waves crashed over her, drowning her in ecstasy.

He released his bite and laved his tongue across her nipple. "Gods, woman, I need you."

Somehow, she understood what he needed, and at this moment, she'd give him anything. She swept the hair from her neck, and she turned her head. "Take what you need, I offer freely."

His tongue glided over her pulse as his cock slammed into her. He suckled her neck, a light pinprick and his fangs buried deep. She dug her nails into his back. The eruption started as a slow burn, the need to sink her teeth into him nearly made her crazed. His cock swelled and stretched her. Her entire body became more sensitive, the wave moved from her neck, down her body leaving bumps in its wake. When it finally reached her throbbing core, she exploded, her teeth clamping onto his chest, and she screamed.

When he withdrew his fangs, he threw his head back and yelled. His cock pulsing hot seed into her. They both climaxed for what seemed like an eternity and when the last of their orgasm ebbed, Marcus rolled to his back, bringing her to rest on top of him.

She was exhausted, but sat up to give a frantic look at his chest.

He brushed the hair from her face. "What's wrong, love?"

"I bit you. Oh god, I'm so sorry. Wait...there's no mark."

"I heal quickly." He cupped her face and pulled her to him. A soft kiss brushed her lips. "You can sink your teeth into me anytime."

She fell to his chest, too weak to move. "That was incredible," she mumbled as sleep overtook her.

CHAPTER THIRTEEN

HE FINGERED THE LONG, silky locks of her hair while she slept pressed against him, hardly able to believe he'd tasted her last night. Freely, she gave herself, and after all that had happened, the reactions his body had to her blood were undeniable. Besides the intense orgasm, his mind completely connected to hers—every thought, dream and heartbreak part of him.

Muscles tensed when he learned of her ex-fiancé John and how he had broken her. Part of him wanted to kill the man for ripping her heart out. The other half, thankful he'd left because she belonged to him.

Mine.

He kissed the top of her head. The corners of his lips curled upward when he imagined her belly one day swollen with his child. Children meant the world to her. He wondered how she would react to the news that once converted to a guardian, her body would mend itself. She could have a house full of children if that was her desire.

My beautiful bride, I promise to protect you with my life.

SOMEONE SPOKE and she opened her eyes to find a handsome guardian staring at her.

"Good morning, who were you talking to?"

Marcus pressed his lips to hers. "I was merely thinking out loud. I didn't mean to wake you."

She rolled away, stretching her arms overhead. "You didn't." Her mind was a jumbled mess, busy trying to digest what she'd learned last night. Had he told her he was an alien, she probably would have had an easier time coping. Might have even asked to see his space ship. *Why am I having a hard time processing this? I mean, I never thought about creatures living right here among us. Me? The mate to a guardian angel? It's laughable at best.* She slapped her arm over her eyes. God, she had a headache and was afraid of what this all meant.

"Cassie, honey, your emotions are giving me a headache as well. What can I do to help you?"

She jumped. "You're reading my thoughts again?" That pissed her off.

He pressed his lips against her forehead. "They are reverberating off my brain." He sat up and placed his fingers on her temples. "Let me take care of you."

Soothing warmth radiated across her scalp and soon the pain receded. She sucked in a deep breath and released it slowly. "You did that, didn't you?"

"Yes. I can't stand to see you suffer."

"Thank— wait a minute." She sat up, the sheet dropping to her waist and exposing her bare breasts. "What do you mean by reverberating off your brain?"

"I have a blood bond with you." Eyebrows waggled.

She grabbed the sheet and pulled it up to her neck then smacked him on the arm. "Be serious. What do you mean blood bond?" Panic was beginning to set in.

He leaned back against the headboard and crossed his arms over his chest. She glanced down to the tent forming under the sheet. "I was enjoying the view, but if you'd rather talk. I know all your thoughts, memories. Everything. I can now connect with you tele-pathically."

She glared at him, still clutching the sheet to her chest. "So, you can read my mind whenever you want? Why didn't you tell me this before I offered myself?"

"Would it have mattered? After all, we belong together. Besides, we are able to block our thoughts, allowing entry to only those we wish. You simply need to learn how."

With a huff she grabbed the T-shirt he'd given her last night, dropped the sheet and pulled the shirt over her head. She slipped out of bed and padded to the window. Pulling the sheer aside, she stared outside. Sunlight dappled through thick forests, and a soft breeze carried the scent of pine through the open window. This was the first time she'd seen her surroundings.

"Where are we, Marcus?"

His warm body slipped in behind her and he enveloped her with his arms, bringing comfort. So, why was she still fighting panic? "This is my home. It's called Vandeldor. Another realm that exists beside yours."

She sucked in her breath, another world? How much more could her mind take? "When can I go home?" She needed time to think. Absorb all this new information and decide about this mate business.

He spun her around until she faced him. "I told you, it is too dangerous."

Did she want to chance facing those...things again? But she had a life, a job, and responsibilities. "I have a life back there. I can't simply disappear. People will worry." Her gaze dropped to his chest. She couldn't look him in the eyes. "I need time to think, time away from you."

"No, I will not allow you to go back. You could be taken or worse. If it's space you need, then I can stay with Gwen, but you will stay here."

She pressed her lips together and shoved him away. Storming across the room, she grabbed her jeans and pulled them on in a jerking motion. "Allow? So now I'm to be your prisoner?" She fisted her hands, wanted to deck him. *How dare he!*

"Woman, there will be no placing yourself in danger." His eyes grew dark and stormy, fangs descending. She'd struck a nerve but didn't care. If he meant to scare her, it wasn't going to work. She already knew he would never harm her. But damn it, she was not going to lose her freedom no matter what. Shoving her chin out, she hoped to radiate confidence. "If you don't take me back, then I will find someone here who will."

A low rumble emitted from his chest. "I will kill anyone who touches you."

Had he growled at her? Seriously? "I'm not your personal possession. You took my thoughts, my memories, all without my permission. Now you take my freedom. I'm grateful for what you've done for my sister, but you are too much for me right now. Too overpowering." She stormed from the room and headed to where Jill still slept. Tears burned her eyes, but she refused to let them spill. Damn it, she would not back down.

Marcus finally relented and took Cassie and Jill back home but with the agreement his conditions were met. Guards were posted outside, and she promised to call for him if anything strange went on. She approved, actually felt comforted knowing protection was close by. It was also the only way she could come home.

Jill slept in the guest room, unaware of the night's events. She worried about her sister, but Marcus had insisted Jill was fine and needed more time. Cassie threw herself on the couch and cried. The look of pain on his face when he'd left had scorched her. She'd not realized the extent of their bond, still didn't understand it. Only knew she never meant to hurt him, but she needed time to think.

She was so tired. Her eyes fluttered shut and sleep overtook her.

"Wake up!" someone yelled in her ear.

"No, let me sleep," she mumbled, wanting to curl into herself and stay there forever. Maybe if she slept long enough, she would wake to find it had all been a nightmare.

"Damn it, Cassie, wake the hell up," the voice shouted. She felt a sudden pinch on her arm.

"Ouch," she yelped and finally opened her eyes. Jill stood staring down at her. Those blue eyes that had looked so lifeless earlier were bright with irritation. She shot up and drew her sister into her arms. "Oh Jill, I was so worried about you."

"I'm fine, but what the hell happened? Last thing I remember was some man sinking his teeth into me, and then I blacked out."

Cassie motioned toward the kitchen. "Let's go make some tea. This is going to be one of the longest, strangest stories you've ever heard." She placed the kettle on to boil while Jill pulled up a chair at the table. Starting from the beginning, she explained everything she had seen and learned including the trip to another place. She explained what she knew about being Marcus's mate and only left out the mind-blowing sex and blood-sucking. When finished, she raised her cup and took a sip of tea, waiting for Jill to laugh hysterically.

It never happened.

The corners of her sisters mouth twisted upward. "So, you're the mate of a vampire. When do you get your fangs?"

Cassie nearly spit out her tea. "What? Do you truly believe all of this?"

Jill's gaze narrowed. "You were not on the receiving end of that bite. Yes, I believe every word of it. You and I both know there are things that exist, which we simply cannot explain away."

"Well, I must say I'm surprised. I'm not sure I believe it, and I was awake for the entire show. At least, I think I was awake." She shuddered. "And by the way, I have no intention of getting fangs. I..." Her sentence was interrupted by the doorbell. "I wonder who that is." Her voice lowered as she shot Jill a fearful glance then moved toward the door. Pressing her eye to the peep hole, she got a good look then jumped back with a gasp.

"Who is it?" Jill asked, worry etching lines across her face.

"It's Marcus," she whispered.

Jill's eyes widened. "Well, let him in."

"No, I don't want to see him."

"Oh hell, Cassie, he's a vampire. It's not like you can hide from him. Let's find out what he wants," Jill said, her hand reaching for the doorknob.

She slapped her sister's hand away. "Since when did you become the vampire expert? Who says I can't hide?"

"Ladies, stop your arguing and open the damn door," Marcus yelled from the other side.

Jill smacked Cassie on the arm. "See, dumb shit, he knows you're here."

Cassie pursed her lips. "It doesn't mean I have to open the door. Besides, he can't come in unless invited," she stated, crossing her arms over her chest and giving a nod of satisfaction.

"Really, love, you need to stop watching those damn Dracula movies," Marcus replied.

Both women spun around, mouths gaping open, to find him sitting on the couch. Relaxed, with both arms draped along the back, a sly grin painted across his lips. *Shit.* Cassie's heart skipped a couple of beats. Handsome as ever, wearing dark jeans and a black T-shirt that showed every bulge in his chest. His stormy eyes looked deep into her soul and she knew she was in big trouble.

"Marcus," Jill shouted as she ran to the couch and planted a big kiss on his cheek. "I can never thank you enough for saving my life. I owe you big time."

He brushed his hand over her face. "I am glad to see you are well and you do not owe me anything. I would do it again without hesitation."

Jill smiled. "Thanks again. So, Cassie tells me you're a vampire. I was wondering if..."

"What are you doing here?" Cassie let out a huff.

Marcus's eyes softened as he looked at her. "I needed to see you."

"Well, you saw me. Now you can leave." Hurt flashed in his eyes.

God, it broke her heart, but it had to be this way. She needed time to think.

His shoulders sagged. "I'm sorry you feel that way. Will you at least give us a chance?"

Her eyes watered. "I need time away from you. Maybe... Maybe you will be given another mate who is more suitable."

He stood and headed for the door. Grasping the knob, he opened it to leave, but turned back to face her. "No, I was already given a second chance with you. There will be no other." He stepped through and closed the door behind him.

"What the hell, Cassie?" Jill shot back as she ran to the door and flung it open. "Shit, he's gone, just vanished."

"It's better this way."

"Why do I get the feeling you've already made up your mind?"

"I just don't know. This is all too weird, don't you think?" Cassie sighed. "He will break my heart and I just can't go through that again."

"You forget who you're talking to. I know you, and this is a decision you'll soon regret."

Cassie crossed the room and kissed her sister on the cheek. "I need to go shower. You're welcome to stay." She headed for the bathroom, stripped and stepped into the steaming mist. Tears blurred her vision as she leaned against the wall and cried. Her heart shattered. She would never give it to another. She tried to convince herself it was better this way. They were too different.

"ROMAN," Odage shouted, tapping his fingers impatiently on his throne. Where the hell was that pain in the ass? "Roman!" he roared, agitation growing with every second he waited. Finally, his lieutenant scurried into the room and dropped to his knees before Odage.

"Yes, my liege?" His voice quivered as he stared at the floor.

Odage bared his fangs and snarled. Already shifting partially into his dragon form, something that happened to him when angry. "Where the hell have you been?"

"I-I am sorry, my liege. We are having a problem. One of the females refuses to eat."

Odage stood, and two strides brought him to the bottom of his dais where he stood with legs apart, hands on his hips and a look of disgust swathed his face. "Get up, you imbecile." He paused, waiting for Roman to stumble to his feet. "I will deal with her. Now, I have a very important task for you."

Roman lifted his eyes to meet with Odage's. "Yes, my liege?"

"You will go to the Vutha Mountains in Vandeldor and seek Caleb. Give him this message." He held out a small envelope showing a dragon crest on one side. "I will send you through a gateway to the other realm." The gateway materialized to his left. Cerise light spun with golden hues, forming a sphere large enough for a man to walk through. Roman looked backward at Odage before entering.

"How will I get back, my liege?"

"Do not fret my *miulkar*, minion. Caleb will send you back. Now go." He watched Roman enter the sphere and disappear. The gateway snapped shut with a sizzle, sending electrical pulses throughout the room. Odage absorbed the energy, his body returning to its full human form. He inhaled then turned and left the throne room, maneuvering down the narrow passages of the cavern system until he reached the holding cells. He scanned for the demon who cared for the women. Spotting her coming out of one of the cages, he called out, "Lileta."

Her hips swayed as she sashayed toward him. Raven hair fell in silky strands down to her plump, round buttocks. She wore black pants that clung to her hips like a second skin, and full breasts strained against a flimsy red and gold lace demi-top. Golden cat-like eyes gazed into his.

"Yes, my liege?"

His blood boiled then shot right to his groin. Lileta was a Kothar demon whose beauty demanded attention. Men wanted to possess her. He, however, couldn't touch her. Kothar body fluids were poisonous to dragons. Intimacy with her would prove fatal. With that in mind, he would admire her from a distance. Instead, he focused on the engraved silver bands wrapped around her wrists. They, along with the black magic laced in the metal, were the only thing keeping her from killing him. As long as she wore them, she was weak as a mortal.

"Where is the one that refuses to eat?"

"This way, my liege." She stepped toward the cell where Veronica was housed.

No longer alone, there were ten abducted, impregnated women to keep her company. Veronica still had several months before she gave birth to his first child and he couldn't afford to have her miscarry. Entering the cell, he touched her stomach, the boy healthy and growing normal caused his chest to swell with pride. Soon he would have a nest of young.

"Why do you refuse to eat?"

Veronica looked at him with fiery eyes. "A monster grows inside me."

Since she remained lucid enough to realize what was going on, he would need to give her more of his blood to calm her. "You dare to call my child a monster?" If it hadn't been for the fact she carried his child, he would have eaten her heart right there.

She lifted her chin. "Yes, and I can't stand the thought of gazing upon it when it's born. I thought I might starve it to death."

Fucking bitch. He had become too complacent with her. Clawed fingers grabbed her face and squeezed, digging nails into flesh.

"Do you know how a dragon is born? No? Let me explain. He will claw his way from your womb, his talon's shredding your insides. If you're lucky, you will be dead before he rips open your belly completely and enters the world." He paused, enjoying the terror reflected in her eyes. "I would have spared you the pain by putting you to sleep but not now. You will feel my son's escape from your pitiful body. I would suggest you reconsider starving him, or he will begin eating your flesh from the inside." He tossed her onto the bed and stormed from the cell.

"Lileta, double her dose of blood wine, and if she still refuses to eat, force-feed her."

"Yes, my liege."

CHAPTER FOURTEEN

MARCUS LEFT Cassie's home with his heart in his hand. Her emotions confused him. She wanted him yet struggled, afraid of the unknown, and still convinced she was unworthy of his affection. No doubt these were remnants of her ex, the bastard. She also feared losing her identity and becoming captive in a world she didn't understand. His heart ached, wanted desperately to comfort her, but realized she needed time. Perhaps if he gave this one thing, he could win her back. He would wait, give her time to become accustomed to the idea then come back for her. He would also have to try not to be so overbearing. It would be difficult because he only wanted to protect her, but he would work at it. With nothing left to do, and his mate being guarded, he set out to find Odage and stop the dragon's reign of terror. He flashed back to where they were attacked, hoping to find some kind of clue left behind. The sun would be setting in a few hours. Maybe he'd get lucky, and the bastard would show up himself.

When he arrived at the warehouse, he flared out his senses. Someone watched him. *I'll ignore them, make them think I'm unaware of their presence.* Whoever it was lurked inside, that much he knew, but their identity remained a mystery, their signature cloaked. He searched the grounds where the minions attacked, but found nothing. Next, he moved toward the abandoned warehouse, a dagger in his palm and a Glock tucked into the waistband of his jeans. His grip tightened on the dagger. *Odage, you motherfucker, show your face.*

Marcus, where the hell are you? Aidyn shot into his mind.

He certainly didn't want to talk to Aidyn but realized he couldn't ignore his king either. *I'm searching the area where the fight occurred. Someone is watching me, and I aim to find out who.*

I sense by your mood things didn't go well with Cassie?

No. Great, the last fucking thing he wanted to discuss. He entered the abandoned warehouse that years ago had been a hub of activity, but now stood a skeleton of its former self. There were two stories and the presence who was watching him hid on the upper floor. The sun moved across the horizon, and Marcus slipped into the shadows, remaining out of sight yet cautious since most immortals were adept at hiding.

Marcus, I am sorry about Cassie, give her time. Is someone still watching you?

Yes.

Let me send you some backup.

No! I do this alone. He reached the other side of the warehouse. Since the stairs were still intact, he didn't dare flash to the upper level because he had no idea what surprise awaited.

Fine, but keep in touch with me. I want to know the minute you find something. And Marcus?

What?

That's an order.

He furrowed a brow. *Yes, my lord.* Then pulled the Glock from its resting place and sheathed the dagger. The bullet would slow down any immortal long enough for him to take their head. He set his foot on the first step, testing to make sure it remained sturdy. Once assured it would hold his weight, he moved in stealth mode taking two steps at a time until he reached the top floor. The last of the remaining sunlight filtered through broken windows and cast dancing shadows on the wall. Sensing someone on the other side of the room, he raised the gun.

"Come out where I can see you."

Slowly, the shadows moved, and a figure emerged from the darkness. "Step closer," he demanded.

A hooded figure stepped out of the shadows into the last of the flickering sunlight. He blinked, but the vision remained. "Holy Christ," he whispered. *Aidyn!*

The figure turned and moved back toward the shadows. He quickly followed, even though his head spun and his mind played tricks on him. There was simply no way. "Wait." He heard a whimper then moved to stand in front of the dark stranger, grabbing both shoulders, he pulled the person into the last of the sunlight. "What kind of fucking game is this?"

Tears streaked down a dirty face. Tattered clothing covered in blood hung loose over a delicate frame. Golden locks matted to her head. "No game, I swear." The reply came as a mere whisper.

He looked closer. Frail and thin, chocolate eyes once filled with life were now dull and filled with pain. "It's impossible." Now convinced the curse had overtaken him. The darkness on his soul showed his past sins and had sent him to hell. He looked around half expecting the prince of darkness to make some flashy entrance. "How is it you're here?"

The figure before him gazed at the floor. "I... I'm not sure."

"Wrong answer," he snarled. "There's no fucking way in hell." The vision played out in his mind. Blinding pain stabbed at his brain. "What kind of illusion is this, and who's behind it?"

The woman's head snapped up to look at him. Her face twisted with pain, but eyes blazed with anger. Her fists clenched. "Of course, you watched me die. It was your blade that killed me!" Her body trembled as she ran toward him, fists pummeled his chest as the rage seeped from her voice. "I loved you, but you took my life from me.

Look at me! Three hundred years I have wandered not knowing what to do, barely existing because of you!"

He grabbed her wrists to stop the assault. She no longer looked at him but sobbed. Her body convulsed with every tear that spilled. "If you are indeed who you claim, then why not contact me or your brother? What about your mother?"

Her gaze lifted to meet his, long lashes moist with tears. "How could I when I knew you didn't love me."

Gods, her scent. It was true, but how he had no idea. He fell to his knees, unable to stand it any longer. "Eliza, please forgive me. I never meant to hurt you. I thought you were lost to me."

She knelt in front of him. "Tell me, mate. Do you love her?"

She spoke of Cassie. Gods, how fucked up his life had become in a matter of seconds. Did he love Cassie? The answer was buried deep. He hardly knew her, yet their connection was strong. He could love her easily if given a chance. "No."

Eliza peered at him through slits. "I think you're lying. Perhaps I will take her head just as you did mine." The cold metal snapped. He looked down in disbelief at the silver bands shining on each wrist. How the hell had he allowed this to happen? His strength ebbed and weakness surrounded him. Only seconds remained before he'd become as fragile as a mortal. *Aidyn! Watch over Cassie.* The connection broke. "What are you doing?"

Eliza stood and beckoned someone from the corner. Demons appeared and dragged him to his feet, now too weak to fight. "Why, Marcus darling, I am repaying you for all those years of love and kindness you showered on me." She flashed from the room.

A WEEK HAD GONE by since Cassie last saw Marcus. One long, lonely week. On several occasions, she stopped herself from calling out for him, knew he would respond and come back. She tried to go on with life, but that had proved easier said than done. Her mind wandered, which wasn't such a good thing since she worked in a hospital. People counted on her, their lives put at risk by her inability to concentrate so she requested a temporary leave of absence, stating personal reasons. Mental problems would have been more accurate.

A knock sounded at the door. It was five in the afternoon, and she wasn't expecting any visitors. Cautious, she approached and looked out the peep hole. *Damn.* The vampire Cassie had seen earlier when they were attacked by demons lurked outside. Knowing she couldn't avoid him, she slowly opened the door.

"What do you want?" she asked.

"I only wish to speak with you."

She stepped back to let him in. "I don't suppose I have much choice anyway. If I refuse, you'll just poof your way in." Her voice was filled with sarcasm.

Aidyn threw his head back and laughed. "Poof? I don't poof."

A delicate brow raised, and she pushed a stray strand of hair from her face. "Excuse me. I'm afraid I'm not up on the current vampire lingo."

He chuckled as he sat down on the couch and patted the cushion next to him. "Cassie, come sit next to me so we may talk."

Deciding it might be better to keep her distance, she chose the chair directly across from him. "I think I'll sit here."

He let out a breath as if annoyed. Maybe she shouldn't push him. After all, a vampire could pretty much do whatever he wanted. Still, she couldn't help it. She'd woken up in a foul mood earlier in the day, and nothing she did seemed to help. Actually, not true, she had been in a foul mood since Marcus had brought her home and she had told him to go away.

"So, I can assume you're here to talk about Marcus?"

His features softened. "First, tell me, how is your sister?"

Feelings of guilt washed over her for being such a snit. "Jill is doing very well." She lowered her gaze to the floor. "Of course, she is mad at me over the deal with Marcus."

"I can't say that I blame her. You didn't truly give him much of a chance."

She looked up and met his chocolate eyes. Perfection. Chestnut locks framed his youthful face in tousled waves. A tight fitting black T-shirt molded itself to every muscle. When he moved, the shirt actually rippled. Odd, she felt no attraction. Was this how she would feel with all men now? Empty?

"Cassie, I want to be extremely honest with you. I am here to ask for your help."

She tucked her legs under her and curled up in the chair, certain this would be good. "What kind of help?"

"Marcus is missing. We have lost all contact with him. I am not even able to connect with him telepathically."

Her heart skipped. "He's probably spending some time alone and ignoring you." It made sense too. If he felt anything like she did right now, then that's exactly what he would do.

Aidyn shook his head. "No, you misunderstand. Let me tell you some things about Marcus."

She leaned forward, unable to help herself, wanting to know everything about him. "Why was I chosen to be his mate?"

He lifted his shoulders. "That is one answer I do not have. I am guessing it's because you have some psychic abilities."

She tilted her head. "How did you know?" True, sometimes she could read people. Not their minds, but knew things about them. It spooked the hell out of her.

"I can read your mind."

She gasped. "What do you mean you can read my mind? Get out of my head!"

He held up a hand. "Cassie, I am not intentionally reading your mind, but you have left it open to me."

"I don't understand."

He leaned back on the couch and tapped his fingers on the cushion. "All guardians are telepathic. We often communicate with each other this way. However, we have to make a mental connection by touch or blood in order to read a human's mind. I, on the other hand, can read any species. I would be happy to teach you how to put up mental blocks to prevent this."

"Oh that might be a good thing to learn. Why is it you have these special powers and not the others?"

"Because of who I am. Now on to Marcus..."

She must have looked dumbfounded because he stopped mid-sentence and took a deep breath. "Cassie, I am a product of a god, meant to lead powerful warriors, protect the human race and keep peace among all immortals. I need strength and yes, on many days, arrogance. Now, let me finish. I am going to start at the beginning. I know he told you that many of our women died in the Demonic war." He paused, waiting for her to acknowledge. When she nodded in confirmation, he continued. "But he did not tell you about Eliza."

Her chin rested on her fist, waiting to hear more. "Who is Eliza?"

His expression became slack. She sensed it difficult for him to talk about, but he focused his gaze on her. "She was my sister. Three hundred years ago when Drayos started the war, he took our women, used them like breeding stock. When we found them, they were nothing but soulless creatures. We beheaded them."

She slapped her hand over her mouth, tears threatened to spill. "I'm so sorry." She choked. It seemed cruel and barbaric.

He gave a nod of acceptance then continued. "Eliza was Marcus's destined mate. He had not bound her to him yet because she was young and he wanted her to live her life first. He is the one who killed her."

No longer able to hold back the tears, she let them slip down her cheeks. Poor Marcus, how he must have suffered. She tried to imagine the pain but would never understand what it must have been like. Another piece of her heart shattered for him. *That must be what he meant when he said he had already received a second chance.* Now, she had taken that away from him as well.

"Yes, Cassie, he did suffer, greatly. His mother had been

abducted. His father had to kill her. I was there when his father begged Marcus to end his own life."

Cassie was unable to comprehend the pain and loss he had suffered. And now she had caused him even more pain. She was the worst, most selfish person in the world. She sniffled and looked to the guardian who sat across from her. "Something tells me you're not finished."

His gaze lowered to the floor. "No. Drayos cursed all the men. We were created from light and dark. The light is the guardian, the dark the warrior. The curse imbalances us, eventually taking away the light and leaving us in darkness. We become no better than the evil that attacked your sister."

Bile rose in her throat, it tasted of fear. "What does that mean, exactly?"

"If Marcus becomes consumed by the dark, his soul will be lost. It means I will be forced to kill my friend."

She must have misunderstood. "Is this what's happened to him? Why he is missing?"

"No, not yet but I fear he is close. My last contact with him was disturbing, to say the least," Aidyn said.

She pulled her legs out from under her, planted her feet on the floor, and leaned forward. Fear licked her skin like an animal about to devour its prey. "What happened?"

"He claimed Eliza was alive and they were together. His last words to me were to watch over you."

She ran shaky fingers through her hair. This made no sense. "Can you live if your head is removed? I mean. How does that work?"

His lips pursed together. "No, we cannot reattach our heads. My sister is dead. This is an impostor. Someone means to harm Marcus."

"So how am I supposed to help, exactly?" She chewed her bottom lip. What if Aidyn was wrong and Eliza lived somehow? She didn't like to think of Marcus with another woman, not that she held any claims. After all, she'd thrown him out.

He touched her arm. "You are now his mate and you have a connection to him. I hope to be able to use it to find him."

"Did you tell me all of this to make me feel guilty?"

"No. I thought you might want to know that the man you love is going to die if you don't come to your senses."

Ouch, that stung. "Nothing like being blunt," she retorted, turning her head away. She simply wanted to curl up and forget everything.

Aidyn moved in front of her in a flash. He grabbed her chin and forced her to look at him. "Yes, I will use whatever means necessary to save him. Including your guilt. Be thankful I don't bend your mind to my will."

"W-what do you mean by that?"

He let out an arrogant laugh. "Cassie, I am an extremely powerful man, not even my brethren know half of what I am capable of. I could make you live an eternity of lies, remembering only what I want you to know."

If he meant to scare her, it wasn't working. Her vision saw what was in his heart. A man who would do anything to save his friend and she couldn't fault him for that. Hell, if only more people had this much dedication, maybe the world would be a little better place to live.

"You may have the power, but you also have a heart. You would never do that to me."

He smiled. "We are going to get along just fine, little one."

CHAPTER FIFTEEN

CASSIE WRAPPED her arms around her waist, trying to find comfort. Waves pummeled the sandy beach, the sea was full of turmoil, the same as her. Had she been standing on the beach, she might have stepped into the angry water and let it carry her away. Instead, she watched from her perch tucked high on a bluff in Aidyn's home. After his recent visit, she'd agreed to come to Vandeldor and try to help find Marcus. Everyone welcomed her with genuine warmth. A surprise considering it was she who had sent Marcus away. If she had not done so, he might be with her now.

Gwen tried to help Cassie connect with Marcus, but so far, they had failed. Lucan, a dark and mysterious vampire, had attempted to teach her how to fight. Guns, daggers, hand-to-hand. Aidyn wanted to make sure she was able to defend herself if needed.

On this day, two weeks after Aidyn's visit, she stood in his living room and waited for her escorts. Recon work done by a few demons indicated Draki activity in the Carpathian Mountains. Aidyn believed Odage was behind Marcus's disappearance. Gwen was sure if Cassie got close enough she could break through whatever blocked their communications and connect with him. Either way, Cassie wanted to help. If his friends were worried about him, then there was cause for her to worry as well.

"Cassie, stop being so stubborn and admit you love him." Aidyn's voice caused her to jump.

Arching a brow, she peered at the king. "You're putting your own thoughts into my head. I don't love him. Besides, who's to say he's not happy with his mate Eliza?" Just speaking the woman's name made her want to run a stake through the bitch's heart. She had been assured, however, that only worked in the movies.

Damn it.

Aidyn snorted. "You're a stubborn woman, Cassandra Jensen. It's no wonder the gods chose you. Only problem is, Marcus is even more difficult. Believe me, he would never have left you for this long. Something is wrong."

She started to make a rebuttal when another figure appeared next to the king. Tall, dark and handsome with much emphasis on the dark. The scowl upon his face made her wince.

"Cassie, this is Seth. He will accompany you on this mission." Aidyn's mouth curled into a grin.

She regarded Seth with a wary eye. Cassie guessed him to be over six-foot tall. His dark hair was cut short, and his Mediterranean blue eyes stared deep into her soul.

She turned to Aidyn with a shiver. "Are you sure he's safe?"

He threw his head back and laughed. "The only thing you need to worry about is being bored to death. Seth is not much of a social butterfly." He leveled his gaze and stared into her eyes. "I trust him with my life, and I trust him with yours."

Still, she wondered about the vampire. From where she stood, he looked like a cold, heartless killer. It didn't help her demeanor any that they still waited for one more to join them. A shudder ran up her spine. She'd been told a demon would round out their team of misfits. *God, I hope he doesn't have red skin and horns.* She stiffened when someone entered the room. Wanting to sneak a peek, she peered through slits. Of course, he looked nothing like a demon. Who the hell created these immortals? A horny goddess who hadn't been laid in centuries? Similar to the vampires, he stood over six feet tall. His raven hair was pulled back with a leather tie, and his body was solid muscle and sinew. Pale golden eyes reminded her of a cat.

Aidyn spoke first. "Baal, I am glad you agreed to this assignment."

Baal gave a slight bow. "My condolences on the death of your mother. Queen Daria was a remarkable woman. She served as a staunch ally in the fight against the slave trades. My people are grateful for any help you can give us."

Aidyn slapped Baal on the back. "You've nothing to fear, my man. We will continue to assist you in this endeavor."

Aidyn turned toward Cassie. "Cassie, this is Baal."

Again, the demon gave a slight bow, a twinkle in his eye. "So you're Marcus's mate. My friend is an extremely lucky man."

Her cheeks grew hot. "Thank you."

"You have been briefed about where we are going?"

"Yes, but do you really think this will work?" She knew the plan. Both Gwen and Aidyn believed she could create a telepathic link with Marcus even though she wasn't a telepath. She had doubts but would try anything. She only hoped that her heart didn't get broken in the process. Aidyn might be wrong. What if Marcus was happy with Eliza? She tried to convince herself she didn't care. *And you're a big fat liar too.*

Baal shrugged his broad shoulders. "Who knows, but we will try. Are you ready?"

She grabbed the backpack with her supplies. "It's now or never."

Baal took her hand then looked at Seth. "While you're cute and all, I don't swing that way. No hand-holding, so take my arm."

Cassie furrowed her brows. "He can go through the portal on his own, right?"

"No portals for me, doll. I can flash us right out of this realm and into yours." He gave a head nod in Seth's direction. "Damn vampires gotta carry an amulet with them every time they want to leave home. Dumbest thing I've ever heard of."

Her body tingled with a thousand tiny pinpricks, and the room faded away to total blackness. She wondered if she would ever become accustom to this kind of travel.

MARCUS OPENED his eyes then quickly slammed them shut. His retinas burned like they'd been sandblasted. *Damn it!* Again, he tried, this time more slowly. First, he peered through lashes. When the pain subsided, he opened them a bit more until—what felt like an eternity later—they opened completely.

The room was small and bare, with no furniture except for the bed he lay on. The only lamp hung over his head and flickered like a moth caught in a bug light. Upon closer inspection, he realized he was surrounded by rock. *I'm in a damn cave?* He tried to sit up but found his arms chained to the wall. *What the hell happened?* His brain recalled Eliza and silver bands. Sure enough, when he looked up at his wrists, he saw the glint of silver. Okay, so he hadn't imagined it, but Eliza was dead.

"Well, lover, I see you're finally awake."

He strained to follow the voice. When he focused in on the beautiful woman, he found Eliza staring back at him. All cleaned up, her golden strands shimmered in the light. Her skin looked as if she'd washed with the morning dew. Skin-tight jeans and a yellow T-shirt that showed off her bra-less breasts covered her body. Her strawberry nipples pressed into the fabric, looking as if they were trying to make an escape. *Fuck, I'm in trouble.*

"How is it you're alive?" he asked.

"Marcus, Marcus, my unfaithful mate," her voice sang out like an angel as she approached the bed. She reached up and ran a red nail down his cheek. "I will tell you my secrets in due time, but first, I have other plans for you. You are my mate, and I will forgive your indiscretions once you bind us together." She squeezed his cock through his jeans, and he sucked in a breath, waiting for a reaction, but nothing happened. Slowly, he exhaled. Eliza was no longer his true mate. Cassie had been given that position.

"Look, I thought you were gone. We had to kill all the women that day." Gods, had they somehow been wrong? Could they have been saved? His stomach rolled and threatened to spill its contents at the thought of such a horrific mistake. No, there had to be another explanation.

Eliza unsnapped her jeans and pulled them past her rounded hips. Once they were to her ankles, she stepped out of them then crawled up on the bed and straddled his lap. She grabbed the end of her T-shirt and pulled it over her head, tossing it to the floor. She kneaded her breasts and rubbed against his cock. The only thing between them was his jeans and her red lace panties.

"The only thing that's dead, Marcus, is the innocent little girl you left behind." She narrowed her gaze. "And it seems your cock as well." She pushed aside her panties and dipped a finger inside, letting out a moan as she worked in and out. "I have spent three hundred years without a man because of you. The only pleasure is what I give myself." She moved her finger faster and pinched her nipple with her free hand. Her moans became louder and her breaths more shallow until she screamed out in pleasure. When she regained her composure, she slid up his chest and wiped her juices over his lips. Gods, she tasted sweet but not as sweet as Cassie, never that good. *Keep telling yourself that, and maybe you can keep it together.*

"Your body's on fire right now. Don't fight it. Just think how wonderful you would feel sliding your cock deep inside me. Be warned, I will make your body crave mine until you beg me to mate with you. And beg me, you will." She slid off and walked from the room, her round, firm ass taunting to be touched as she made her exit.

CASSIE HAD LEFT with Seth and Baal only a few hours ago and now made a quick mental check of her faculties. *I must have a brain*

tumor. It was the only logical explanation she could come up with for why she stood in the wilds of Romania with a vampire and a demon. She shifted her backpack, thankful she was healthy and fit. They currently made their way along an old abandoned mining road. The plan: to trek as far into the forest as they could before sundown then make camp for the night. She knew the camp was only for her bene-fit. These two men had excellent night vision and the stamina of a teenager. She, on the other hand, would have to rest.

"So doll, what do you do in the human world to fritter away your day?" Baal asked.

She laughed, glad the demon had come along. At least, he was someone to talk to. "I work as a nurse at a children's hospital. What does a demon do to pass the time?" Not sure, she actually wanted to know.

He raised a brow then flashed a white smile. "You're a brave girl for asking. I actually own a casino in Las Vegas. I prefer the nightlife. You know—good food, wine and women, not necessarily in that order."

She rolled her eyes. Baal looked more like he should be one of the strippers, no doubt his body would put them all to shame. "A casino, huh? It sounds fascinating. So tell me more about these slave trades."

He continued to walk ahead, not looking at her. "My species is the most powerful of the demons. Ironic, isn't it, that we are also the most captured. Our abilities are sought by other immortals. Often, we are used as sex slaves, our services purchased by unsuspecting humans or other immortals." He waggled his brows. "We are excel-lent lovers."

Her cheeks heated, so she stopped, pulled out her water bottle, and took a swig. "That's terrible. I mean, that they use your people for slavery."

There was sadness in his eyes. "Yes, my sister was kidnapped five years ago. She was only sixteen at the time. I have never given up searching for her."

"I'm so sorry. I pray that you find her."

He smiled. "Thank you. You should also pray for those who took her. When I find Lileta, her captor's death will be slow and painful."

She had no doubt this man was capable of unspeakable acts.

Seth slid in next to her. "Do you need a break, Cassie?"

Baal slapped his thigh and gave a snort. "Whoa, he speaks."

She touched her chest. These were the first words Seth had spoken since they left Vandeldor. "Uh no, I'm fine but thanks for asking."

"Very well then," he replied and continued walking.

She returned her bottle to the side of her hip and turned to Baal. "Is he always this quiet?"

"'Fraid so, doll. Didn't anyone tell you about his abilities?"

She shook her head. "No. What ability is that?"

He moved closer and lowered his voice. Not that it mattered. Cassie understood vampires had exceptional hearing. "When he drinks blood, he acquires the memories of his meal. Normally, he can purge them from his system, but since the curse, he has been unable to do so. Those memories have been with him for three hundred years. Can you imagine?"

She couldn't stop her jaw from dropping open. "No wonder he walks around like a black cloud hangs over him." There was no way to conceive what it must be like. Part of her gained a new respect for the quiet man.

"Makes me wonder how much longer he can cope." Baal shook his head. "It's a pity, the fucking curse Drayos placed on them." He looked Cassie in the eyes. "Maybe they'll all get lucky and find their mates. I think it will be their only salvation."

She furrowed her brows. "I don't understand. If they are warriors, then why would their gods allow this to happen?"

"Who knows why the gods make the decisions they do. It is what it is, and we are left to deal with the mess. Zarek pulls the interference card, says it's not good for evolution. Bastard!"

"Why are you whispering?"

His brows shot up to his hairline. "Really? I don't want the prick knowing I'm talking about him. He just might show up."

She gave a mental shudder, Zarek didn't sound like anyone she wanted to meet anytime soon. "But, isn't he your god also?" *I'm so confused by these 'gods' they keep referring to.*

"Yes, doll, doesn't mean I have to worship the ground he walks on."

"Oh."

CHAPTER SIXTEEN

MARCUS'S THOUGHTS wandered back to Cassie. He should have stayed away from her but had been weak. The connection between them was stronger than he ever imagined, much stronger than the match with Eliza. He wondered why Zarek decided to choose a human over one of his own kind. He certainly didn't deserve a woman like Cassie and feared he would be overcome by the curse, his soul possessed by pure evil. He'd become nothing more than a blood junkie, taking for the unadulterated pleasure like a heroin addict.

Time passed at a snail's pace, only indicated by Eliza entering the room to torture him with her sexual exploits. So far, he'd been able to put his mind on other matters, keeping his body's reaction to her a non-issue. How much longer he could do that, he didn't know. He prayed for as long as necessary. His skin was now hyper sensitive to touch, and his cock ached for release. The term blue balls held a whole new meaning. Something he wouldn't wish on even his worst enemy.

He scanned the room, looked for anything to aid him in escaping this hell hole. He found nothing. Then there was the hunger, he couldn't remember the last time he had food or blood. His belly ached. Every time Eliza entered the room, he thought of tasting her, in more ways than one. *Maybe I should just mate with her and be done with it.* Part of him felt he owed her. Hell, he did owe her. There was no question about it. However, visions of Cassie would dance through his mind. He wouldn't give up on them.

He tried again to free his wrists from the shackles and failed. There was no escape, weakness plagued him. The door opened, and Eliza entered for another round of pleasure. His fangs dropped at the sight of her, if she got close enough, he'd drain her.

"Marcus, darling. I feel your hunger," she cooed while she climbed on top of him. "We must really do something about that." Her fangs extended and she bit into her wrist, letting droplets of precious blood splatter onto his stomach. "Oh silly me, I am such a klutz. Hmmm, the smell of blood has made me hungry. Maria!"

A young girl appeared in the doorway. He guessed her to be no more than eighteen. She wore a peach-colored bra and matching thong, the color complemented her olive skin. "Yes, my lady?"

"Come closer, Maria."

The girl obeyed and moved toward the bed. Was Eliza actually going to let him feast on the girl? He licked his lips in anticipation. His belly rumbled, begging to be filled. Once Maria stood beside the bed, Eliza reached up and moved the girl's raven locks away from her neck.

"Doesn't she look lovely, Marcus?" Eliza slipped Maria's bra straps past her shoulders and exposed her firm, round breasts. "Maria, I'm hungry."

The girl moved to sit on the edge of the bed, facing Marcus. Eliza caressed the girl's breasts, causing her to moan softly. *Son of a bitch.* She really was going to do this in front of him, again!

"You want her, don't you?"

Yes, yes, he did. In that instant, his cock grew stiff, and his stomach growled. *Shit! Why now?* Why did he become aroused for this young girl and not for Eliza? Damn his body for betraying him.

"Marcus, you are aroused for her." Of course, she would notice, sitting on his lap. Her eyes turned into molten lava as she leaned over and sank her fangs into the girl's neck.

Maria gasped while Eliza drank and continued to massage the girl's breasts. Marcus inhaled the coppery scent, his gaze fixed on the blood that trickled down her neck. The girl continued to moan in pleasure until she screamed out in ecstasy. Eliza should have stopped but didn't, she took deeper pulls.

"Eliza, what the fuck are you doing? Stop!" He fought against his restraints to no avail. He heard Maria's heart slowing, her breaths became shallow. Eliza was killing her. Again, he pulled, tried to focus all his energy on freeing himself. The restraints held. *Helpless, I'm fucking helpless to stop her. Zarek! Where the fuck are you?*

Eliza took one last draw of blood then released Maria to fall into a heap on the floor. He looked at the innocent girl, and his vision glazed over. If he could have reached Eliza at that moment, he would have killed her again. "You bitch! We are guardians, sworn to protect."

She licked the remaining blood from her lips as she moved off of him. "You are a guardian, not I." She walked toward the door and called to someone standing outside. A demon entered, grabbed Maria by the arm, and dragged her from the room. Marcus would kill him too for disrespecting the poor girl.

"What the fuck are you?"

She picked at her red fingernails. "Really, darling, you're so moody." She sighed, her hands dropping to her side. "You chose to be a warrior rather than a husband. You left me to wait rather than bond with me."

He stared at her in disbelief. "I am a warrior, and I thought you were too young. I didn't want to saddle you with a husband and possible children at such a young age."

She sneered. "Thanks to your lack of attention, I gave my heart to another. Yes, I loved Drayos, and I intend to avenge his death. You will suffer for what you did to me." She wrapped her fingers around his chin and squeezed. Her nails bit into his flesh, sending warm liquid running down his chin. "As far as the girl you killed that day? It was Drayos's magic, he used another and made her look like me."

He watched her leave the room, vowing under his breath that one way or another she would pay. He had once loved the woman, but now he was filled with hatred. So much hatred, bile burned his throat. How could someone so innocent turn so ugly? No, she wanted to blame him for what happened, but her heart had been turned black long ago. He knew guilt should plague him. No doubt Drayos turned her against her own people. However, he refused to feel it. He had to find a way to free himself then slaughter her. He thought of Aidyn. The man had suffered enough. How would he react to the knowledge his sister lived? He would be happy beyond belief, but when he learned who she truly was, it would crush him. No, he would kill the bitch before his friend ever learned the truth. Somehow, he had to hide this from his friend.

SETH DECIDED to make camp near a small lake located off the abandoned logging road. Cassie sat on a fallen tree near the water's edge and pulled off the hiking boots. Her feet were tired and aching, so she dipped them into the water. With her face turned up toward the sky she swore there was a hiss when her feet hit the water.

"May I take your backpack for you?"

She jumped, surprised by Seth's soundless approach from behind. So eager to get her boots off, she'd forgotten she even wore a pack. "Thanks. That would be wonderful." She reached for the clip and undid the cinch around her waist. Seth helped pull the pack down her arms and off her. She was in excellent shape, but the day's hiking had worn her out.

He gave her a sidelong glance. "You need to come up by the fire, Cassie. It is not safe down here."

She looked behind her. Baal already had a fire going and stood with a sword perched over his shoulder. Her posture went rigid. Something wasn't right. "What's going on, Seth?"

"Draki passed through here, probably two days ago."

"Is that bad?" *What a stupid question, of course it was.* She was well aware of the possibility a conflict between the vampires and dragons could break out anytime.

"I would rather not cross paths with them." Seth glanced up at the darkening sky as if searching for something. "No doubt if they are in the area, there is a good chance Odage is as well." He leveled his eyes on her. "It is very dangerous here. You need to try and make contact with Marcus tonight."

"Okay." She didn't want to tell him yet. She'd been trying, without success, ever since they arrived. She grabbed her boots and followed Seth to camp. Hungry and tired, her feet tangled beneath her, almost sending her headfirst to the ground. If not for Seth grabbing her arm, she would have done a nosedive in the dirt.

A faint smile crossed her lips. "Thanks. Again."

He tipped his head then escorted her to the fire. She took a seat on her sleeping bag, glad to be on her ass instead of her feet. Upon reaching into her backpack, she pulled out a bottle of water and a chicken pesto MRE. She frowned, hoping the container of food didn't taste like cardboard.

"Where's Baal?" she asked.

Seth looked up from poking the fire. "Hunting."

"I'm probably going to regret this, but what do demons eat exactly?"

He replied in his usual monotone voice. "Raw meat."

She wrinkled her nose. "What about you, did you bring your bag of blood?" She knew he was able to eat food but needed blood to keep his strength.

He stopped poking at the fire but kept his eyes on the ground. "No, it must be fresh. I thought Marcus explained that to you." He must have sensed her fear. "Do not worry. I ate well before we left. I will be good for a week or more."

Cassie gave a sigh of relief. *Thank god.* "So tell me more about the slave trades. How do they capture such powerful demons?" She and Baal had never finished their conversation on the subject, and she was curious about it.

He continued to poke at the fire, never making eye contact with her. "They place a band of silver on them. It weakens them considerably. They are then placed on the auction block for sale."

"So why can't they just remove the silver band?"

"It has magic placed on it. The only one who can remove it is the owner or another Kothar whose magic is powerful." Seth rose and walked over to Cassie. He knelt down beside her and handed her what looked like a bracelet. "This is the silver band. It is our weakness, as well. Keep this safe and use it if needed."

She looked at the bracelet, running her fingers over its polished surface. "What's this mean?" She referred to the scrollwork covering the surface. It looked like some sort of hieroglyphics.

"A Kothar demon made this piece. The scrollwork is the spell cast over it. Once you place this on a vampire's wrist, he or she will not be able to remove it. Only another Kothar can do so."

"What will it do to the vampire if I use it?"

"It will weaken him enough to save your life."

She bit her bottom lip. "I'm confused. Why would a Kothar do something to hurt his own people? And second, why do I need it?"

Seth got up and walked back to his seat. "History has shown people will often sell their own, demons are no different. As for you, we do not know what has happened to Marcus. If he loses to the curse, you may be in danger."

Baal walked back into camp, sat down and stretched his long legs out as he reclined back on a log.

She took in the view through her lashes. His muscular legs were covered with dark jeans. He wore leather biker boots and a black fitted T-shirt. She almost wished she felt something for the handsome demon, but the most she could do was admire his looks. He didn't evoke the feeling of safety and comfort that Marcus did. She flipped back the sleeping bag she sat on and crawled inside. Her eyes slid shut and she tried once more to reach Marcus.

Cassie?

Marcus, is that you? A soft caress touched her cheek.

You must go back, love. It's too dangerous here.

Where are you? Are you hurt?

Do not worry over me, go back. He leaned down and kissed her. Her lips parted, allowing his tongue to dance with hers.

"I've missed you," she moaned.

Si itov wux, my sweetness.

His hands brushed her nipples, she gasped. "I need you. I..."

"Cassie."

What the hell? Marcus was fading. She reached for him and cried out, "No!"

"Cassie."

"What?" she yelled, realizing she was being shaken. She opened her eyes to find Seth bent over her.

"Are you all right? You were talking in your sleep."

Sleep? She'd been sleeping? Then that meant it was only a dream, he didn't actually talk to her or touch her.

"I am sorry, but Aidyn is here to speak with us."

She looked around, tried to get her bearings. Still in her sleeping bag and the fire now cold. The sun peeked out over the horizon. Seth, Baal, and Aidyn stood looking at her. She dropped her face into her hands. *Oh god, how much did they hear?* She had to be blushing but crawled out of her sleeping bag, grabbed a change of clothes, her toiletry bag and a towel then headed toward the lake. She wanted nothing more than to drown herself and avoid any embarrassing questions. For now, she'd settle with cleaning up and brushing her teeth.

Sensing someone behind her, she stopped in her tracks and whirled around to find Baal following her. Placing a hand on her hip, she glared at him. "Why are you following me?"

He threw up his hands in surrender. "Sheesh, a little grouchy in the morning, are we?"

Guilt shook her. She hadn't meant to be such a snit, but her head still reeled from earlier. "Sorry, I just need some alone time."

He smiled. "I understand. I'll have some coffee ready, how would that be?"

"I would love some, thanks. I won't be long." She hurried the rest of the way to the lake, making sure she was out of view before pulling off her clothes. After the dream she'd had, an ice-cold dip was exactly what she needed. She was still unsure of what had happened. It had seemed so real. She would swear Marcus had been there with her. *I really am losing my mind.*

She dove in, letting the cool water caress her heated body. She contemplated staying under but knew there was no use in hiding. With a sigh, she swam back to shore, and grabbing some shampoo, she quickly washed her hair. Maybe being clean would help her sense of humor. After toweling off, she dressed then brushed her teeth. Her stomach growled, reminding her she was hungry, so she gathered her things and headed back to camp. The aroma of rich coffee made her mouth water. Baal greeted her with a smile and a steaming cup.

She smiled back at him. "Thanks, and sorry for being a grouch."

His eyes twinkled. "No worries, doll. I'd be a little testy too if I had to leave such a wet dream."

Her jaw dropped. "Is nothing sacred around you people?" she whispered, hoping Aidyn and Seth wouldn't hear. They seemed to be caught up in their own conversation anyway.

"Not really, but you'll get used to it. You need to practice putting up those mental blocks."

She scrunched her brows. "I would have thought to be safe in my sleep."

"Cassie."

She turned toward Aidyn's voice, making a mental note to continue this conversation with Baal at a later time. "Aidyn, why do I feel like you're here to bring bad news?"

He tilted his head. "You are very astute, little one. I'm afraid the dragons have declared war on us. We must get you to safety."

"I don't understand. You want me to leave?"

"Yes, Cassie, it's not safe for you to be here. If you are found here with us, it could mean your death."

"But what about Marcus? I thought I was here to find him." Panic started in the pit of her stomach and moved up to the back of her throat. She had to find him. She could not leave him.

"You are now my first concern." He lowered his eyes. "I promised him."

"No! You can't do that to him. I refuse to go. I want to continue the search."

Aidyn crossed his arms over his chest. "You have no choice. You will be taken through the gateway as soon as you're packed up."

Tears welled up in her eyes. How could he give up on his friend so quickly? She would not. "You can send me home, but you can't stop me from coming back here and searching on my own. I will come back here, I promise you that."

His features softened. "I see you have finally come to your senses. Very well, I will give you three more days, but that is all. I can't spare any more warriors to guard you, and I need these two back at home. Good luck. I, more than anyone, hope you find him."

A gateway opened behind Aidyn, he turned to Seth. "Remember, three days. I don't care if you have to bring her back kicking and screaming."

"Yes, my lord," Seth replied.

Aidyn walked through the gateway, leaving them there to stare at the space where he'd once stood. Cassie had three days to find Marcus. Panic caused her mouth to dry out, and she threw up her coffee. *What the hell is wrong with me?* A flush crept across her cheeks, and sweat beaded on her brow.

"Cassie, are you all right?" Seth asked, touching the back of her neck.

"It's just nerves. I'll be fine...really." She walked to where her belongings were and started to pack. "We should get going. Three days isn't much time."

CHAPTER SEVENTEEN

MARCUS OPENED HIS EYES. The raging hard on pressing against his jeans nearly cut off his circulation. He searched the room and discovered he was alone. *Thank gods.* He steadied his breaths and tried to calm his body. Somehow, he'd managed to connect with Cassie, stepped into her dreams.

Dream-walking, something he'd only heard of but had never done. Hell, he wasn't even sure how he'd accomplished it. He sensed her nearby, maybe proximity held the key. He'd tried on several occasions since being captured to link with his brethren and Cassie, but the silver bands blocked him. Fear wrapped around him like a ten-foot python, squeezing the life from its prey. He warned her to go back. If Eliza found her, Cassie would be killed. If Cassie died, he'd be the one to start Armageddon and not Odage. There would be no stopping him. He would turn this world to ash. *If you can hear me, sweetheart, run! I can't help you now.*

Voices echoed from the hall. Great, Eliza stood outside the door. Would she kill another innocent? *I swear to the gods I will kill you for good.* No longer did he regret taking her life three hundred years ago.

The only regret he had now was not knowing he'd slain the wrong woman.

"Marcus, darling. I have a treat for you, a dear friend I want you to meet. Oh wait...you already know each other. Silly me." Eliza gave a wave of her wrist then stepped aside. Behind her, a large, hulking Draki marched into the room.

Odage.

He tugged on his restraints, and blood ran down his wrists where he opened old wounds. "Eliza, that bastard killed your mother!"

She turned to Odage with a raised brow. "Really?" She clapped her hands together. "I'm sure the bitch deserved it."

Who the fuck is this woman? He couldn't believe she would act this way. She'd loved her mother. Somehow, Eliza had become infected. It was the only explanation he could come up with.

Odage walked to the side of the bed. "How nice, Eliza has you all wrapped up for me." He waved his hand and four Draki moved forward. Eliza stepped up with the key for the lock.

"Wait. Before you move him, we might need this." She slapped a silver band on each ankle. What little strength he had melted away. He was screwed in a big way. Eliza removed the chains, and then each Draki grabbed a limb. He wanted to fight, but darkness fogged his eyes.

CASSIE WAS anxious to renew the search for Marcus. The sun shone bright across a clear blue sky, indicating another warm day. She found the August weather in Romania enjoyable. Seventy-five degrees, the perfect temperature compared to the scorching nineties back home.

Seth and Baal approached her with their packs already loaded up. Baal reached down and picked up her backpack. "Here, let me help you with this."

"Thanks." She smiled, sticking her arms through the straps then hooking the belt around her waist. "So where are we headed?"

Baal gave a nod toward the mountains. "Up there. There's a lot of caves, and it's a good place to start."

She pulled her hair back into a ponytail and donned a ball cap. Her gaze followed Baal's. The mountains looked like they were miles away, and they only had three days. Biting her bottom lip, she said, "I hope we're not walking."

He gave a devilish grin. "I'm going to flash us there."

"Why can't Seth flash himself?"

This time Seth spoke up. "If there are any dragons around, they will sense my power and know we are here. They will not think much of the energy used for the demon to flash."

"I guess that makes sense. Okay then, let's get this over with."

"Since we know this location is safe, I'll take Seth first so we can make sure it's secure up there. I'll be back in a flash." Baal snorted. "I'll be back in a flash, get it?"

She rolled her eyes. "I get it. You should be on Comedy Central...really."

Baal grabbed Seth's arm, and they both vanished. Before Cassie could gather another thought, he returned.

She touched her chest. "Crap! You scared the hell out of me."

Baal shrugged. "Sorry, doll, next time I'll wear a bell." He linked his arm through hers. "Ready?"

"Yes." Ready to find Marcus and get this trip from hell over with.

Her head spun. It seemed flashing wasn't any better than the gateway, but at least she seemed to be getting better at it. Seth stepped in behind her.

"Cassie, I think you should rest for a bit." He scanned the sky. "Dragons have been here. I am going to take a look around." He looked at Baal. "Stay here with her."

She watched Seth walk off. *I'm such a burden.* She held back the team with her weakness.

"Can I get you anything?" Baal asked.

"Some water please." She sat on a large boulder and looked out over the forest below. Even though her stomach rolled like she'd stepped off a roller coaster, she was grateful they didn't have to hike it.

He reached into her pack, pulled out a bottle of water, opened it and held it out to her, before taking a seat next to her. He reached into his own pack and pulled out a chunk of jerky.

"Want some?"

She looked at the offending piece of shriveled up meat and wrinkled her nose. "No, thanks."

"Suit yourself." He bit down and ripped a huge hunk from his snack.

Cassie chewed her bottom lip. "Tell me, do you happen to know what *si itov wux* means?"

He stopped mid-bite and pierced her with his gaze. "It's a very old language. Draconic, not many speak it anymore. Is that what Marcus said to you in your dream?"

Heat rose up her neck to her cheeks. She picked at some gravel and prayed like hell he hadn't whispered some dirty love talk. "Yes."

He reached out and touched her arm, she looked back at him. "*Si itov wux* means I love you."

She closed her eyes. It meant nothing really. Her imagination conjured up some erotic fantasy because she did not want to love him. Did she want him to love her? Yeah, a part of her did. A tear slid down her cheek, and Baal reached up with his finger and wiped it away.

"Don't worry, doll, he'll be fine."

She stood and turned her back to Baal. "It was only a stupid dream anyway. It wasn't real."

"No, it was real."

She spun around. "What do you mean?"

"Immortals can dream-walk, although those that usually do are what you call nightmares. Somehow, he managed to find you in your dream state." He scratched his chin. "His connection to you must be very strong."

Life got weirder by the minute. Dream-walking vampires? What next? She shuddered to think about it. "Someone needs to wake me up from this dream. None of this can be real."

He threw back his head and laughed. "Doll, it doesn't get more real than this."

She glared daggers at him. This wasn't funny. As a matter of fact, she decided when she got back home she would pay a visit to Dr. Story and beg him to put her in a straitjacket.

Baal shifted. "Oh shit!"

Cassie rushed to his side and caught a view of Seth, his sword drawn. "Now what the hell?"

"I felt it too. Did you happen to get a look at them?" Baal asked as he reached for his weapon. He looked at Cassie. "Grab your knife, use it only if you have to. Remember, go for the heart."

Her heart beat against her chest. The first thought that came to mind was the dragons had found them. Next thing she knew, three men flashed in front of them, but it was what flashed in next that made her stomach hit the ground.

MARCUS WOKE and peered through slits. He tried to pull up his memories of what had happened while he worked to force his eyes open. Damn, last thing he recalled was Odage and four Draki grabbing hold of him. He'd been overcome by darkness but remembered being dragged across some rocks. His entire back stung from the gaping holes, gravel now imbedded into his skin. Blood trickled down the side of his cheek from the gash on his head. It didn't take long to realize he was in deep shit. His wrists and legs bore silver bands thanks to Eliza.

While his legs were free, both wrists had a shackle that connected to a chain. When he looked up, he saw the chain ran through a ring embedded into the rocks. They'd given him only enough slack to stand with his arms over his head. *Just fucking great*. At least he could lean against the wall. He was in another cave, but where, he had no clue. Still trying to shake the cobwebs from his head, he sensed someone approaching. Unable to tell who, or what they were, he quietly waited, pretending to be asleep.

"Toss the bucket of ice water on him."

His muscles constricted when the freezing water hit him square in the face and chest. He trembled, unable to regulate his body temperature. He forced his burning eyes open, and tried to focus on the image in front of him. When the fuzziness started to fade, he was greeted with a clear view of his enemy.

"Ah, I see you have finally decided to join us," Odage said. "Tell me, did you really think you could outsmart me?"

Marcus spit in Odage's face. "Fuck you."

One of the guards approached and pulled out a *dirise*, an ancient whip, with twenty-one wing-shaped, stainless steel blades that snaked into a wire-wrapped handle. It totaled forty-two inches of pure hell. He swallowed hard and braced himself for what was to come.

The first lash snaked across his bare chest, causing his fangs to pierce his lip. The second, tore across his already sliced up back. Searing pain radiated throughout his body, and blood dripped from dozens of wounds. He gritted his teeth but refused to cry out. Odage would gain no satisfaction from him.

Odage's nostrils flared when he spoke. "You will address me as my liege."

Marcus coughed, his throat raw. "When hell freezes over."

A female voice caressed his skin. "Still stubborn as ever," Eliza said.

Odage threw his head back and laughed. "Hell has only begun for you, vampire. I sense the curse on your soul growing. Soon you will be as evil as I am, but before you turn completely, I will give you one little gift. I will capture your mate and bring her here to you. Then, you can watch as I fuck her."

Eliza jumped and clapped her hands. "Yes, and when he is done, I will drain her. You can watch her die, just like you watched me die." Bitterness dripped from her voice. "Only this time, your little bitch won't be coming back."

He struggled against his restraints. Darkness coiled in his body like a snake ready to strike. He would do just as Odage said. He would become the evil he feared, but he would take immense pleasure from physically ripping both of their heads from their bodies.

"LEAVE HIM FOR NOW," Odage commanded as he headed out of the room with Eliza by his side. "Things couldn't be better. Caleb has arrived, and the dragons have declared war on the vampires."

Eliza gave a nod of satisfaction. "What about the amulet? Your lord and master is getting impatient."

"I have Oroumea looking for it as we speak."

"Ah yes, your new bride. Wise choice bonding with a memory ghoul. I only hope for your sake she finds it soon."

"My liege!"

Odage turned to find Lileta running toward him. "What is it, my pet?"

"The female has gone into labor."

A smile curled across his lips. "Excellent, take me to her." Odage and Eliza followed the slave down the corridor. Screams echoed through the room. Veronica was strapped down to a bed. Two nurses moved around her while the doctor performed his exam.

"How much longer?" Odage asked.

The doctor looked up. "The babe is ready, everything looks good, my liege."

"Excellent." He moved closer so he could view the birth of his first-born son. He looked at Veronica, fear swam in her eyes as she screamed out in pain.

"Are you going to sedate her?" Eliza asked.

"No. I want her to feel the pain of this birth," he spat.

Eliza shuddered. "Even I wouldn't be so cruel. You will pardon me if I decline tonight's entertainment." She turned and left the room.

Odage watched as the first claw poked its way through Veronica's belly. "Gag her, this bellowing is giving me a headache."

The nurse complied and stuffed a cloth in Veronica's mouth. The claw disappeared, and the screaming stopped. Odage looked at the woman, now passed out. *Bitch gets her wish after all.* She would be dead in a matter of seconds and now would never experience it. No matter, his son would soon be entering the world.

The claw pushed back through.

"Yes, that's it. Come out, my son."

A second claw pushed in next to the first and in one swift motion sliced the entire belly open. The doctor moved in to remove the child and cut the cord while the nurses cleaned the babe. Seconds later, Odage heard the most beautiful sound, the wailing of his son.

The nurse turned to Odage and handed him the babe. "My liege, your son is perfect."

He cradled the babe. Sapphire eyes stared back at him. "My son, you and I shall rule the world together. I shall call you Erebos after the primeval god of darkness." The babe smiled at him as if understanding and liking his new name. Odage bit his wrist and held it to the babe's mouth, giving him his first taste of life. Soon, he would be able to eat raw meat, but until that time, Odage would feed and care for his son, trusting no one else to raise his child.

When Erebos had enough blood, he pulled his lips away and smiled at his father. Odage looked at the nurses who were still cleaning up. "Toss her body outside, the local wildlife will make a quick meal of her." He headed out of the room and made his way through the narrow tunnels, moving upward in the maze of rooms.

Once he reached the upper level, he called out, "Roman!"

"Yes, my liege?"

"Where is Caleb?"

"I believe he and a few of your men are out conducting a search of the area."

"Ah good. When he returns, send him to me. I want to introduce the men to my heir."

Roman gave a bow. "As you wish, my liege."

CHAPTER EIGHTEEN

CASSIE COULDN'T SPEAK. Cold sweat trickled down the back of her neck. *What the hell is that?*

The creature stood over seven feet tall. Its muscular legs narrowed to clawed pads, like those of a canine. Its chest protruded, revealing a bony ribcage, and its shoulders tapered into long fingers tipped with pointed nails that dragged the ground. A second pair of grotesque arms jutted from underneath the first set. Shorter in length, but just as menacing. Red almond-shaped eyes stared at her from a large pointed skull, and its mouth, full of razor-sharp teeth, glistened in the noonday sun.

The creature's jet-black skin, slick with moisture, made her want to vomit. Memories of earlier thoughts came back to haunt her. She recalled how nothing would surprise her after meeting vampires and demons. *If I weren't so fucking scared, I'd laugh.*

"Wendigo," Seth whispered.

Is that the name of the man in charge? Her eyes bored into Seth as if he would hear her mental question.

The one who appeared to be the leader stepped forward. "I want the demon."

Seth bared his fangs. "You will need to shop elsewhere for your next slave. This demon is mine."

The man shifted his weight. "Since when do vampires keep slaves? I see no binding ring on his wrist. Therefore, he is mine to take. Look around vampire, you're outnumbered."

Her throat burned. *So these are slave traders?* From the looks of it, they were indeed outnumbered. The beast alone could overtake them. *How the hell are we going to get out of this mess?* She dug her nails into her arm. Nope, her eyes were open, and this was a living nightmare.

"Leave the vampire and the girl, and I will go with you, peaceful-ly," Baal said.

The man scrunched his face, deep in thought. "I don't know. The girl could prove to be a real good time." The other two men laughed and elbowed each other. "She might make a nice addition to our harem."

She forced back tears, couldn't even begin to imagine the terror they would inflict upon her. *What the hell was I thinking when I volunteered to come out here?* She should have listened to Aidyn and left this morning. *Maybe Seth has called for backup.* Her gaze shifted, hoping for a friendly face. They were alone.

"No deal, Diablo. The girl and vampire unharmed." Baal cast an evil grin. "Besides, she is Zarek's mistress. I doubt even you wish to piss off the god."

Seth looked at Baal. "He speaks the truth, she is a gift to my king. I am responsible for making sure she reaches her destination."

Wait. What? This must be some type of ploy, a trick to buy them time.

The man nodded his head. "I don't want to deal with either of them." He narrowed his eyes at Baal. "But you, they will not miss. Drop your weapons." He motioned the beast to step in front of Seth. "If he as much as flinches, kill him."

The creature moved in front of Seth in one step. Its obsidian-colored body towered over him, and saliva dripped at his feet. Cassie noted Seth's discomfort at having that thing so close, it matched her own.

Baal dropped his weapons. *No!* Her heart ached. What would they do to him? She'd grown fond of the demon, so much so, she would call him friend. He sacrificed in order to save them. Tears rolled down her cheeks.

One of the men moved forward and placed a silver band around Baal's wrist. His shoulders sagged, the vibrant life she knew sucked from his body. He turned to her and gave a wink.

"Don't fret, doll. I've survived worse." The other two men each grabbed an arm, and all three flashed away. The only ones left were the ring leader and the beast.

Bumps rose on her body, and dread coursed over her. Would the man go back on his word to Baal? He spoke something she didn't understand to the beast then vanished. Seth swung his sword, but the creature flicked its wrist, flinging the weapon like a tinker toy. It reached out with both hands and sank its claws into Seth's chest, making a slice from his ribs all the way to his groin. The sound of tearing flesh and breaking bones rang in her ears.

"You will not follow us," the raspy voice spoke.

A scream escaped her throat when Seth hit the ground and the beast vanished. She ran to him, sure he was dead. "Oh god, Seth!" His eyes focused on her, he opened his mouth, but no sound came out.

Frantic, she ripped off her T-shirt. "Can you heal from something like this?" Knowing the vampires to be excellent healers, she still doubted even they could regenerate from this. His entire chest and abdomen lay open, his insides exposed.

"I-I can, but I am too weak to open a gateway to get you home."

"Then we'll wait. How long will it take?"

"We have no time." Her gaze followed his toward the sky.

"Holy shit! Are those what I think?" They circled high above like vultures waiting for their prey to die. "What the fuck else can go wrong today?" Seriously pissed, she worked faster at covering his wounds, careful to make sure she bound him tight enough to keep his insides from spilling out.

"What do we do? We can't just sit here and wait for them to come and kill us. I'm in no mood to die today."

Seth coughed, and blood trickled down his chin. "You must slip away. If you get away from me, they may not find you. Hide in the forest until Aidyn comes for you. It is your only hope."

"No! I will not leave you here to be murdered."

"Cassie, your destiny is to save Marcus, not die here with me. Now go!"

As if to bring the point home, a ball of fire exploded a few feet away. She looked up, the dragons circled closer. Their gargantuan bodies blocked the sun, causing shadows to blanket over her. *Think! There has to be a way out.*

She looked back at Seth. "If you feed, will you have enough strength to get us out of here?"

He looked at her, perplexed. "Perhaps, but I will not ask you to sacrifice."

She glared at him. *Stupid vampire.* "Why not? It's my choice to make." She offered her wrist.

"Remember, I will take your memories."

She pulled back. "You mean I will forget everything?"

His body was racked by a coughing fit, precious blood spewed from his mouth. She gently placed a hand behind his back and propped him up so he wouldn't gag.

When his body finally calmed, he whispered, "No, but I will know everything about you. Every intimate detail."

She knew what he tried to say. Her darkest secrets would become his. Every detail of those precious moments spent with Marcus would be shared. She wanted to blush, but their lives were in danger.

"Promise you'll never reveal them?"

He gave her a droll look. "I never drink and tell."

"What? Now you get a sense of humor?" She was unsure if she should laugh or cry when two large fireballs exploded next to her.

Rocks tumbled down the side of the mountain. The dragons drew closer. *Hell!* Once again, she offered her wrist. "Take it or we both die," she yelled.

Still he refused. "I will have to take you close to death in order to gain enough strength. Even then, I am not sure it will be enough. If I fail, you will die."

Fine, he would learn just how stubborn she could be. Another fireball hit too close for comfort, this one rattled her teeth. She drew her knife from its sheath and with a clean swipe, slit her wrist. She then grabbed Seth by the back of the head and forced his lips to her wrist. "We're both going to die for sure if you don't drink."

Fireballs crashed, starting an avalanche. Sweat trickled between her breasts from the intense heat surrounding them. Seth continued to drink while she prayed it would be enough. Her body betrayed her as the orgasm built, then her vision blurred, she closed her eyes and thought of Marcus, wondering if she would ever see him again. *I'm so sorry I failed you.* It was in that moment of darkness that she realized she loved him.

MARCUS PASSED out from the pain and loss of blood. Odage had come back a second time and commanded his servants beat him again. This time, his legs and feet bore wounds from the *dirise*. His left eye was swollen shut, and his lips were cracked from where they repeatedly punched him. Every inch of his body was cut and bleeding. He hurt like hell.

He opened his one good eye and tried to focus, but his vision was fuzzy at best. Still chained, any strength he had was terminated by the silver bands. He could hardly keep his head up. Someone whispered his name. He jerked, and his eyes rolled from side to side trying to see who entered the room. There was no one, the only company he had was his chaotic mind and the pool of blood spreading under his feet. Panic latched onto his spine and crawled like a black widow and then, recognition. He recognized his mate's orgasm.

What the fuck!

It was quickly followed by her slowing heartbeat. She was in trouble. Her life force slipping away. *Cassie! Love, what's happening?*

No response.

He viewed darkness, and her mind calmed. They were killing her. Had Odage gotten to her? No, he would have carried out his promise. Brought her here for him to witness her rape and death. Then who?

Aidyn, you promised me! Was his king dead as well? Aidyn would die protecting Cassie, he knew that. *Am I the only one left?*

A faint heartbeat. *She still lives.*

He bellowed at the top of his lungs. "Zarek, you fucking bastard. If she dies, I will kill you myself!" He twisted and fought his restraints. Spittle ran down his chin, he hissed in anger. He was worthless as a guardian, deserved the beating Odage gave him.

Silence, deafening silence.

She's dead. Tears slid down his face and mingled with the blood at his feet.

"Odage, you prick, come show me what you've got." Marcus yelled out, hoping to bring him back for more.

His wish granted, Odage appeared in the doorway. "Vampire, you look like hell. What is it you wish?"

"Come on, you bastard, kill me."

He stepped closer. "Tsk, tsk, now why rush things when I'm having so much fun?"

He spat at Odage. "You're a fucking loser. You send in your lackeys, why don't you finish the job yourself?"

Odage picked up a bat that had been sitting by the door. "You like pain, vampire? I will give you what you ask for only because it pleases me to do so." He swung, hitting Marcus in the chin, the sound of breaking bones filled the room. Another swing hit him in the chest, breaking every rib on his left side. Marcus grinned, he wanted more pain. Anything to make him forget Cassie.

"You're a fucking wimp, Odage." The words barely audible from the swelling of his face.

Odage took another swing, cracking Marcus in the head. The final blow knocked him out.

BRIGHT LIGHT SHINED in Cassie's face and brushed warmth over her tired, cold body. She wanted to move toward it, but something stopped her. When she finally opened her eyes, everything looked blurry. She tried to sit up, but her head throbbed. *Ouch!*

"Lie still." A soothing voice sang. She'd heard that voice before but couldn't place where. She searched her mind, looking for the last memory she had. Fireballs, something about fire and dragons? Impossible, dragons were a myth. Oh wait, her mind moved back to someone sucking on her wrist. She wrinkled her nose in disgust. Forcing her lids to part, she decided it was safe to open her eyes all the way. Gwen stood looking down at her, her brown eyes filled with compassion.

"Cassie, I'm going to help you sit up." She slipped her arm under Cassie's back and helped Cassie ease into a sitting position. Grabbing a couple of pillows, Gwen then propped them behind her for added comfort. Next, came a cup of tea.

"Here, drink this herbal tea. It will help with your headache."

"Thank you." She sipped the warm liquid, and a hint of lemon danced on her tongue. Cassie looked around the room. The walls were colored a pale green and low light filtered through the window. Peace surrounded her like a blanket and made her feel at home. "What happened?"

Gwen took a seat on the edge of the bed. "We almost lost you. As a matter of fact, your heart stopped for a brief moment. Luckily, Seth gained enough strength to get you both to the forest where he opened a gateway and called for help. Any later and we would have lost both of you."

It all came flooding back to her now. She looked down at the bandage wrapped around her wrist. Visions of Seth nearly gutted like some animal haunted her. "Is Seth all right?" She actually liked the quiet vampire.

"Yes, it will be a few days before he heals completely, but he will be fine."

Her mind raced, wanted to know how they had brought her back from the brink of death. She would have needed blood, lots of it. She didn't feel any different but then again, what did it feel like to be a vampire? She would have asked, but there was a knock on the door and Gwen excused herself.

Voices moved closer and she recognized the male voice before he entered the room. A smile broke across her lips as Seth's large frame shadowed the doorway. "Can I come in?"

"Of course, you can." She observed the dark circles under his eyes, his color pale. He also walked slightly hunched over. She waited for him to take a seat in the chair next to the bed. "How are you? Gwen said you were healing, but you must still be in pain."

He nodded. "I am healing slowly. That damn Wendigo nearly gutted me."

"Is that what that was? God, I hope I never see one of those again." She shivered at the mere thought of the vile beast and how easily it had nearly sliced Seth in two.

"You look well, Cassie."

Sure, he was being polite. She moved to smooth her hair, it was a rat's nest. "Thanks, I feel pretty good. Which brings me to the question of..."

Seth held up a hand. "Yes, it was human blood we used."

A breath escaped. She wouldn't be sporting fangs anytime soon. But something else nagged at her. Her memories. "Seth, about my memories," she hesitated, trying to find the right words.

He looked into her eyes. "Never be ashamed, it was not your

fault," his voice more authoritative, no longer the tight-lipped vampire. "Should you choose to mate with Marcus, your ability to have children will be corrected." His features softened. "His loss will be our gain. Besides, even if you remained barren, Marcus would love you anyway."

"Thank you." She brushed away a tear.

"Now, besides coming to see how you were doing, I also wanted to thank you. You saved my life, and I will be forever in your debt."

Relieved for the change in subject, she answered, "I think we saved each other. I have never been gladder to be in a vampire's home than right now." She picked at the quilt, her nerves frayed. "I'm still worried about Marcus. Do you think we've lost him?"

"Cassie, I promise you I will continue my search for him. I will not stop until I find him."

She gave a weak smile. "Thank you, Seth." She believed he would too. After everything they'd been through, a bond grew between them. She looked at him like the brother she never had. *I hope you find him alive.*

"What about Baal?" Her worry for him was as real as the worry she carried for Marcus. The man had surrendered himself in order to save Seth and her.

"Baal is much stronger than you realize. He has always hoped to be captured. Maybe now he will find his sister."

It was hard to swallow this whole nightmare. She'd grown fond of Baal. Hell, who was she kidding? After getting to know many of the vampires here, they felt like family to her. Family...she missed Jill and needed her sister right then. Perhaps she could go home for a visit.

CHAPTER NINETEEN

HUMAN. The scent of human blood saturated his nostrils. His brain told him to scan the area for prey. Marcus obeyed and snapped his eyes open. His vision adjusted to the dim room instantly and found he was still chained to the wall. Every muscle throbbed, and several bones were broken. He needed blood to speed the healing.

A shadow moved in the corner. "Who's there?" His throat felt raw, like he'd swallowed a thousand razor blades.

Two women moved into view. He sensed one to be a Kothar demon and the other a human. The demon moved toward him, her raven hair pulled back into a braid that fell to her waist. As with all Kothar, her beauty took his breath away.

"My name is Lileta, I am sister to Baal."

Shit, Marcus had not seen her since she was a small child. Now a grown woman, she had gone missing as a teen, and Baal had been searching for her. "Lileta," he whispered. "What are you doing here?"

"I am Odage's slave." She pulled the human closer. "I am here to help you. This is Beth, and she is one of Odage's prisoners. She has agreed to help by feeding you, but we must hurry before we are missed."

Beth stepped forward and pushed her wrist to Marcus's lips. Sweet deity, she smelled of heaven. He flicked out his tongue and licked parched lips, his fangs extended. He brushed his tongue along her vein once, twice, then sank his fangs deep. He moaned as the sweet nectar of the gods ran across his tongue. The first swallow started the healing of his smaller wounds and his headache eased. He wouldn't be able to take enough to heal completely, but this would be a start. He took three more long pulls then closed the wound. He stopped before Beth reached her climax, they didn't need her screaming her pleasure up and down the halls.

"Thank you."

"I will come back as soon as I can, but I can't promise when that will be," Lileta said. "Please tell Baal where to find me when you get free from here."

"I will, and we will free you. You and Beth."

"There are other humans and slaves too, you must free us all," she replied, closing the door behind her.

He smiled for the first time in weeks. He had an ally in this hell hole and now stood a chance of escaping. The smile faded, his head tipped. *What is this I feel? Can it be?* It was the heartbeat of his mate. Cassie lived. His determination for escape renewed with an intense vigor.

AFTER SETH LEFT, Cassie made her way to the living room. Gwen sat in an overstuffed chair flipping through a Vogue magazine. She was the type of woman who made others green with envy. Chocolate tresses were pulled back into a ponytail that fell to her mid-back. A pair of slim-fitting jeans and a yellow tank top covered her sun-kissed skin. The woman held inner beauty as well, her kindness and generosity were something Cassie had seen in few people.

"Somehow, I didn't expect to find you reading Vogue," Cassie said.

Gwen tossed the magazine to the table. "I'm glad to see you're feeling better. Aidyn asked to see you when you were well enough."

Good, she wanted to see him as well. But first things first. "Gwen, I understand you have the ability to see the future? Tell me, is Marcus still alive?"

Gwen hesitated before answering, which caused Cassie's nerves to frazzle. "I can, but I don't have control over my gift, which really ticks me off. I haven't seen his death, but then again, I haven't seen much lately. My heart tells me he is still alive. We will find him, Cassie." Gwen reached out and gave her a hug. "Are you ready to see the king?"

"Can we walk, though? I feel the need to stretch my legs."

"Of course, it's a nice walk from here, and it's pleasant out." Gwen led the way out the front door. "We'll walk along the beach."

Cassie gasped when she stepped outside. In front of her, waves of aquamarine splashed against a diamond-studded beach. The most surreal sight she had ever laid eyes on.

"It's beautiful, isn't it?" Gwen scooped up a handful of sand and let it sift through her fingers.

"Beyond words. I've never seen anything like it. Is it safe to swim in?" She bit her bottom lip, imagining all kinds of weird creatures that might swim in a vampire ocean.

Gwen let out a chuckle. "Of course. The sea life is no different from your own, really. It's called the Lejir Sea. It means Blood Sea in our language."

Cassie wrinkled her nose. "The name doesn't make it sound very safe."

"No, I guess not." Gwen gave a sigh. "Marcus wanted to be the one to show you the beauty of his home. I wish he were here in my place."

Me too.

They continued their walk along the beach. Cassie removed her shoes, wanting the sand between her toes. The sensation more like silk, nothing like the gritty stuff back home. She hoped Gwen's feelings were right and Marcus was still alive. After walking a few minutes, she noticed a rocky bluff that emerged on her left. Looking up, her gaze caught a large home located on its peak. White, with a clay roof and several levels, reminiscent of the stone homes she had seen in Greece. "Whose house is that?"

"That would be the king's," Gwen answered.

"Duh, I guess that should've been obvious by its size. How do we get up there?" She'd been in the home before but had been flashed inside, never seeing the full beauty from the outside.

Gwen arched a brow. "We take the stairs."

They had stopped in front of a set of stairs carved into the rock. She looked up, her mouth gaping. "Holy shit." She then looked at Gwen. "Come to think of it, why do you have stairs?"

Gwen gave her a curious look. "We like to walk. We only flash when necessary. Besides, the children don't have the power to flash until they are older."

"You have children?"

A forlorn expression covered Gwen's features. "There was a time when children's laughter could be heard all throughout Vandeldor. Both vampire and Draki. Today, there are only a few children because of the lack of females."

"I'm so sorry." Somehow, her apology didn't seem like enough. She shared the emptiness they all felt. "I guess we had better head up."

She lost count of the number of steps after fifty or so. When they finally reached the top, she turned in a circle, taking in the landscape. The view made her head reel. The ocean with its glistening beach to her left and mountains framed by lush green forest behind her. Understanding struck. This was the reason vampires chose to stay here more than in her world. The place held a magical, peaceful feel.

They crossed a patio and entered the house through elegant French doors. Cassie found herself stepping into a large room with polished stone floors and colorful Asian rugs that were laid out like artwork. Two overstuffed, burnished leather couches sat in front of a massive fireplace and beckoned her to curl up with a good book.

Her gaze was immediately drawn to the painting over the fireplace. A handsome man who looked much like Aidyn sat in a relaxed posture on a large thrown. The most beautiful woman Cassie had ever laid eyes on sat in his lap. Her golden hair piled gracefully on top of her head. Curls escaped around her porcelain face, and eyes the color of the sea stared back at her. The man's arms lovingly embraced her.

"I see you're admiring my parents."

She spun to find Aidyn standing directly behind her. She swore she saw moisture in his eyes. Pain knifed through her at the loss he still experienced. She'd been told he'd lost his mother a few months ago and was now the only living member of his family. The burden he carried weighed heavy on his shoulders. Her sixth sense was a curse. She didn't want to know things about people. It just happened.

When he spoke again, his voice commanded attention. "Gwen, I will ask you to leave us."

Gwen bowed. "Of course, my lord."

Aidyn directed Cassie to take a seat. "Can I get you something to drink?"

"No, thank you, I'm fine." She sank into the couch. Aidyn took a seat across from her, one arm slung over the back of the couch. She still wasn't used to the power that rolled off him. It was so thick in the room she swore she could reach out and touch it.

She watched as Aidyn inhaled deeply then tilted his head, his brows knitted together. "Cassie, you are with child."

Her mouth dropped open, her voice momentarily lost. "W-what?"

He leaned forward. "I didn't mean to spring it on you like that, but yes, I can sense the babe."

"How? I mean I know how, but it's impossible." She rubbed her hands over her face and mentally counted backward. It had only been three weeks since the last time they'd been together.

"Not possible, I mean I can't get pregnant."

"Apparently, you can and have."

"What do I do now? I can't have a half vampire baby in a normal hospital. How do I explain this?" Her eyes filled with tears. "Oh god, will the baby be all right? I mean, seeing how I'm human." She jumped up and began to pace, whirled around. "Are you sure? I mean Gwen said nothing. Wouldn't she know?"

He tapped his index finger on his knee, patiently waiting for her tirade to end. "Are you finished? Good. Now, where to start? Gwen would only know this if she had seen the vision, which obviously, she has not. As I said, I can sense the babe. You forget I am the most powerful man here. As for the rest..." He let out a sigh. "I am not sure how the child will grow and survive with a human mother. It has never been done before." He got up and crossed the room to where Cassie paced and grabbed her by the shoulders. "I will find the answers, I swear. Seth has already begun his search again for Marcus."

She threw her arms around Aidyn and sobbed. He held her tight, gently stroking her hair. "Shhh, I understand you're frightened, and I wish it were Marcus here instead of me. However, I promise I will take care of you. We will all take care of you."

She pulled back and looked up at the tall vampire king. No wonder he was chosen to lead his people. "You are also the most arrogant man here," she snorted, then her face turned serious. "Thank you, I know I can trust you." Her heart told her things would change forever. She would have to leave everything behind and start a new life, with or without Marcus.

"So, what next?" she asked.

After a long discussion, Cassie sat in a chair, her mind a flurry of thoughts. Aidyn had sent her home, giving her two days to get her life in order before he came back for her. She would quit her job. What else could she do? No one knew how this pregnancy would progress or what strange things might occur. She'd taken three at-home pregnancy tests, unable to believe what Aidyn had told her. This wasn't supposed to happen, and yet a guardian and three tests said it had. She now carried the child of a warrior of a god.

She was alone and terrified. What did it all mean? This miracle was bigger than all of them. She just wasn't sure how she fit into this picture. She caressed her stomach. "Well, pumpkin, it's you and me for now. Your mama is a dumb ass and sent daddy away."

The front door flung open, and Jill hurried in. "What the hell's been going on? Did you find him?"

Jill had wanted to go with her on the search for Marcus, but Cassie insisted she stay behind. It was one thing to put herself in danger, but she would not endanger Jill ever again. Not after almost losing her.

"No." It was the only word she managed before she began to sob.

Jill ran over and hugged her. "Tell me what happened."

After several minutes of telling the story about the dream and the Wendigo, then ending with the dragon attack and almost losing her life, she sighed. "And that's not all."

Jill had slipped into the chair across from her during the story, her face a mask of disbelief. "What the hell else could go wrong?"

"I'm pregnant." She caught Jill's expression. "Yeah, I had that same look."

"How the hell did that happen?"

She snorted. "Do I really need to explain?"

Jill waved her hands in the air. "No! I know how it happens, but I mean...well, hell, who knew vampires could have children?"

Certainly not her. The thought never crossed her mind when she'd slept with Marcus. She was never supposed to conceive. At least, that's what the doctors had told her. "I think this was a shock to everyone, me especially."

"You're getting an abortion, right? I mean you can't have a vampire baby, not with the father MIA."

"Absolutely not! This child is a miracle." She would die if it meant this child would live. Cassie believed everything happened for a reason, and there must be a logical reason behind this whole mess.

"Besides, Aidyn has promised to help me. Matter of fact, I need to talk to you about that."

Jill clutched her arms to her chest and sucked in a breath. "I have a feeling I'm not going to like this."

"Aidyn is moving me to their home in New York. I can see a doctor there that knows about them. Of course, no one knows for sure how this pregnancy will go, but we'll take it one day at a time."

"I don't understand. Why doesn't Aidyn take you to his home?"

It would be difficult, leaving her sister. However, she saw no other choice. They'd still stay in touch by phone and email, which would be impossible to do from another realm. "They are at war with the dragons. I don't fully understand it, but somehow Aidyn has kept them protected. However, he fears if they find me, they will try to use me against them." She moved next to her sister and put her arm around Jill. "Gwen is going to stay with me, and you can come visit anytime." Tears spilled down her cheeks as she hugged her sister tight. "I'm going to miss you."

"Damn it, Cassie, I know this is the right thing for you to do, but I'm going to worry myself sick. I'll come to visit you real soon. When are you leaving?"

"Tomorrow night. Aidyn will come for me and take me to New York." She tilted her head in thought for a moment. "Hey, maybe when you want to come and visit, he can just pop you over."

Jill put on a big smile. "Ohhh, that sounds like my kind of ride."

Cassie still had a lot to do before Aidyn arrived. He'd told her not to worry about expenses, but the idea of not pulling her weight didn't bode well. He'd then offered the idea of renting her home from her so they could use it as a base in New Orleans. She would tell the neighbors she was renting it while away. That way she wouldn't have to worry about her home being empty or the lack of cash. It seemed like the perfect deal.

CHAPTER TWENTY

CASSIE HUNG UP THE PHONE. Finally, all her loose ends were tied up and quitting her job had been the last thing on the list. Of course, her boss he had been upset at losing her but didn't push the issue. Now, she flopped her tired ass on the couch, exhausted by the day's events. Gwen was expected to pop in any minute, but she needed a few minutes to relax. Allowing her eyes to close, and thoughts of Marcus to drift through her mind.

I wish you could hear me. You're going to be a daddy.

She desperately wanted him to answer her, tell her everything would be fine. Maybe he was happy with Eliza, and Aidyn was wrong about everything. Even though Aidyn insisted Eliza was dead, Cassie still held doubts. Tears threatened to spill, but she pushed them back. She would make a life for her and her child with or without him.

"Cassie?"

She sat up. "In here."

Gwen swept in from the kitchen. "How are you feeling?"

"Do you mean mentally or physically?"

"Both."

"Mentally, I'm a wreck. The world as I know it has gone to hell, literally. Physically, I feel fine. No morning sickness yet."

"I wish there was something I could do for you." She smiled. "I have to admit I'm thrilled about being an aunt." She touched Cassie. "You know I will help you any way I can."

"Yes, I know. The most important thing now is to find Marcus. I need him and this baby needs him."

A disturbance rippled through the air followed by a bright light that formed in the center of the room. The light shifted, taking the form of a man.

Gwen walked toward him. "Argathos."

His steely voice echoed in the room. "Gwen, I am sorry that I could not come sooner."

Cassie rubbed her arms. The power that ran off this man measured tenfold to Aidyn's. So this was a god? She expected an old man with milky hair and a beard, but he wore faded jeans and a gray T-shirt. Thick, mahogany hair fell past his collar, accenting his high cheekbones. Dark-brown eyes lent to the exotic look. Like the other immortals she had met, he towered over her. His lean muscle mass flexed with each movement. She shook her head, apparently the gods didn't believe in being unattractive.

Argathos moved away from Gwen and approached Cassie. "Cassandra, I am pleased to meet you."

She was unsure of what she should do—bow or kneel? "Uh, you will have to pardon me. I have no idea what protocol is when meeting a god."

He flashed her a smile then searched her eyes. "There is no need for such nonsense with me. I don't require your obedience." He turned his attention to Gwen. "Leave us. I wish to speak to Cassie alone."

Gwen did as asked and flashed from the room, leaving Cassie with Argathos. He reached out and took both her hands in his then closed his eyes. "Don't fear me, I only wish to see your future."

"What do you see?"

"I am not allowed to give too many details. Your daughter is extremely important to the guardians. She will grow up to be a strong woman. However, what you have to teach her is the most important. Your life will be in danger if you do not convert and become one of the guardians."

Bile rose, burning the back of her throat. "I'm going to die?"

He released her hands, his gaze never departing hers. "The pregnancy will weaken you. Aidyn can help ease the burden on your body, but you need your mate." He raised a brow. "Your daughter is a full guardian even though you are human. That is what you wanted to know?"

"Thank you. Can you tell me where he is?"

"I cannot."

Her brows knitted. "Can't or won't?"

He smiled. "You catch on quickly. You also worry about things that have no merit."

"I don't understand."

"You question his commitment to you. If you want to save him, you must search your heart."

Damn it with the riddles. She looked down at the floor and thought about his comment. *Why am I really here?* She recalled Marcus telling her they were chosen to be together. She realized this was bigger than any of them, bigger than the god who stood before her. She loved Marcus. There was no sense denying it. He'd been right, their souls somehow connected. She loved a man she hardly knew, and her life was about to get even more complicated, but she would fight. Fight for his life and that of her unborn daughter.

She looked back up at the god with resolve in her eyes. "I love him."

He smiled once again. "Be warned, the road you are about to travel will not be easy."

She snorted. "It's been full of potholes already. I'm becoming accustomed to the bumpy ride."

He touched the top of her head and warmth spread through her body, bringing with it a sense of peace she hadn't felt in months, maybe even years.

"Always remember your destiny and fight for it. When challenged, stay your course and you will prevail. I leave you with a gift." He faded away.

"Wait! What? I so don't need this right now."

Gwen flashed back into the room. "You okay?"

"No, your god left me with a gift." She ran her fingers through her tangled hair. Shit, when was the last time she'd combed it?

"What kind of gift?" Gwen asked.

She threw up her hands in frustration. "Hell if I know, he didn't say. You have any ideas?"

Gwen sighed. "The gods sometimes have a flair for drama. Maybe Aidyn will be able to tell, we should— we need to leave. Now." Gwen grabbed Cassie's arm and flashed. Their bodies sucked into a black hole, and Cassie had no idea where they were going and why so sudden. Not until she found herself in the center of a beautiful expansive room overlooking a lake. She assumed it must be the home where she would be staying. When she turned to take in her surroundings, she found Gwen next to her.

"Sorry for the abruptness of our departure. Lucan sensed demons in your neighborhood, and we were not about to take any chances," Gwen said.

Cassie collapsed in the nearest chair. "Yes...of course." When next she looked up, she was greeted by a smiling face that belonged to Daniel, she guessed.

"Welcome, Ms. Jensen," Daniel said.

She moved from her seat and walked to Daniel, extending her hand. "Please, call me Cassie, and you're Daniel?"

He took her hand and gave it an eager shake. "Yes, ma'am, I mean Cassie." He peered around the room. "You didn't bring any luggage?"

Gwen stepped forward and gave Daniel a hug. "We had to leave rather abruptly. Lucan should be along any minute with her things."

She placed an arm around both Daniel's and Cassie's shoulders. "How about we give our guest a tour."

The three of them moved about the two-story home. It was beautiful, and Cassie had no doubt her every comfort would be looked after, still her heart was empty. When they stopped in front of one of the five bedrooms, Gwen pulled her aside.

"This is the room Marcus uses when he stays here. Would you like to have this one?" Gwen hurried on. "Of course, if it makes you uncomfortable, we can choose a different one."

Cassie stepped inside, his scent still hung in the air. "No, I want to stay here." She spun around to look at Gwen. "I'd like some time alone, please."

"Of course." Gwen exited the room, pulling the door shut behind her.

Cassie spotted something lying on the chair across the room. She moved closer and found it to be Marcus's jacket. She picked up the leather and pressed it against her cheek. Guilt slapped her in the face. Guilt at the argument they'd had and how she'd treated him. She should have been more understanding, but damn it, she thought he had meant to take her freedom. Now she realized he only wanted to protect her. She had since learned these men were overprotective but meant well. After learning their history and all they had lost, she understood.

She hugged the jacket. *Marcus, I'm so sorry.*

MARCUS HAD FALLEN ASLEEP, his body healed from Beth's blood. In the distance, a female cried. He strained to hear and realized the sound came from inside his head.

Cassie?

Marcus, is it really you?

Sweet deity, woman, are you all right? He thought for a moment he'd lost his faculties. How did he communicate with her but not his brethren?

I'm fine. I'm in your room in New York. Aidyn sent me here with Gwen. My home is no longer safe. I'm not even sure how, but I think Argathos has something to do with us being able to communicate. Marcus...are...are you with Eliza?

Funny she would ask that when she was the one who had the orgasm. He shouldn't jump to conclusions, after all, she nearly died, and he had no idea what happened back home. *It must be serious if Aidyn has moved her,* he thought. She was safe, and that's what mattered at the moment. *Cassie, yes, Eliza is here, but it's not what you think. She is in league with Odage, and they are holding me prisoner.* Somehow, he needed to speak with Lucan. He had a plan, and if it worked, he would be out of this hell hole and holding her in no time.

Marcus, are you injured? Where are you? I will come for you, and I will kill that bitch if she has hurt you!

He smiled. *I worry about you. What has happened that you have been moved from your home?*

Nothing, I'm fine.

She lies. Why does she lie to me? He thought, needing to compose his emotions. *Listen, sweetheart, I have a plan. Can you get to Lucan?*

Sure, I guess so.

Good, speak to him and tell no one else. Here is what I want you to do.

PUTTING ON HER GAME FACE, Cassie dropped the jacket and left the room. Marcus had explained that if Lucan was able to connect with her then he might be able to find Marcus through the connection she now had to him. It was a long shot but one she was willing to take.

Like a mouse, she scurried down the stairs and found Daniel in the kitchen.

"Hey, Lucan just showed up with your things. I was about to bring them up to you," Daniel said.

Sweet, Lucan was already here. Maybe she could do this without anyone knowing. "Great. Is he still here?"

"He went outside to check the grounds."

Even better. She would sneak out and find him. "Thanks, will you take my stuff up? I'm going to get some fresh air."

Daniel shrugged. "Sure thing."

She slipped out the kitchen door. The setting sun blanketed the horizon with hues of reds and oranges. She did a quick visual of the lay of the land. Not having been outside the house yet, she was unsure of where to go. She pushed her shoulders back and took a determined stride around the house. Nothing. Where the hell was he? *What if I've missed him?* Her eye caught sight of a boathouse down by the lake. She did a quick look around then headed through the grass toward the water. Half way she stopped, and her hair stood on end. Someone watched her. She spun around but saw no one behind her.

"Lucan?" Maybe the vampire was still on his rounds. The only sound to penetrate the dusky sky were the croaking frogs. She licked her lips, her throat suddenly parched. Determination made her turn around and continue to the boathouse.

"Going somewhere, pet?"

Cold arms encircled her, holding her firm. Before she could scream, blackness surrounded her.

CHAPTER TWENTY-ONE

CASSIE AWOKE, lying on a strange bed. She sat up and found herself surrounded by four walls of bars. The stench of rot filled the air and the only sound was the drip of water in the distance. Carefully, she placed both feet on the floor and moved toward the door where she grasped the bars and pulled. Locked. Outside the cell were four stone walls, reminding her of the caves she had visited as a child. Bumps danced across her skin from the cool, damp air.

Marcus? No answer. Tears threatened. *No, I have to remain strong, no matter what.* She rubbed her stomach. *Well, pumpkin, it's just you and me again. How do I keep ending up in these terrible situations?* Like it or not, she was here, wherever the hell that was.

"H...Hello?"

Her throat tightened when heavy footsteps moved closer. Taking several steps backward, her legs hit the bed. Her stomach churned and threatened to heave lunch from earlier. All control abandoned when her body started to quiver. She swallowed. *I have to face my fears. Maybe it's not as bad as I think. Right, and you're not the mate of a vampire either. Ha!*

A dark shadow moved into view. "So you have awakened. Welcome." The gruff voice caused her lips to tremble.

"Who are you?" She moved closer to the bars, wanting to get a better look at her captor. "Why am I here?"

The shadowy figure lunged for the bars, causing her to shriek and jump backward. Before her, stood the same man she'd seen vanish that night in her neighborhood. Marcus called him Odage. His menacing laugh grated on her nerves. "I should have taken you last time we met. Had I known who you were...well, let's just say our meeting would have ended with your lovely mouth wrapped around my cock."

"You didn't answer me, why am I here?" She refused to give in to her fears. There was more to protect than just herself.

"You are to become part of the slave market. A pretty young human like you will fetch thousands. Demons will come for miles to fuck you." He licked his lips. "The thought of teaching you how to please a man excites me." He placed both hands on the bars, his blues eyes penetrating deep into her soul. "Interesting, you are with child. This could prove extremely useful indeed."

Panic gripped her and threatened her sanity. Adrenalin spiked, causing her heart to race. No one touched her child. She would find a way to escape. "You harm me or my child, and you will die."

He laughed. "And who is going to kill me? You?"

Her brows furrowed as she stared at him. "The guardians."

Odage laughed again. "They have to find you first. Perhaps you'd like to see how your mate fares? Then you can tell me all about how the guardians will be coming to your rescue." Another set of footsteps moved closer. Softer and quicker than the last. A woman only slightly taller than Cassie's own five-foot-six frame stepped closer. Golden hair spilled down her back, and brown eyes glared at her. She didn't need any introductions to know who this was.

Eliza.

The woman ran a red fingernail along the bars. "So you're the bitch who thinks to steal my mate?" Her fangs extended when she hissed at Cassie. "A mere human who is much too weak for a man like Marcus." She walked to the other side of the cage. "He fucked me, you know. Was unable to resist me when we were together."

Cassie's eyes burned, could it be true? No, this woman was a vindictive bitch.

Eliza laughed. "It's the child he wants, you fool! You're only a vessel to carry it. Perhaps he and I will raise her together."

"You cannot have my daughter!" She placed a protective hand over her stomach. "Besides, you're the one who tortured Marcus. You don't do that to someone you love. He would never have had sex with you."

"Stupid girl. I never said I loved him, only that he's mine." She ran her hands down her waist, stopping at her hips. "Look at me, I'm immortal. I'm perfect. Are you so sure he didn't take me hard and fast? After all, the male can't resist his mate. They're like animals, and oh does Marcus fuck like one, especially when he's taking your blood."

He had been so passionate when he had taken her blood. Maybe he did have sex with Eliza. After all, she had been his mate before her, not to mention she was beautiful. Her skin flawless and her curves perfection. The type women loved to hate but wanted to be like. *Why the hell would he want me? I'm so stupid to think a man would finally love me.*

"Of course, he doesn't love you. He used you. Told you lies about how you were his chosen and it was all for a good time. That's all." Eliza opened the cage door and stepped in. "And I forgive him for that."

Cassie had nowhere to go, already pushed against the bed frame. *I can run past her out the open door.* But Odage stood outside, she'd never make it. *Fuck it, try anyway.*

"You can't escape me," Eliza said.

Cassie clutched her head; intense pain made her skull feel as if it would explode. She cried out before falling back on the bed.

Her head pounded. *What the hell did that bitch do to me?*

"Get up, we're leaving." Eliza grabbed Cassie by the arm and dragged her off the bed.

Her head in a fog, she didn't have the strength to fight. Hell, she could hardly stand. It was like she had gone on a drinking binge the night before and now paid the price. Her stomach rolled, threatening to empty any contents that remained.

"Where are you taking me?"

Eliza cast a wicked smile. "To hell."

"I thought I was already there."

Eliza laughed. "Not yet, my dear human." She slapped a pair of shackles and chains around Cassie's wrists. "Just in case you get any crazy ideas about trying to escape." Eliza grabbed the chain and jerked, leading Cassie from the cage. They moved past Odage who licked his lips when she passed him. Her stomach revolted, but she managed to keep from vomiting.

She had to follow behind Eliza as they slipped through a narrow corridor. Light came from the room they exited, the only thing in front of them was blackness. The stone of the cavern walls scraped her body. A stinging sensation told her that her skin was covered in tiny cuts.

Marcus? Silence greeted her.

"He will not answer you, he doesn't want you," Eliza said.

Well, since you're invading my mind, here's one for you. Fuck you, bitch! Sweat trickled down her forehead and into her eyes. She reached up and wiped her face with the hem of her shirt. Eliza hadn't been kidding when she said they were going to hell. The air grew hotter by the minute.

After what felt like an eternity, a faint light blazed in front of them. Her heart raced, fearful of what awaited her. When they exited the tunnel, cool air brushed her skin. A sigh of relief escaped her lips until she took in her surroundings. Eight holding cells. A quick count told her four women occupied two of the cells, the rest sat empty. A couple of the women were pregnant, and she wondered if the others were as well but didn't show yet.

"What is this place?" Not sure she actually wanted an answer.

"It's Odage's maternity ward. Don't worry, you won't be staying here."

Eliza tugged the chains, dragging her across the room to an opening. A set of steps led down a narrow passage. At least this time it was lit, so she didn't have to worry about tripping down the stairs. The farther down they went, the hotter it became, and her shirt clung to her like a sweat rag. Eliza stopped in front of another entry, pulled out a key and shoved it into the lock. When she pushed the door open, Cassie saw the silhouette of a man shackled to the ceiling, his arms stretched over his head and his back pressed against the wall.

Recognition dawned.

"Marcus!"

His head raised, steel eyes caught hers then looked away. He didn't utter a word, let his chin drop back to his chest.

Eliza pushed her through the door and led her to a corner of the room. She removed one manacle from her wrist, ran it through a ring embedded into the rock wall and placed it back on her arm. She could only crouch in the corner.

Eliza stepped in front of Marcus, her finger lifted his chin. "Darling, look who I brought."

Cassie held her breath, waiting for his response.

His face showed no emotion. "I could care less."

"But lover, I thought you wanted her," Eliza purred.

"I have no use for her, you are all I want." His voice was thick with desire.

Cassie's heart shattered. *No, please tell me this isn't real.*

As if to answer her request, he licked his lips. "Eliza, love. Kiss me."

Eliza obeyed, brought her lips to his. Their kiss, long and passionate had Cassie wanting to look away, but disbelief forced her to watch. When they finally parted, Eliza looked at her.

"I told you he didn't want you. Don't worry, precious, we have men already lined up requesting your services." Eliza laughed as she exited the room, leaving them alone.

"Marcus, that was just a trick. Right?" He refused to answer, dropped his head and closed his eyes. Her lip trembled. "Talk to me, please." He turned his head away from her, still not speaking. She curled into the fetal position on the floor and wept.

THE PAIN he experienced when he told Cassie he didn't want her and kissed Eliza, had been worse than anything Odage could have done to him. He knew what they were up to. They thought to get to him through her. It had taken every ounce of strength to pretend he didn't care. Her sobbing in the corner ate him alive. At this moment, he wanted to yell the truth—he loved her. But he wouldn't risk her life or that of his daughter's.

He sensed the babe growing inside her. Soon her belly would swell with their child, something he'd never expected. Damn it! Where was Lileta? If she would only come and release him, he would get them all out of there. On cue, he heard the door unlock, his breath held captive in his lungs. Odage entered. *Fuck!*

He moved toward Cassie, unchained her and pulled her to her feet. Marcus bit through his tongue. *Show no emotions.* He dared not even communicate with her telepathically. Odage dragged her, stopping in front of him.

"I'm taking your mate, vampire. Soon, I will begin her training."

Marcus raised his head, looked the Draki in the eye. "I'm sure you will find her pleasing. By the way, she is an expert cock sucker." Betrayal stared back at him, she'd never forgive him now. He'd live with that, had to. Odage didn't hide his displeasure.

"You lie, vampire, I think you still want her."

"I cannot lie, remember?" Except when it came to protecting his mate. Nothing was off the table when it came to his female. She would remember he told her the same thing once before. His heart squeezed in a vise from the tears in her eyes. His ruse was working. Odage's anger rose. He pulled a dagger from his boot and slid it into Marcus's stomach, twisted for good measure.

Marcus gritted his teeth through the pain while Cassie screamed. Even after he had ripped her heart out, she still cared for him.

Odage dragged a whimpering Cassie out the door. As soon as the lock engaged, Marcus pulled on his chains, he would chew off his hands if he had to in order to save her.

CHAPTER TWENTY-TWO

SOMEHOW, she had to get away from him. Cassie's mind was a frenzy of thoughts. Odage led her back toward the stairs, so it was now or never. She followed behind him, and when he came to a halt, she swung the chain over his head. It landed at his neck, and she pulled with every ounce of strength she had.

It wasn't enough.

His fingers curled around the chain and pulled it free. He turned and backhanded her, sending her through the air to land with a hard thud on her ass.

"Fucking bitch, try that again, and I swear to the gods I will remove his head while you watch. When I'm done with the vampire, I will slice that child right from your womb." In two steps, he was in front of her. "Get up."

She quickly jumped to her feet, not daring to check for any injuries. He grabbed her arm and shoved her in front of him, forcing her up the steps. When they reached the top, he pushed her through the door. She landed back in the room with the other women. Again, he grabbed her arm and dragged her to an empty cell, then shoved her in and closed the door.

"Lileta," Odage shouted.

A beautiful dark-haired woman entered the room. "Yes, my liege?"

"Give this one a dose of blood wine." He pointed toward Cassie.

The woman bowed her head. "As you wish." She exited the room.

"Obey me, and it will make life much easier for you." He turned and left.

Cassie looked around her cell. Two sets of bunk beds and a small bathroom were all the comforts afforded her. Footsteps told her Lileta approached. The woman entered the cell with a wine glass in hand. Paused and glanced around before she moved closer.

"You must drink this, it is only wine." Her voice lowered. "I did not add the dragon blood as Odage commanded. You need your wits to escape."

She narrowed her eyes. "Why should I trust you?"

"Because I'm helping Marcus escape, he will come for you."

Cassie tossed her head back. "Ha! I think you're mistaken."

Lileta held out the glass. "He protected you. If Odage and Eliza believe he cares for you, they will use it against him."

Did she speak the truth? Something seemed familiar about her. She searched her memories. *She doesn't look familiar. What it is?* Her eyes widened. "Your name is Lileta?"

"Yes, why?"

"Do you have a brother?"

Her eyes filled with tears. "Baal. I have not seen him in many years."

Cassie slapped her palm to her mouth. "Dear god, I was with him only a few days ago. He was taken by the slave traders while we were out searching for Marcus."

Lileta closed her eyes. "No, I cannot bear the thought of his capture."

Heavy footsteps echoed into the room. "Is she giving you any grief?"

"Take the glass," Lileta whispered.

Cassie grabbed the glass and put it to her lips, taking a sip.
"No, my liege."

"Good, have her cleaned up and ready to depart in one hour. We will all be leaving this place." The door slammed behind him.

"Dear gods, I don't think I can free Marcus in time." She gave Cassie a shove. "Quickly, into the shower while I get you some clean clothes."

Cassie entered the bathroom and began stripping. Her mind swirled, Marcus had only been pretending. She would have been relieved except a new set of problems presented themselves. Where did Odage plan to take her?

MARCUS'S HEAD still pounded after what he'd done to Cassie. She was alive, but for how long? His thoughts were disrupted when the cell door opened and Lileta slipped into the room, alone. She moved as stealthily as a cat toward him, a large tool in her hand. "Odage is moving us. I have come to free you, but we must hurry. He plans to take your mate away from here." She reached up and cut the chains, his arms fell to his side, and he collapsed to the floor.

"Quickly." Lileta reached for him and helped him to his feet. "Unfortunately, I can't remove the silver bands."

He struggled to stand. "I'm weak from the knife wound Odage gifted me with. I can't help Cassie unless we get these bands off. Wait...where the hell is he taking her?"

"I don't know, only that he gave me an hour to get everyone ready. That was thirty minutes ago."

He followed Lileta from the room, down a narrow corridor then slipped through a door that led them into a maze.

"We must take the back way, no one uses these corridors."

After several minutes, they walked through a door and into a small chamber that housed only a bed and nightstand. "This is my room." She led him to the bed and had him sit.

"I need to get rid of these bands. I can't communicate with my brethren."

Lileta gave him a pained look. "If I could remove them I would have taken my own off. The best I can do is provide you with a way out." She shifted toward the door. "I need to go check on your mate, wait here."

Marcus paced the small room. He needed to see Cassie, hold her in his arms, and beg her forgiveness. He stopped mid-step when Lileta returned.

"Where is she?" His voice panicked.

Lileta wrung her hands. "She is gone, Odage has taken her already and started moving the others. We must hurry before he looks for me."

"Fuck," he growled.

She moved back toward the door and peered out. "We need to get you out of here before they discover you're missing as well." She motioned for him to follow and led him to a room filled with racks of wine.

"He has a fucking wine cellar?"

She turned her head to gaze at him. "Yes, he gives the women blood wine to control them."

"Rotten bastard." He stopped when Lileta pressed her hand against the back wall and opened a secret passage. "Nice."

"I don't think Odage even knows it's here. I discovered it a few weeks ago myself."

"How the hell did you find it?" He gained a whole new respect for this demon. She proved resourceful, even with her power hindered by the silver. He only wished Cassie was with him.

"I was looking for it. I remembered these caves once belonged to Drayos, and it made sense that he would have several hidden passages." The door closed, leaving them in complete darkness. At least his vision didn't seem to be impaired by the silver.

"This is as far as I can go. I'm sure if you follow the tunnel, you will find a way out." She turned to walk away, but he grabbed her wrist.

"You're not coming with me?"

"No, he can track me and will kill us both. Besides, the women need me, just promise you will find us."

"I swear it. But what is Odage up to?"

"He is keeping human women to bear his children. His first child was born only a few days ago. The mother is dead."

He ground his teeth, his fists clenching into tight balls. "I'll kill the fucking bastard."

"He has also bound himself to a memory ghoul. She seeks the amulet of Tobor for him."

"What the hell does he want with the amulet of life?"

"I don't know, I can only say he is being controlled—" She shivered. "—by someone very powerful."

He kissed her cheek. "Thank you for everything, but I must ask one more favor of you."

"What is it?"

"Please watch after my mate, she carries my child. And...and tell her I love her."

"I will." Then she disappeared back through the door.

He prayed she wouldn't be found out and punished for her role in his escape and Cassie remained safe until he could find her.

A ROAR SHOOK the entire mountain, rocks spewed into the air like a dog shaking off fleas. The villagers who lived at the foot of the mountain made the sign of the cross and ran for cover. Steam escaped his nostrils as he took one breath in then exhaled. Odage's vision burned red with fury. The vampire was gone. There was no way he had escaped on his own, someone helped him. He stormed through the caverns, smashing fists into walls as he went. His body hung in a state of metamorphosis, stuck between man and dragon. His mind, in such turmoil he was unable to make a complete shift to either form.

"Roman!" Two voices echoed out. The timbre of the beast lower and grating against the skin.

"Y-yes, my liege?" Roman came forth and knelt before the half beast.

Odage moved in front of the minion, lowered his head to within inches of Roman's. His fangs exposed, spittle flew into the man's face. "Where. Is. The. Vampire?"

Roman's body trembled, his eyes cast to the floor. "I-I don't know, my liege. H-he was there when I last checked on him."

"And when was that?"

"Only a few hours ago...my liege."

"You are such a disappointment, minion. You let the vampire escape." The crimson body of his dragon emerged. A long tail snaked around the room, and claws sprouted from each toe. The shift complete. He sucked in a breath and let out a roar of flames, burning the man who knelt in front of him. His tail flicked the charred remains across the room.

He continued to move to the upper level of the cavern slowly, as his body morphed back to its human form. *Caleb, come to me.*

His commanding officer formed in front of him. "Yes, my liege?"

"Caleb, status report."

"Camp is set up, the women moved, and the men are ready to dig on your command."

Odage stopped in mid-stride. "Excellent, I can always count on you. Let us leave here then. Have a few men stay behind and search for the vampire." A wicked smile snaked across his lips. "He won't go far, I have something he wants."

Caleb bowed. "As you wish, my liege."

MARCUS FOLLOWED the passageway's twists and turns as it led

up the mountain. Light could be seen ahead, but he would have to wait for the cover of darkness before he dared make his escape. He hated like hell to sit and do nothing while Odage got away with Cassie, but between the knife wound and the silver, he was too weak to help even himself. He crawled into an alcove and went to sleep.

His eyes snapped open, and he had no idea how long he'd been asleep. He crawled to the front of the alcove and peered out. A faint light with pinkish hues danced off the rock. The sun was almost down, it was time to leave. Once outside, he found himself planted on a narrow ledge with no way to detect his enemy. The silver blocked everything. He would have to fight the old-fashioned way.

He crawled along the ledge for several yards until he spotted a Draki walking toward him.

Grabbing a rock, he crouched, and when the Draki walked past, he jumped on his back, smashing the pointed end of the rock into the back of the man's skull. The shifter slipped to the ground, the trauma not enough to kill him so Marcus rolled him off the edge of the cliff. He'd still live, but it would take him days to regenerate from the numerous broken bones the fall would leave.

He stood, looked around and saw no one else, so he moved forward down the trail, certain there would be at least one more Draki on the mountain. He stumbled and nearly fell, the knife wound leaving a trail for the enemy to follow. In his weakened state, he wasn't even sure where he was going. Only that he needed to get off the mountain. *Maybe I can get back to the forest and at least catch some game for nourishment.* It was his only hope.

A Draki jumped out and swung his sword. Luckily, Marcus's reflexes were quick enough he was able to duck before losing his head. However, the motion had set him off balance, and he fell to the ground. Weak and without weapons, he would never survive a direct assault. The Draki flexed his arms to make another swing. Marcus was too weak to roll out of the way, but he made eye contact with the dragon.

"I'm not your enemy."

"Tell that to my brother who lies in a broken heap at the foot of this mountain."

Marcus coughed up blood. "I only defended myself. We did not start this war with you."

The Draki's eyes swirled dark. "You started it by accusing our leader of murder. We will finish it." He swung but never made contact. His head flew through the air.

Marcus looked up at the hand held out to him. "It's about fucking time you showed up."

"Such gratitude, my friend," Aidyn replied.

He accepted the king's hand and stood. "I need to get these off," he said, holding out his silver encased wrists.

Aidyn flashed a wicked grin. "Lucky for you we have just the tool for that."

"Figures you'd be lying around on the job while we do all the work." Baal stepped from behind Aidyn.

He let a breath escape. "Am I ever glad to see you." He held his wrists out to Baal who placed his hands on the silver, chanted and the cuffs fell to the ground.

"Thanks, I owe you one. Would you mind taking care of the other ones too?"

Baal scowled. "You just want me to kneel at your fucking feet." The demon dropped to his haunches and repeated the process with the ankle cuffs then stood. "Now, shall we go get your mate?"

CHAPTER TWENTY-THREE

MARCUS PACED Aidyn's office while the other warriors sat and watched. He had taken blood and was almost back to normal. Now he needed his mate. He was edgy and ready to snap. He needed the fight. The blackness in his soul shifted as if to agree.

"I need to find Cassie."

Aidyn looked up from his desk. "As soon as Baal gets back with the intel we need."

Marcus snarled then sighed. "Aidyn, I need to speak with you privately."

The king arched a brow. "Now?"

"Yes."

Aidyn waved his hand in the air, indicating everyone was to leave. "What is it?"

"Eliza is alive and in league with Odage."

Aidyn worked his jaw. "Explain."

"She captured me. Said she'd loved Drayos. Apparently, he used some kind of magic to change another into looking like her three hundred years ago. I killed the replica."

"I am sorry for all the pain my sister has caused you. I can't understand how or why she turned, but I will kill her myself this time."

"I can't let you do that." There was no way in hell he'd allow his friend to bear that burden. It was bad enough when he did it the first time, when Eliza had been his mate. Now, he would have no problem taking her head.

His friend held up a hand in protest. "No, it is my duty. You have Cassie and a daughter on the way. I will do this."

"But—" Marcus was cut off before he could continue.

"No." Aidyn's eyes flickered to black. "I command you to step down."

Shit, Aidyn pulled rank. He tipped his head. "Yes, my lord."

"Good." Aidyn walked to the door and summoned the rest of the team. This time, Baal entered with them.

"I'm glad to see you back among us, Marcus," Baal said.

"How is it that you're here? I heard you were captured."

Baal's lips curled into a wide grin. "Aidyn came up with a plan just in case I was captured. I gave him my blood, therefore, he could track me. Once I was sold, Aidyn came with a "get out of jail free" card and sprung me."

Marcus frowned. "I don't understand. We can't drink Kothar blood, and what the hell is a "get out of jail free" card?"

Baal laughed. "Seems your king can drink anything. When he," pointing a thumb in Aidyn's direction, "showed up, he kicked some serious ass. Leveled the compound and killed—wait for it... a fucking Wendigo."

Marcus clenched his jaw, his teeth ground together so hard he thought they might turn to dust. "What the hell were you thinking?" Marcus glared at Aidyn, almost daring him to a fight. "You could have been killed!"

Aidyn shrugged. "I wasn't."

Marcus threw his arms in the air. "Oh for fuck sake. You're the king, and it's my responsibility to see to your army, such that we are." He held up his hand. "Yes, I know I was...detained. Still, Lucan is next in command when I'm not here. You should have sent him in your place."

"If you two ladies don't mind, I'm afraid I have bad news," Baal said.

Marcus braced himself for the worst. No, he would know if Cassie was dead. "What?"

"They have taken her to hell." Baal delivered the bad news.

"Mother fuck."

THE AIR GREW thick with heat. Cassie looked around and realized she was no longer in her cell, but now walked through a tight, dark corridor. Small beams of light burrowed through tiny holes in the rock, giving off a faint glow. When had she left the prison cell? *Oh yeah, now I remember.* That bitch Eliza had come for her. She scrubbed her face, and the fog in her brain finally lifted. How long had they been walking?

"Where are you taking me?"

"I told you before, hell."

"Why?"

Eliza sneered at her. "You ask too many questions."

Bitch.

They walked for another hour in silence. Exhaustion wore on her. She couldn't remember the last time she'd eaten, or slept, for that matter. Her feet were killing her, and she was unsure of how much longer she could continue. Finally, they exited the small corridor and moved into a lush, tropical forest. Exotic flowers in vibrant reds, oranges, and purples bloomed near a waterfall. Her mouth watered; she was dying of thirst. As if on cue, Eliza produced a bottle of water from a pack she carried.

"Here," she said, handing Cassie the bottle. "We will rest for a while." Then led her to a patch of grass near the water where she tossed the pack to Cassie. "There's food in there, take what you want."

She gave Eliza a suspicious glance, wondered if she should trust her. She opened the pack and found some energy bars, apples, oranges and more water. Deciding on a bar and an orange, she sat on the grass and pulled the wrapper from the bar. Taking a bite, she moaned in delight. Who knew a piece of cardboard could taste so good?

She wiped the sweat from her brow. "Feels like hell, but it's not what I expected it to look like."

Eliza's lashes fused together. "Stupid human, this isn't hell. It's a gateway meant to fool the souls passing through." She pointed a finger at the water. "Look down there."

Cassie's gaze followed the bony finger. In the translucent water swam what looked like mermaids. She frowned and leaned forward. When one jumped from the water, she scooted back in horror. The bottom half of the body was fish and covered in green scales. The top half was a red, leathery texture. They lacked hair on their heads, which accentuated the large, pointy ears. When one jumped close to her, it snarled, exposing a full set of razor-sharp fangs.

"Care to go for a swim?" Eliza laughed.

She clutched her chest. "I think I'll pass. What are those things?" Why did she insist on asking stupid questions?

"Those are your worst nightmare. If you happen to decide on a swim, one will latch onto you, pulling you into the depths and devouring your flesh over and over again for eternity."

And to think, she had considered Eliza her worst nightmare. "I thought people were already dead when they came here."

"Yes, but the soul can still feel, still hurt." Eliza stood. "We must go, you will carry the pack." Then Eliza jerked the rope around Cassie's waist, dragging her to her feet.

ALL THE WARRIORS including Marcus swore. They were forbidden to enter hell ever since the curse Drayos placed on them. Going there would call to the darkness in their souls, causing the evil to emerge. Once in hell, they would never come out.

Marcus yelled, punched the wall beside him. His heart shattered into a million pieces. Was she all right? "What the fuck am I supposed to do? I can't stand around here and do nothing. Who knows what they are doing to her."

"Zarek!" Aidyn bellowed.

Marcus threw his dagger across the room, sticking it to the wall. He then stalked toward it, pried it loose, turned and tossed it again. He had just invented a new way to pace the floor.

Zarek flashed into the room, his features as violent as a spring storm. "Your mate is in hell."

"I fucking know that! How do I get there?"

Zarek clenched his fists. "Quadira!"

Within seconds, a woman flashed into the room. Quadira—the goddess of fire, Zarek's wife, and the mother of the dragons—stood before them. Her burnished copper hair hung in a braid down her back. The emerald green of her gown bringing out the color of her eyes.

"Why are your children not kneeling before me?" She looked at Zarek, her fangs bared.

"Because wife, your children are not playing nice in the sandbox. One of your own has stolen a mate who also happens to be with child."

She knitted her brows. "Seems to me, husband, one of your children has removed her from this realm."

Everyone knew Quadira had created the dragons. Long before any immortal or human walked the earth, dragons filled the skies.

"Fix this," Zarek commanded.

Her peaches and cream skin turned pink. "It is forbidden for us to interfere in their games." She crossed her arms over her large breasts and lifted her chin in defiance.

Zarek moved in front of her. "Those are my rules, and I will break them any damn time I wish. Do not forget, my dear, that all gods, including you, bow to me." He brushed a finger down her cheek. "Now love, you, as well as I, know the importance of the guardian's mate."

Tears welled in her eyes. "I have lost control of Odage." She bowed her head. "I am sorry."

Zarek pulled her to him and brushed a kiss on her forehead. "We will prevail," he whispered.

"What about my mate?" Marcus yelled out.

Zarek stepped aside, and Quadira motioned to Marcus. "Come."

He slid in front of her in two steps, his eyes leveled on her. If she expected him to kneel, she could go fuck herself. She was to blame for this mess as far as he was concerned. She touched his shoulder. Heat seared his skin and caused it to blister. The darkness screeched and tried to move deeper into his soul. "What the fuck did you just do to me?"

"The only thing I could. I have forced back the darkness, but it is temporary. You can enter hell, but your time will be limited."

Marcus blinked. "How long do I have?"

"Twenty-four hours."

Fuck. That wasn't much time to find Cassie and get back before the curse completely overtook him.

"I know Baal is going with you, but I would feel better if I could go as well," Aidyn said.

"I will go with him." A rough voice spoke from behind.

Everyone turned with weapons raised. "Who are you?" Marcus asked.

"I am Gabriel. I was sent here by Zarek to accompany you to hell."

Marcus narrowed his gaze on the man who stood across the room. He was taller than anyone there, his dark blond hair streaked with golden highlights and messed into spikes on top of his head. He wore only a pair of faded blue jeans and black boots. His chest was bare, showing off corded muscles and sinew. His left bicep bore a black tattoo of Anubis's head, the only color was in the eyes. They matched the same icy blue as the man who now stared at him. The most important feature this stranger had was the pair of black wings that arched high from his back and reached down to the floor. The feathers shimmered with colors of black, blue and purple.

"Why did he send you?" He'd heard of Gabriel, but in all the years he'd lived had never met him. He was Zarek's personal protector, a winged warrior of death, a being that could walk between heaven and hell.

"I am to aid in your mission. If you fail, then I am to kill you." A burst of power rolled across the room as if to make his point. Yeah, he got it, loud and clear. Well, at least the angel didn't mince words. He had to admire Gabriel for that, although he wasn't sure if he liked anything else about the angel.

Marcus turned to Aidyn. "If I don't make it and angel on steroids here—" He pointed a thumb in Gabriel's direction. "—comes back with only Cassie, promise you'll take care of her."

Aidyn clasped him on the shoulder. "You will come back, but yes. She will be protected and so will your daughter."

Relief overtook him. "Thanks."

Aidyn stepped out of the way and allowed each warrior to say goodbye and wish him luck. Gwen was the last to approach him. "Brother." She hugged him. "I love you and wish you well. You will be successful."

"If you're done with the sappy stuff, we should be leaving. Your clock is ticking," Gabriel said.

CHAPTER TWENTY-FOUR

ODAGE WATCHED from the tent while his slaves dug through the sand. He slipped on a pair of sunglasses and stepped outside to take a closer look. "Gods, I fucking hate sand," he muttered under his breath. His gaze caught sight of raven hair flowing in the hot breeze. Oroumea, his wife, was in the thick of things, moving amongst the slaves and trying to locate the amulet. She was proving extremely useful.

"My liege." Odage snapped out of his thoughts and turned toward the silken voice. Lileta stood before him with his babe wrapped in a blanket. Odage reached out and took his son from her arms.

"Leave us," he growled at her. He knew fucking well she was responsible for helping the vampire escape. For now, it was his own little secret until he decided on a fitting punishment.

"Ah, my son, look up there." Odage pointed at the numerous dragons that filled the sky. Erebos's eyes followed his father's finger, and the babe smiled. "Yes, Erebos, one day you will be able to take flight and soar with your kind." Even though the child was only a week old, he had already shown signs of partial shifting. At the rate he was growing, it wouldn't be long before Odage could teach him to fly. The babe watched as a majestic blue dragon hovered in front of them then landed gently in the sand. When the dragon's massive head reached down and nuzzled Erebos in the belly, the babe squealed with delight.

"Caleb, I think he likes you. When the time comes, you will teach him to fight."

Caleb shifted into his human form. His immense body stood level with Odage, and his bronze skin glistened in the sun. Caleb was a callous man but loyal to a fault, which was why Odage had made him second-in-command. He noted how Caleb's dark blond hair was in total disarray, sticking out here and there and in some places plastered to his face.

Caleb bowed his head. "I would be honored, my liege."

"You look like you have been fucked hard and left for dead."

Caleb's brown eyes swirled with flecks of emerald. "That would be putting it mildly."

Odage knew if anyone deserved it, it was Caleb. The man had lost his mate during the war with Drayos and had since become a coldhearted bastard. "Did you at least leave any women for the rest of the men?"

Caleb grinned. "Oh yes, my liege, I don't think that will be a problem. The women here are extremely giving."

Odage rubbed his chin. He might have to make a trip into town later. If his ghoul of a wife thought him to be faithful, then she was going to be disappointed. Odage would use any female that caught his attention. As a dragon overlord, it was his right to take whatever he wanted.

"Good. Now make sure no humans come within fifty miles of this camp. We would not want anyone to stumble onto our little dig here."

"As you wish, my liege." Caleb shifted back into his dragon and took to the sky. Once again, Erebos cooed as he watched the dragon take flight.

Odage smiled at the boy. "Soon, my son, soon." Then he turned and walked back into his tent. He laid Erebos down on the bed. It was time for his feeding. Odage bit into his wrist then held it to the babe's mouth. Erebos suckled with enthusiasm until his eyes grew heavy and finally closed. Odage sealed his wound then left the babe to sleep.

Suddenly, darkness closed in around Odage, and a chill snaked up his spine. *Fuck!* He knew what was coming next, his master would be wanting an update on the amulet.

"Odage," the darkness whispered.

"Yes, my lord?"

"Where is the amulet?" The darkness now wrapped around him and squeezed.

"It is here, my lord, we only need to uncover it."

"Excellent. I understand you lost the vampire, Marcus." The darkness reached into his chest and grabbed his beating heart. *Shit!* Sweat trickled down Odage's nose. Surely, he wouldn't kill him when Odage was so close to the amulet. Or would he?

"One of my slaves helped him escape. She will suffer considerably for her foolishness." Odage now regretted not killing her on the spot. Perhaps if he had done that, it would have appeased the darkness.

"You should be more mindful of your servants. Perhaps you need a lesson on how to punish them?"

"I will deal with her, my lord, make no mistake about it."

The darkness continued its hold on Odage's heart. "The vampire's mate is on her way to me. Once I have the amulet and the girl, I will be able to leave this realm."

Odage shuddered, not sure he wanted to meet the darkness. "I look forward to it, my lord." He knew once the amulet and Cassie were together, her sacrifice would open the gateway allowing hell to pour into the human world.

Odage stepped outside the tent and summoned Oroumea.

"What is it, my love?" she asked, brushing sand from her feet before entering the tent.

"Stay here with the child. I have work to do."

Oroumea wrinkled her nose. "I am not a babysitter. Call your servant to take care of the child."

He pulled his wife close. "I know you're not fond of infants, but I need this favor." He kissed her neck, hoping a little seduction might help.

She rubbed against his erection, making him clench his teeth. "Very well, I take it the slave is to be punished for her deceit?"

"Yes." He pushed her aside. "I must go." He shoved his sunglasses up his nose and exited the tent. His booted feet left deep impressions in the sand as he strode toward Lileta's tent.

Caleb. Odage wanted his right-hand dragon there, as well. She would fear them both before this day was done. He would also have to find a new slave to care for Erebos, lest Lileta dare to take her anger out on the boy.

Yes, my liege?

Come down here and bring the dirise. *We have some punishing to do.*

I'll be there momentarily.

Seconds later, Caleb landed beside Odage, taking his human shape. The *dirise* hung from a leather holster on his hip. Odage noted that Caleb looked more refreshed, his hair at least combed this time.

"Bring the slave to me," he commanded, taking the *dirise* from Caleb.

Caleb disappeared inside the tent and seconds later, exited with Lileta being dragged behind him. He stopped in front of Odage and pulled the slave to stand before him, pinning her to his chest, facing Odage. "Here she is, my liege."

Odage grabbed her chin and squeezed. "I should kill you for your betrayal. I may yet."

Lileta pulled from his grasp. Her golden eyes glowed with fire and her breaths came in rapid succession. "Do me the favor. I would rather die than remain your slave." She spit on Odage's boot then tried to wrestle free of Caleb, but he held tight.

Odage looked down at his boot then back at Lileta. "You wish to die? Then I think you shall live and suffer every day for it." He met Caleb's gaze. "Tie her to the whipping pole."

Caleb dragged Lileta over to a tall wooden pole sunk deep in the ground. He reached for the leather straps that were fastened at the top and tied her wrists over her head. He looked to Odage for further instructions.

"Rip her top off," Odage snarled while he swung the *dirise* back and forth. Caleb did as directed. He extended a claw and sliced off the pink T-shirt she wore. Leaving her with only a pink lace bra.

"The bra as well."

Caleb shredded the bra, leaving her bare from the waist up.

Lileta looked at Caleb through fused lashes. "Bastard." She spit in his face. He glared at her then turned his back and walked away, never bothering to wipe his face.

Odage stepped forward and raised the *dirise*, its sharp blades glistening in the sunlight. In one fluid motion, he brought forty-two inches of pure hell down, slicing across her back. Lileta flinched but never muttered a sound. Blood trickled down her chin from where she bit her lip. Odage struck again, this time catching part of her right breast. Blood poured from her wounds as the sun beat down on her.

"You will obey me. I am your master."

She met his gaze, eyes filled with hatred. "Never."

Odage swung the *dirise* over his head in a circle like a lasso then brought another sharp slap across her back. Her long, raven hair now matted against her bloody skin, but still she refused to whimper, not even a tear escaped her golden eyes. He had to give her credit. She was a warrior and took a beating like one. He'd known many men in his life that had screamed like a small child from a beating less than what she had just received.

"I should leave you out here for the vultures to pick at your bones."

Caleb leaned over and whispered something in Odage's ear. The shifters lips curled into an evil grin as he looked at Caleb. "Granted."

AS CASSIE MOVED BEHIND ELIZA, her skin pebbled. Someone followed them. She turned her head and wished she hadn't. Behind her were two demons. Their black, shiny skin glistened in the light. Tusks protruded from their mouths, luminous eyes cast an eerie glow. They walked on hooves, and large claws protruded from their hands. Their height equaled her own.

"Ummm, there are some disgusting things following us." She wondered how they were going to get out of this mess. It seemed unlikely Marcus would be coming for her. She'd tried to reach him, but there was no answer.

"Ignore them."

Right, easier said than done. Especially when one of them yelled out.

"Give us the human female."

"Yes, give us the female, and we will let you pass," the other hissed.

Eliza stopped and whirled around. "Back off, bitches, she belongs to High Lord Lowan."

The creatures shrieked and began to back up. "Yes, take her. Leave us please." They sang in unison.

Eliza stood for a moment to make sure the beasts fled then jerked on the rope. "Come."

Cassie tripped and nearly fell but managed to right herself before she hit the ground. She doubted Eliza would have stopped but dragged her to their next destination.

"Who is Lowan?" Again, another question she wasn't sure she wanted the answer to. Then again, best to get to know all your enemies.

"He is High Lord, and my and Drayos's son." Eliza flashed a wicked grin. "He is most anxious to meet you."

Cassie bit her bottom lip. Yeah, she couldn't wait to meet him either. Not. "So, he sends his mother to do his dirty work? Why didn't he just come and get me himself?"

"He cannot leave his world, yet."

Fantastic, so if she could get away from him, he would be unable to chase after her. Then she only had to worry about bitchtilda here. Of course, how she would escape here was another problem altogether. *What is this?* They were coming up to another cave. She was really getting sick and tired of caves.

"Don't touch the walls," Eliza warned.

"Do I dare ask why?"

"Flesh-eating spiders."

Cassie stopped dead. She had a real fear of spiders. "Do we really have to go in there?" She started shaking uncontrollably. Hyperventilation wouldn't be far away if she didn't regain composure. She tried to remember her breathing exercise, one Dr. Story had taught her. She had worked with one of the psychiatrists at the hospital on her phobia. *Breathe in, breathe out. In with the good, out with the bad.*

"Why, you have a fear of spiders, don't you?"

"Yes, and flesh-eating isn't helping."

Eliza walked into the cave and left her standing outside until the slack in the rope ran out, then with a jerk, she went stumbling into the darkness. Eliza had produced a torch, Cassie almost wished she hadn't. At no time did she want to see the creepy crawlies that slithered along the wall. Instead, her gaze focused on Eliza's head and imagined the numerous ways to remove it.

Cassie wrapped her arms around her waist. It was the only way to keep from touching the cavern wall and the spiders that lurked there. "How much farther?" She felt like she'd been walking forever. Tired, hungry and her back was killing her. At this point, she was just downright cranky.

"Stop your damn whining, or I'll leave you here with the spiders."

That was it, the last damn straw. She grabbed the rope and jerked with all her might. Success, Eliza fell on her ass. "I have had about enough of you, bitch."

Eliza jumped up and was in her face before she could back away, slapping her so hard she stumbled backward. "I should gut you right here." Fangs reflected the glow of the torch. "If my son didn't need you to leave this realm, I would."

"What do you mean he needs me? For what?" She had a bad feeling about this, her gut told her to gather as much information as she could. The guardians were going to need it, and she planned on leaving here. Alive.

"We don't have time for this." Eliza grabbed Cassie by the arm and shoved her out front. "You go first, I'll cover your back." She flashed a mouthful of white teeth.

Cassie grabbed the torch and marched forward. *Screw this, I want out of this god forsaken cave and now.* Once again, she tried to find a telepathic link, not caring that Eliza might eavesdrop. *Marcus? Aidyn?* Odd, rather than the silence she always heard before, now she got static. Maybe that was a good thing, perhaps she was closer to establishing a link with someone. Eliza hadn't made her usual remarks either. Could it be Eliza hadn't heard her this time? She tried to remain calm, not wanting to get her hopes up.

She caught a faint light ahead. It looked like the spider cave was coming to an end. She forced her tired legs to move faster, wanting out of the confines of the narrow tunnel. When she stepped through the opening, she froze. Her eyes took in the bleak surroundings.

"Lovely, isn't it?"

The light she had seen came from rivers of lava. Small fires burned, and thick, hot goo bubbled to the surface. A combination of rotten eggs, burning flesh, and blood assaulted her nose. More than she could bear, her stomach rebelled, tossing its contents onto the jagged rocks nearby. While her gut was racked with spasms, screams filled her ears until she thought they would bleed. If this wasn't hell then god help her, for this was worse than she ever imagined.

"Tsk, tsk, such a weak stomach you have."

God, that voice grated on her nerves. Visions of tossing Eliza into the burning inferno made her smile. Had she not been attached to the bitch by a rope she might have given it a go. Another jerk on the rope and bitchtilda had Cassie following behind her. *I swear to the heavens. Wait...why didn't I think of this sooner? Argathos.*

She held her breath, would the god heed her call?

Cassandra. The voice caressed her mind like a whisper. Excitement coursed through her veins, she clasped a hand over her mouth to keep the squeal of delight from escaping, lest Eliza suspect something. So far, the bitch seemed clueless.

Oh Argathos, I'm in terrible trouble. Please help me.

Cassandra, I am unable to enter that realm, but there are three who come searching for you. Are you hurt?

No, not really... Who's coming for me? She hoped with all her heart that Marcus's name would roll off the god's lips.

Marcus, Gabriel and Baal search for you. They are in that realm right now.

Tears filled her eyes. Marcus was coming for her, or maybe he was coming for his daughter. She didn't care, he would save them both. *Eliza is taking me to her son, Lowan, some high lord or something.*

Have you spoken with Marcus?

No, you're the only one I've been able to connect with. Static. Damn it, had she lost him? *Argathos?* Panic caused her to trip over a rock and fall to the ground. It was then she noticed the demons, all different shapes and sizes but all disgusting just the same. She spotted a woman tied to a burnt tree. The woman yelled to her, pleaded for Cassie to help her as a demon raped her. She tried to look away, but her body refused to move.

"Eliza, we have to help her," Cassie yelled.

Eliza looked at her, and for a moment, Cassie swore there was a hint of sadness in the vampire's eyes, but then it was gone. "She is only a tortured soul. There is no help for her now." She tugged on the rope. "We're almost there."

Cassie continued to stumble over rocks, her body hot and fatigued, the humidity so stifling she could hardly breathe. She kept her gaze to the ground. Otherwise, she bore witness to the atrocities played out by the demons. Souls tortured by rapes, burnings, and hacking off of limbs. The screams continued to fill her ears. She knew that even if she managed to somehow survive, she would never be the same.

"We're here."

She slowly moved her gaze upward, her vision filling with horror. *Marcus, please hurry.*

CHAPTER TWENTY-FIVE

MARCUS, Gabriel, and Baal headed straight into the depths of hell and now were surrounded by demons. A scream pierced his ears. To the right, a soul was tied to a blackened tree and body parts were being hacked off. He looked away. He had no sympathy for the damned. Shit happened when you bargained with the devil. Besides, it was Gabriel's job to save those that were truly innocent, only tricked by greedy demons. His only concern was his mate.

Gabriel produced two swords and tossed one to Marcus and the other to Baal. "Here, you will need these," he said, producing another for himself.

Marcus gave it a thorough inspection, noting that it held an odd gleam. "What's it made of?"

"It is the blade of the Xarizith and will serve you well."

He was impressed, the blade of ice would indeed cause severe pain to any demon. "Thanks, now lead the way." He itched to kill something, but more important, he needed his mate, and time was something he didn't have much of.

The three men moved past pools of fire and lava. He tried to ignore the screaming, but it grated on his already thin nerves. His lungs burned from the sulfur that hung thick in the air. Out of the corner of his eye, he spotted four demons approaching them.

"We have company."

"Yes, they have been following us for some distance." Gabriel turned to face him. "I will question them about the human."

Marcus's lips curled into a snarl. "That human has a name, and you will address her as Cassandra." He swore the next person to disrespect his mate would feel his wrath.

Baal gave a snort.

Gabriel's face showed no emotion, just as it had since he showed up. His eyes merely darkened then he turned to face the demons. "Stop where you are. You will tell me what I wish to know."

The demons cackled, their forked tongues flicked out to taste the air. The largest of the four spoke first. "You do not scare us, angel."

Marcus sized up the other three. They stood a good foot taller than him and bore horns on their arms and legs, their skin covered in green scales and their eyes glowed red. He decided taking off their heads would prove enjoyable. He raised his sword, and in the blink of an eye, he removed the demon's head.

"Wrong answer." He looked at the other three. "Now, who among you cares to answer our questions and live?"

Baal stood, sword planted in the ground and leaned on it. He looked at his nails. "The vampire here is in a foul mood. I'd play nice if I were you."

The other three seemed to have a change of heart. "We play nice." They sang in unison.

"Good. Have you seen a human female down here?" Gabriel stuck the point of his sword into the demon closest to him. The green skin burned from the ice, and the demon screamed, jumping backward. "Nooo. But we heard that there are two females making their way here."

Marcus moved in, his turn to poke the demon. "Where are they headed? Think carefully before you answer, demon." He prayed for the information he desperately wanted. He had to find Cassie. He would not fail her.

"To our massster."

"Who is your master?" Gabriel asked.

"Loooord Lowan."

The three men looked at each other.

"I have never heard of him," Gabriel said.

"I sense several more demons approaching," Baal offered.

"Yes, they hope to overtake us. It would seem you may get your battle after all, fang boy," Gabriel mocked.

Marcus gave Gabriel a mental fuck-off for reading his mind. He hadn't blocked himself, wanted to stay open for Cassie. So far, that had proved fruitless. "I'll take up the rear, you deal with these dick wads." He spun around to face the threat that came up from behind. *Oh shit.*

Demons came in droves, and Marcus sliced and hacked off their heads with the blade of Xarizith. When he thought their numbers dwindled, more came. "How are you faring back there, angel boy?"

"I fare well and you?"

"I'm managing, but how many do you suppose there are?"

"Hundreds, I'm sure. We haven't even seen the meanest of them yet. These are merely minions of the many lords," Gabriel said.

"Just fucking great, how much time do we have left?" Marcus asked, shoving the Xarizith into the black heart of a demon, slowing him down enough to whack his head off.

"Fourteen hours, can you keep up the fight?"

"With one arm tied behind my back." Damn, too much time lost already. *Will I ever be a good mate?* Maybe if he hadn't failed Eliza, none of them would be in this mess right now. Then again, he wouldn't have Cassie either. He would give her up if it meant her safety, if only he could go back in time and fix his mistakes.

"Would you die for her?" Gabriel asked.

"For Cassie? If it meant she could live, and be safe? Without hesitation."

"Interesting," Gabriel shouted back.

Marcus sent another head rolling to the ground to reside with the hundreds of others already there. "Wouldn't you die for a loved one?"

"I don't love."

Baal and Marcus exchanged glances.

"So, angel, have you ever had the pleasure of a woman's body?" Baal asked.

"Yes, I have sex. I am a man and have desires same as any. I just have no desire to love, what's the point?

Warriors.

Marcus slashed another demon's head, surprised when Argathos made contact. *Have you found Cassie?*

She was able to contact me. Eliza is taking Cassie to Lord Lowan, her son.

Marcus glanced back at Gabriel, fear etched on his face. Eliza had a son with Drayos, and the bastard now had Cassie.

Do you know where he resides? Gabriel was the one to pose the question.

No, but the women are in the realm where you are now. However, you're several hours away from them yet.

Great and there seemed to be no end in sight, the demons kept coming. The warriors were now back to back. "We need a plan," Marcus said.

"I agree." Gabriel spread his enormous wings and took to the air, tossing Marcus his sword. "Give me a second."

"You got it," he growled and ran into the fray, a sword in each hand, slashing and stabbing and sending demons screaming. His muscles burned. The thought of Cassie with that bitch kept him on his feet.

"Lowan must be the son of Drayos and Eliza," Marcus said.

Baal danced around a demon before slicing his head off. "Half demon and half vampire. What a fucking nightmare he must be."

The ground crackled and hissed, the warriors found themselves surrounded by ice, demons frozen in their tracks. Marcus and Baal looked at each other, a grin curling their lips.

Baal waved his sword in the air. "Whac-a-mole time."

Swiftly they moved through the demons, whacking off heads in a double-fisted action. When finally, none stood, they stopped and took a deep breath.

"Shit, hell really has frozen over." Marcus shook his head. "Never thought I'd see the day." He looked up at Gabriel who still hovered above. "Why the hell didn't you do that earlier?"

"It weakens me."

A ferocious roar reverberated through hell's sky. Marcus looked up. "Holy fuck."

The biggest, ugliest demon he'd ever seen floated above them. Its wings were at least twenty feet and moved up and down, sending a dust cloud swirling into the air. Its two heads snapped at Gabriel, showing razor-sharp fangs.

"Can you get that thing to land?" Gabriel looked pale, but Marcus could only assist from the ground.

Gabriel barely got out of the way of the demon's enormous tail. The sharp horn that protruded from the end nicked his leg. "The demon is even worse on land. Better to fight him from up here." He produced another sword, but before he could react, the demon whipped its tail again and managed to shred one of Gabriel's wings, sending him spiraling to the ground. Marcus heard the shattering of bone. The angels other wing stuck out at an odd angle. The warrior of death was out of commission, it was up to Marcus and Baal to finish the beast off.

The demon landed in front of Marcus, its two heads dripping venom on the ground and causing the ice to snap and hiss. *Note to self, stay away from the venom.* He raised both ice swords and prepared for battle, while Baal stood to his right.

He gave a glance at his friend. "How do we defeat this thing?"

"I haven't the foggiest."

Marcus pursed his lips into a thin line. "It's your realm. You're supposed to know these things."

"Hey, I've never had to fight one until you came along."

Gabriel, can you hear me?

Yes.

How do we kill it?

Do not attempt to remove either head, it only grows back and pisses it off more. You must puncture the heart.

Great, where's the bastard's heart then?

Center of the chest.

His gaze narrowed on the location Gabriel spoke of then he looked at Baal. "Up for some fun?"

"We only need to watch out for two heads and a tail. Walk in the park."

Out of the corner of his eye, Marcus caught Gabriel on his feet. A broken wing dragged behind him, but his arms waved in the air. "Over here, you slimy bastard."

Just the distraction they needed, now to get the timing right. The demon moved toward Gabriel, his injuries too much for the beast to resist. *Yes, that's it, a little farther.*

When the demon leaned down to devour the angel, Marcus and Baal flashed in front of him, both shoving their blades deep into the beating heart. The beast screamed as ice ran through its veins and crystals formed on the demon's crimson skin. Seconds later, it shattered into a million tiny fragments, raining snow down on their heads.

Marcus looked back to find Gabriel lying on the ground. Quickly, Marcus moved toward the angel and dropped down beside him. "Will you heal?"

Gabriel clenched his jaw. "Eventually. I hate it when my wings get clipped." He tried to sit up, but Marcus pushed him back down.

"Let me see if I can help you." He slid his eyes shut as he placed his hands on Gabriel's chest. His energy searched for internal injuries, and when he found none, he opened his eyes. "Roll over, I need to touch your wings."

Gabriel knitted his blond brows together. "No one touches my wings."

Baal snorted. "Sensitive fuck, ain't he?"

"Stop being a cry baby and roll over," Marcus said.

The angel obeyed. With a little help, he managed to roll onto his stomach. Marcus placed a palm on each wing. Sending white light and energy, he concentrated on mending the torn muscles and knitting together broken bones. After several minutes, he opened his eyes and admired his handiwork.

"Can you move them?" He stepped back so Gabriel could stand.

Gabriel lifted his wings and extended them to their full glory. He turned to Marcus and tipped his head. "Thank you, it would have taken me weeks to recover from that."

"Great, now can we get the hell out of here and find my mate?"

HER GAZE MOVED UPWARD, the towering castle of bones seemed to go on forever. Skulls of various shapes and sizes formed an archway leading to an entry. She recognized several as being human, the rest were probably demon since many had fangs or full sets of razor-sharp teeth. She'd tried to push her fear aside this entire time, but now it knocked her over like an avalanche. There was no getting around where she was or what might happen to her.

"My son is anxious to meet you." Eliza's voice snapped her out of her stupor. She pushed her shoulders back and raised her chin. She could at least give the appearance of confidence even if she had zilch.

Eliza pushed open the over-sized, black wooden doors, revealing red marble floors. The combination of reds and burnt oranges seemed fitting considering where they were. She took one small step, trying to slow down her frantic heartbeat as she wondered what sinister being awaited her inside these hideous walls. To her surprise, Eliza turned and untied the rope. Dare she run? She looked behind her into the darkness. The only light came from the burning fires and lava rivers. She'd never make it.

"Go ahead, run for it. You won't get far before you're caught. I'm sure the demons will enjoy torturing you before they return you to Lowan."

When Cassie turned back and looked at Eliza, Cassie noticed her lips curled around her fangs and her eyes had turned as black as the sky outside. Scary as the woman looked, Cassie decided it was probably better to take her chances here and wait for help to arrive. She stepped across the threshold then nearly jumped out of her skin when the heavy doors slammed shut behind her. She took in her surroundings. The marble floor stood out against alabaster walls and ceiling. A large mural covered the wall to her right and depicted demons in various sexual acts, as if she hadn't seen enough already. Chandeliers of gold and crystal hung from the ceiling. Their light danced through the air like glittering diamonds. If she had been anywhere else, she might have appreciated the décor.

Footsteps echoed on the marble, causing her to shift from one foot to the other. Her throat felt like someone had taken a meat grinder to it then forced her to swallow lighter fluid. She watched as a dark shadow moved closer until it took human form. Still too far away to see his features, but close enough to make out that he wore black pants and a black T-shirt. His exposed skin looked like human flesh.

Okay, at least he doesn't appear to have lizard skin.

One booted foot in front of the other, he stepped closer, now only a few feet away. It was obvious he was built for killing, bigger than any of the other immortals she had met. His biceps so tight they looked like they would shred through his skin at any moment. She looked up when he finally stood directly in front of her. His eyes...they were... black, all black. When she looked into them, her reflection stared back at her. Quickly, she diverted her gaze but not before she noticed the thick scar that ran from his left temple, down his cheek, ending at his top lip. It made his appearance all the more sinister.

"Welcome to your new home, Cassandra." His baritone voice chilled her skin even though it was hot in the room.

She raised her chin. "Thanks for the offer, but I think I'll decline."

He ran a long fingernail down her cheek and across her lips. "Oh but when I show you the pleasures I have in store for you, you will be begging me to stay."

CHAPTER TWENTY-SIX

THE THREE WARRIORS had been walking for what seemed like an eternity. Flashing was out of the question since they had no idea where to go exactly, or what they might encounter once they arrived at their destination. The decision was made to go it the old-fashioned way. Unfortunately, this gave Marcus too much time to think about how he'd failed Cassie. Never again. Once she was safely back home, he would bind her to him immediately. Then he would always know where she was, not to mention she would become a guardian and with that came strength. He knew Lucan had taught her some self-defense, he would further her studies. He would see to it that she could kick every warrior's ass but good.

"Have you any idea how much farther?" He clenched his jaw so hard he nearly snapped a fang.

Gabriel shot him an icy look. "No."

"I don't like this, where the hell are all the demons?" He knew they'd been traveling for several hours but had yet to encounter any more demons. Something didn't feel right. "How much time do I have left?"

"Vampire, now who is the cry baby? Are we there yet? How

much farther?" Gabriel mimicked a small child using a high-pitched whine.

Marcus stopped in his tracks and got in the angel's face. "Angel or no, I'll rip those fucking wings right off your back." He drove home his point by jabbing his index finger into the winged warrior's chest.

Gabriel produced his Xarizith sword and wielded it over his head. "Nothing says I have to wait for you to turn to the darkness before I kill you."

That was all it took to push Marcus over the edge. He pulled back his right arm and let loose with all his strength. His fist made contact with the angel's left cheekbone and sent Gabriel sailing backward. Before the angel could shake off the sucker punch, Marcus was on Gabriel, assaulting the angel's stomach, knocking the winged warrior on his ass.

"Get up, pretty boy, and fight like a man."

Gabriel jumped to his feet, his black wings stretched to their full width. He leaped into the air and flew forward, giving Marcus a swift kick in the chest, sending Marcus to the ground with a heavy thud.

"You fight dirty, angel!"

Gabriel landed on top of Marcus and pinned his arms to the ground. "I like to win."

Marcus reached out and bit Gabriel in the arm. "So do I."

The two warriors continued to roll and punch each other for several minutes. Both were covered in blood from the various cuts received from the other. Marcus was now on top, his dagger in hand and poised at the angel's throat.

He hesitated, something was off. "Why are we fighting, angel?"

"Because you attacked me."

He pressed the blade into Gabriel's skin until blood seeped from the wound. "Because you threatened me." *Still, something isn't right about this.* His mind felt like it was shrouded in a black fog. He shook his head, trying to clear his thoughts. "No, we are warriors on the same side. We have a mission, but what is it?"

"I...I cannot remember." Gabriel pressed his palms to his head as if in pain. "Get off me."

Marcus stood and stepped away from the angel, extending his hand to offer assistance. Gabriel accepted and allowed the vampire to help him to his feet. Both men put away their weapons and dusted themselves off.

"I think we're lost," Gabriel said.

"Are you two ladies done yet?"

They both looked at the man who stood in front of them, arms crossed over his chest.

"Who are you?"

Baal snorted. "I actually signed up for this shit? Marcus, my friend... you, I understand, but angel boy here should not be susceptible to demon magic."

"When did this black mist show up?" Marcus asked.

Gabriel narrowed his eyes, his hands balled into fists. "How stupid I've been. The demon is right, I should have known this would happen and prepared us."

"What? Tell me, I feel like someone's life is on the line, and it's pissing me off I can't remember."

Gabriel nodded to the mist. "It's the mist. Demon magic has messed with our memories, caused us to fight. Someone wants us to forget our mission."

He grabbed the angel's shoulders and shook him. "Gods damn it! What do we do?"

"Give me a minute to work here."

Gabriel brought his palms together as if in prayer, and he chanted under his breath. The angel touched Marcus on the arm, sending heat through his body. A white mist swirled around them. When the mist dissipated, Marcus recognized his surroundings. They were in the other world, on the other side stood the temple of the gods. A place where sacrifices were made and punishments meted out.

"How long will this take?" Marcus asked.

"As long as it takes."

"Maybe we should just go to the temple and ask for help." *Before I rip every feather from your wings.*

"I am your help."

He was getting really tired of this angel and his attitude. Marcus wondered if the god would kill him for beating the shit out of Zarek's personal warrior right on the god's door step. Temptation pushed him in that direction when the fog in his brain began to lift. *Cassie.*

"I remember! Wait, where's the demon?"

"Still in hell, we will find Baal when we return. This time we must keep our minds blocked. We cannot use any telepathy or the magic will overtake us again. We only have eight hours left," Gabriel said.

"Shit, let's go." Not waiting for the angel, he touched Gabriel's arm. "Go!"

In the next instant, they were back in the underworld. Marcus pointed. "Baal went that way."

"Good, I'll fly overhead, so I have a better view."

He nodded in agreement then propelled into a sprint. Being a vampire gave him speed, desperation for his mate increased it tenfold. He was done fucking around. The only thought in his head— protect his mate and daughter. She owned him, heart, body and soul. If anything happened to either of them...well, he hoped Gabriel would kill him before he went on a rampage. There would be no innocents, no one would survive his wrath.

Gabriel dropped from the sky. "Up ahead is a palace. I suspect it belongs to Lord Lowan. We'll need to approach with caution."

Marcus nodded in understanding. "Cassie is number one priority. You must get her out."

"I understand, vampire. I will leave you behind." His blue eyes leveled on Marcus. "Your daughter must not fall into demon hands."

LOWAN OFFERED his arm to Cassie. "Come, let me show you your new home."

She chewed her lip. *How the hell am I going to get out of this?* She had no weapons and no way back to the surface. All she had were the warriors Argathos had said were on their way. But when? She did have her wits and so she would use them to hopefully buy her time.

She reached out and placed a hand on his arm. "I would love to see how you live down here."

His lips curled into a smile. "I think we shall get along fine."

He led her across the marble floor, pointing out the various paintings and murals. Next was the vast library. The room was lined with books from floor to ceiling on three sides. He explained how every book ever written was in this collection. The fourth wall was covered with a stone fireplace, the hearth so vast she could actually stand in it. Several black leather chairs were situated in front of it, offering a refuge to curl up and read. That is if one wanted to spend eternity in hell.

Upon exiting the library, he led her to the ballroom. *Seriously?* Why did she have a hard time imagining an orchestra playing while demons in ball gowns and tuxedos glided gracefully across the dance floor? Did he actually entertain? He certainly had the finest of everything. If she didn't know better, she could imagine herself in some posh estate somewhere hobnobbing with the upper class. All she had to do was look at his black eyes to remind her of where she was.

"So tell me, why am I here?"

He brushed a lock of her hair from her cheek, and she pushed down bile, trying to place happy thoughts in her mind to help her remain calm.

"My lovely human, you are the key to releasing me from this world."

Her mouth fell open. "I don't understand."

"Of course, let me explain. You see, your blood on the amulet of Tobor will open a gateway for me to enter the human realm."

Her palms began to sweat, afraid of what he meant by her blood.

He patted her hand. "Do not worry, a drop of your blood is all I need."

"Why me? I mean I'm no one special, and what is this amulet?"

He sighed. "So many questions. We will talk more about this later."

No, she wanted to talk now but dared not press the issue.

After the ballroom, they moved to the upper floor. Lowan stopped in front of one of the oak doors. "This will be your room, for now." He pushed open the door.

Cassie stepped across cream carpet and tried not to blanch when her gaze caught the black four-poster bed that took up nearly one entire wall. Instead, she focused on the sitting area to the right. Lowan opened another door to reveal a walk-in closet almost as large as the bedroom. Women's clothing from jeans and T-shirts to elegant gowns hung from the rods. Shoes, more than at all the stores at which Cassie shopped combined, lined the floor.

He waved a hand at the racks of clothes. "I wanted to make sure your wardrobe was complete. You should need for nothing."

"Seems you've thought of everything."

"Indeed, only the best for my queen. The women who come after you will merely be my memamosals."

Her brows together. "Memamosals?"

"Wives." His lips curled. "You see, my dear, if you were to bind with your mate, you would most likely become a healer like him. I can't afford to have any more guardians running around. It ruins my plans."

"What are your plans exactly?" She wanted to gather as much information on this sick bastard as possible. Anything to aid the guardians.

He slid up next to her and placed his arm around her shoulder. She had to stop herself from backing away in disgust. "Once everything is in place, I will leave here and enter the human realm. Your people will follow me or die." He reached down and placed his hand on her belly. "Your daughter will grow up to hate the vampires. She may even one day kill her own father."

She bit her lip. Hell would freeze over before she would allow him to have her daughter. She had to find a way to escape, better to take her chances out there than in here. She focused on what Argathos had said, fight for what you want. Fight she would, to her death if necessary.

Throwing on a fake smile, she said. "You do realize that I will die in childbirth as a human. Already my body weakens."

"Of course. You will bind with me. I will perform the ceremony tomorrow eve then you and your daughter will become demon." He grabbed her chin and pinched it between his strong fingers. "Do not think to deceive me, you will not like my method of punishment."

"I wouldn't dream of it. But I'm curious. How do the Draki fit into your plans?" She suspected they were involved. After all, Odage had been the one to kidnap her. He'd threatened she would become a slave, a whore for those willing to pay. Had Lowan been the highest bidder?

He tossed back his head and laughed. "Yes, Odage my puppet. How easy it's been bringing the dragons into my war. They will serve us well. Now, enough of this. It is late, and you need your rest. Tomorrow will be a big day for us both." Once he was gone, she waited several minutes before tip-toeing to the door. Trying to steady her trembling hands, she reached for the knob, grasped and turned.

Locked.

Not surprised, she'd expected as much but still held out hope for escape. Resigned to the fact that this room was for now her sanctuary, she decided a hot shower and some clean clothes would help refresh her. Lowan had told her dinner would be sent up in an hour, so she headed into the bathroom and started the water flowing into the glass shower. Quickly stripping down, she stepped in and went to work on washing away the sweat and grime as well as Lowan's touch. Not wanting to linger least he catch her naked, she hurried and rinsed then shut off the water. In record time, she was dry and dressed in yoga pants and a tank top and combing her hair when Lowan entered, pushing a cart with several dishes into the room.

"Ah, I am happy to see you have freshened up. Now for some nourishment." He lifted the lids off of several silver trays. Fruits, cheeses, meats and a large loaf of French bread made her stomach growl. A silver ice bucket with several bottles of water accompanied the food. He moved the trays to the table and motioned for her to sit. "Eat your fill then rest. I will be back in the morning."

She was busy stuffing a chunk of bread into her mouth when he bent down and kissed her cheek. Nearly choking, she resisted the urge to recoil in disgust. "Thank you for the food." When he turned to leave the room, she exhaled the breath that had been caught in her lungs, then shoved a piece of ham into her mouth. She would keep her strength up and figure a way out of this place. Once he was gone, she moved the trays around, looking for anything that could be used as a weapon. He'd been smart enough to leave no utensils, but perhaps she could use one of the trays and hit him in the head. Tossing the napkin onto the table, she leaned back in the chair. "Boy, am I stuffed." She patted her belly. "Baby girl, I hope you got enough. Who knows when we'll get to eat again." Standing, she gave a stretch and headed for the bed, not wanting to fall asleep but knowing that rest was the best thing for her and the baby. She would take a quick nap to regain her strength then plot her way out of this mess.

CHAPTER TWENTY-SEVEN

EVEN THOUGH HER back was to the door, Cassie sensed someone in her room. She lay perfectly still, afraid to move or even breathe. Was it that bastard Lowan, or had he sent one of his demons to fetch her? She tried to think as the shadows closed in on her. He was at the edge of the bed now, his hot breath tickling her neck. She wanted to scream, but a hand came over her mouth.

"Shhh, love, I'm here."

She rolled to face him. Marcus was real. Tears of joy flowed down her cheeks as she threw her arms around him and sobbed into his chest. She breathed in deep, taking in the salty sea breeze fragrance. It was the best thing she had smelled in days.

"You came for me," she choked out between sobs.

He kissed the top of her head. "Of course, I came for you." He pushed her back, looked into her eyes. "I'm sorry I had to hurt you before, it was the only way. I will beg your forgiveness later."

"I... Eliza said you loved her and..." Her gaze dropped to her lap. "That you two had sex."

He lifted her chin with his finger. "The bitch lies. I never touched her. Except for that one kiss you witnessed." He brushed his lips across hers. "I love you." He spoke against her lips. "I belong to you. Always."

This time his lips pressed harder, his tongue demanding entry. Cassie parted her own and glided her tongue across his, a moan escaped from both of them, but too soon he broke away.

"Are you hurt? Did he..."

She pressed a finger to his lips. "No, he didn't touch me." She watched relief slide across his face. Her heart broke. He looked so fragile right then. What had he been through to get to her? He truly did love her, and she would never doubt him again.

He scooped her off the bed and pressed her to his chest. "We must hurry. I left Gabriel and Baal on watch."

"Baal is safe?" She wrapped her arms around his neck. "Who is Gabriel?"

Marcus opened the door and stepped into the hall.

"Well, it's about damn time. I was beginning to think you two were going to do the ball slappin' dance in there," Baal said.

Marcus swung around, and Cassie squealed, demanding he put her down. "Baal!" She ran and threw her arms around him. "You're safe."

The demon patted her on the back. "Doll, I'm sure glad to see you safe and sound."

Marcus emitted a low growl from deep in his throat. "Demon, hands off!"

Baal quickly put his hands in his jeans pocket. "Vampire, put a cork on your fangs. You know I mean no harm."

"I'm sorry, old friend." Marcus entwined his fingers in Cassie's.

"We have company coming," Gabriel said as he flashed next to Marcus. All three men drew their swords, then created a triangle around Cassie.

"Sweetheart, stay between us."

"Can't you just flash us out of here?" She saw the demons, dozens of them coming from both ends of the hall. The men hacked off heads but not before a few of the demons drew blood of their own.

"Cassie, I can't flash from hell. Gabriel will take you then come back for me." Marcus swung his sword, lopping off another head.

"No, I'm not leaving without you." She was franticly trying to avoid contact with the angel. If he touched her, she would be gone and Marcus would be left here to fight Lowan. If they were to die, they would die together.

Lowan's large figure stormed down the hall. His palms out in front of him. Sparks leapt from his fingertips, arcing across the room, and knocked Marcus to the ground.

Cassie screamed just as Gabriel flashed her from the room.

"SON OF A BITCH, THAT STUNG." Marcus jumped to his feet. It was now up to him and Baal to get out of this mess alive. Gabriel had kept his word. Cassie was out of danger, at least for the moment. He hoped the angel had taken her somewhere far away.

"We're in big trouble, my friend," Baal said.

"No shit, got any ideas?"

"Yes."

Baal chanted. "*si relgr acht wer relgimi ekess troth udoka, adon vi daguam ekess surround udoka.*" His hands formed a circle over his head, then moved down to his waist. Wind rushed past them and swirled, following the contours of the room. Marcus recognized the demon magic. Baal had summoned the elements to erect a force field around them.

"Good going, but couldn't you have kept all the demons on the other side?" Marcus sliced through muscle and bone, sending a demon head to bounce off the invisible wall.

"Ungrateful vampire." Baal whacked off two heads. "At least I kept the bitch and her baby demon on the outside."

"I'm more grateful than you can imagine." He just wanted to get the hell out of there. Claws ripped into his arm and back, and blood dripped to the floor, blending with the red marble.

"Can you flash us out of here?"

"As soon as we kill the last demon."

Marcus understood, knew when they flashed there was that split second when they were vulnerable. Enough time for a demon to take off their heads. A crackling noise hung in the air. Lowan's palms touched the side of the force field, and hairline cracks began to form.

"He's going to break through any minute," Baal yelled.

Marcus fought two demons that clung to him. Fangs sank into his shoulder, their poison pumped into his blood, causing his vision to blur. *I cannot fail!* He sucked in a deep breath and threw the demons off. In a quick motion, he swiveled and removed both demons' heads. Baal's rough hands grabbed him before he hit the floor.

CASSIE CHEWED her lip while pacing the floor. It had only been a few minutes since Gabriel flashed her from Lowan's, but it felt like an eternity.

"Cassie, I'm sure he is fine," Aidyn said.

She stopped and glared. "If he's injured, I hold that angel responsible."

"You couldn't have helped him. Your presence would have only hindered him. He would have worried for your safety."

Aidyn was right. She knew that, but it didn't make the wait any easier. Gabriel had gone back to help while she and the others waited at the lake house. Cassie wondered how the rest remained so calm. She placed a hand on her belly. *Soon, pumpkin your father will be back with us.*

Stopping at the expanse of windows, she stared out over the lake. In the darkness, she saw tiny dots of light along the shoreline. Everyone was tucked in their homes, away from the September rain that had started to pelt the windows. She rubbed her arms against the invisible chill. It wasn't the cold that bothered her, it was something she couldn't grasp or explain.

"Cassie!" The voice she wanted to hear most called from behind her. She spun to find Baal and Gabriel helping Marcus to the couch. She ran and wrapped her arms around him. This was it, this was what she'd longed for, her soul wrapping around his, making her whole once again. She leaned back to get a look at him.

"Marcus, you're injured." He was covered in blood, gouges and bite marks. Some were healing, but many were still red and angry. His face was bruised, and his hair matted with dried blood. She brushed a gentle finger along his cheek as tears spilled down hers. "What have they done to you?"

"Marcus needs blood so he can heal." Lucan stepped in front of them and offered his wrist. Cassie knew that the warrior's blood would help, but he required human blood. Even more powerful was the blood of his mate, her blood.

"No, I will take care of his needs."

Marcus looked at her. "No, Cassie, you don't have to do this."

She took his hand in hers and brought it to her lips, planting a soft kiss. "I want to do this, please let me help you."

"I shall take my leave. I'll post more guards on the premises." Lucan turned into a black mist and rolled from the room. Cassie's jaw dropped, she had never seen him make an exit like that.

Marcus chuckled. "He likes to show off sometimes."

"Neat trick." She turned back to him. "We need to get you into bed."

He waggled his eyebrows. "I can think of nothing I would love more."

She scowled. "I meant to heal, you big dope."

Aidyn and Garin moved forward. "Let us help get you upstairs," Aidyn said.

Garin grabbed Marcus by the arm while Aidyn placed a hand on Cassie's shoulder, and they all flashed from the room.

MARCUS SETTLED into bed with Cassie by his side. He could hardly believe her story, even when she'd retold it from the beginning. Aidyn had come to see her, and how she, Seth and Baal had gone to the mountains in search of him. He held her tight when she regaled him with tales of Baal and his surrender to the slave trader in order to save her and Seth. He would remember to thank his friend. He already owed him more than he could ever repay. He beamed with pride when she told of the Draki attack and how she forced Seth to drink from her in order to save them both. That explained the climax he'd experienced, and her near-death.

He stroked her hair, inhaling her spiced honey scent. "I am so proud of you. You acted like a true guardian."

She blinked, her emerald eyes softened. "Really?"

"Yes." Then he scowled. "If you ever put yourself in danger like that again, I will..."

She pressed her lips into a thin line. "You'll what?"

He nuzzled her neck. "I will die. I nearly died when I felt you slip from me, and I thought I'd lost you." Aidyn had been right, she was a true gift. He stopped nuzzling and looked into those pools of emerald. "I am so sorry for all that has happened. More than that, I'm sorry I had to break your heart." He palmed her cheek. "I had to do it. Odage and Eliza needed to believe you meant nothing to me. It was the hardest thing I have ever done in my life, and now I ask your forgiveness."

She ran her fingers across his lips. "I forgive you, now shut up and kiss me."

He obeyed and pressed his lips against hers. Their tongues collided and performed a sultry dance. His erection rubbed against her thigh. "Baby, I need to be buried deep inside you," he whispered in her mouth.

She cut the kiss short, causing him to moan. "Marcus, you need to heal." She pressed her wrist to his mouth.

He smiled. "Oh no, sweetheart, not that way. Let me show you the pleasures I can bring you." He then ran his tongue across her nipple, causing her to arch her back and moan with pleasure. Yes, he was going to show her how much he'd missed her. He would take his angel to the heavens and make her beg him to stop.

He slid his finger across her moistness. Yes, she was burning up, ready for him. He moved between her thighs and pressed the tip of his cock against her, holding back.

She sucked in a breath. "Yes," she whimpered and tried to push herself against him. He couldn't hold back any longer. He pushed deep inside her and let out a moan. Gods, she was heaven, a perfect fit made just for him. He slid out then back in, slow at first. He wanted to savor her warmth, never wanted to leave this moment. He rubbed his thumb over her nub, causing her to shudder and moan in delight. He sensed she was on edge, her body burning from his touch.

Mine.

"Yours," she cooed. Her encouragements caused him to move deeper, faster until she spilled over the edge, screaming his name. Her body shuddered under him, and she pressed her knees into his hips.

When she finally relaxed, he ran his tongue up her neck. "Are you sure you want this, sweetheart?" Gods knew he wanted it, bad.

"Yes, more than anything. Take all of me, I belong to you."

Her words caused his fangs to extend as he continued to slide in and out of her fiery body. He licked her nipple, grazing a fang across it and causing it to pebble. She pulled his chin up, her gaze meeting his.

"I want to see you."

He obliged and parted his lips, giving her full view of his fangs and the chance to back out. His mind connected with hers. *Do you wish to change your mind?*

No. She traced a fingertip over his lips. *They are as sexy as the first time.*

She turned her head and exposed her neck. He suckled, bringing the smaller vein to the surface then sank his fangs deep. She gasped, her body meeting his, stroke for stroke. He took deep pulls of blood, its rich taste of spiced honey coating his throat. His groin began to burn, his need for release grew stronger with every pull he took. He moved faster, his animal instinct taking over as he pounded into her. She screamed, her body thrashing beneath him as she was sent over the edge, and he followed behind her. His own release erupted. His entire body a raging inferno as he pumped the last of his seed into her. He ran his tongue over the punctures and closed them, collapsing on top of her.

She kissed his forehead. "I missed you." Her voice breathless.

He planted a kiss on her swollen lips. "Cassie, love. Is there something you wish to tell me?"

"Yes." Her emerald eyes glistened. "You're going to be a father."

He grinned. "I wondered if you were ever going to tell me."

"How did you know?"

"I sensed her presence when you were in the cell with me. I've already connected with her." He brushed a kiss on her lips. "I promise to take care of both of you. No harm will ever befall you. I love you, Cassandra Jensen." The next day, he would ask her to be his mate and his wife. That night however, he would keep her tucked in his arms and make love to her all night.

Mine.

CHAPTER TWENTY-EIGHT

CASSIE AWOKE in Marcus's arms. She hadn't slept this well in ages. As she watched him sleep, she realized he was fully healed with no visible signs of his wounds or broken bones. All bruising had disappeared and he was handsome as ever. She wondered, now that he was back, what lay ahead for them in the future. She knew she had to mate with him, otherwise she would die in childbirth if she made it that long. Would he still want to mate with her? He'd said he loved her, but that didn't mean he wanted to commit.

Marcus opened his eyes and smiled at her. "Good morning, sunshine."

She couldn't help but smile back. She was still reeling after last night. "Good morning. You are looking much better."

"That's because of you." He kissed then placed his hand on her belly. "And because of our daughter. I am the luckiest man in the world." He sighed. "However, as much as I want to stay here and keep you naked, we must rise. I need to speak with the others."

"Yes, I have things to share as well."

He frowned. "Like what?"

She kissed him. "I learned things from Lowan that might prove useful."

He picked up a strand of her hair and brought it to his nose. "You are a wise woman. We can talk later after I ravish you." He pressed his lips against hers, sending heat to her core.

"Marcus!"

Cassie moaned. She recognized the voice that called from the other side of the door. Lucan. So much for being ravished.

"Wait here while I kill him."

"You will do no such thing. We can pick up where we left off later."

He brushed another kiss on her lips. "I cannot deny you anything. He's lucky. You have saved him a serious ass whipping." Marcus grabbed the blanket, wrapped it around his waist and headed for the door. When he was gone, his warmth went with him, leaving her chilled. She placed her feet on the floor and grabbed her clothes. Might as well see what's for breakfast. After dressing, she exited the bedroom to find Lucan and Marcus conversing in hushed tones.

"Come here, love," he said holding his hand out to her. When she took it, he pulled her next to him and placed his arm around her waist. "You are a part of us now. It is your right to know what is going on." He kissed the top of her head. "Aidyn has called a meeting. We will go back to Vandeldor as soon as you're ready."

"I'm ready, let's get this done."

"I'll throw on some clothes then we can leave." Marcus stepped from the room and returned minutes later dressed in jeans and a black T-shirt. Lucan opened a gateway, and the three stepped through directly to the king's home. Everyone waited. Aidyn, Seth, Garin and Gwen all sat around a fire in the great room. Aidyn approached.

"I'm glad to see you are in much better shape." He slapped Marcus on the back. "And you, little one. I am most happy to have you back." He kissed her cheek.

Marcus bowed his head. "My lord, I owe you a great debt for looking after Cassie in my absence." He glanced around the room. "I owe all of you."

"It was our honor and pleasure. We are just happy to have you back." Aidyn motioned. "Come join us."

Marcus and Cassie moved to the couch and settled in. He opened a bottle of water and handed it to her. "Go ahead, sweetheart, tell everyone what you've learned."

She took a sip. "Lowan is Eliza's son with Drayos. He told me that my blood placed on some amulet...oh what did he call it?" She wrung her hands.

Marcus took her hand. "Take your time."

"Tobor... yes, that's it. Anyway, somehow my blood and the amulet would open a gateway for him to leave his realm and come to the human realm." She looked at Marcus. "He intends to make us follow him or kill the human race. He is responsible for the war with the dragons as well."

"It's worse than I feared," Aidyn said.

"He was going to force me to mate with him." She touched her belly. "Said our daughter would one day kill her father." Tears streamed down her cheeks. "Will I ever be safe from him?"

Marcus pulled her close. "You're safe, he can't leave his realm, and neither Eliza nor Odage would dare show their faces here." He brushed her cheek. "I'd like you to go with Gwen back to Daniel's home while we talk. She can get you something to eat."

"Okay."

Minutes later, Cassie sat happily stuffing a cheeseburger and fries in her mouth. The sharp flavors ran across her tongue like it was gourmet food. She looked over at Gwen who watched her eat.

"Thanks for going and getting me lunch."

Gwen waved a hand in the air. "Think nothing of it, anything to help my niece grow." Gwen picked up a baby magazine and started flipping through it. "You do realize, of course, that this child will be spoiled rotten? I mean, she will be the first child born in almost two hundred years. And not just by me, mind you, but the men are already talking about the gifts they will bestow upon her. It's actually rather funny to hear them speak about it."

Cassie swallowed a fry then grinned. "I have no doubt that this little girl—" She reached down and patted her stomach. "—will have several vampires wrapped around her little finger. Her father being her biggest fan." It warmed her to think about all the love this child would receive. She knew if anything ever happened to her or Marcus, their daughter would be well taken care of. That she was sure of.

Both women lifted their heads when a presence entered the room. Marcus stepped toward Cassie and kissed the top of her head. "I'm glad to see you're eating. Do you need more?"

She swiped a napkin across her lips and leaned back in her chair. "No, I'm full but give me an hour or so." She certainly had an appetite. If she kept eating like this, she would soon be so big she'd be unable to move. Already she was starting to show, her clothes too tight. Gwen had also been kind enough to bring her back something to wear along with her lunch. She hoped Marcus might take her shopping later.

"Did Daniel's father, Dr. Johnson, stop by to see you?" Marcus took a seat next to her and pulled her hand into his.

"Yes, he said our daughter is growing normally."

Marcus reached out and touched her belly. Closed his eyes and warmth spread over her body. The same white light that she'd seen him cast on Jill when he'd healed her, now shimmered over Cassie's belly. She glanced at Gwen.

"What's he doing?" Her voice low so as not to disturb him.

"He is merging with his daughter. It is the gift of a healer. He can stroke her and talk to her and make sure she is all right."

Cassie stared at Marcus whose silver eyes sparkled. "When you become one of us, you will be able to touch her as well."

Gwen cleared her throat. "I have some things I need to take care of. If you two will excuse me?" She was gone before they could even respond.

"Cassie, I'm sure Dr. Johnson told you about the gestation period for our children?"

He had, and that's what frightened her. "Yes, he said they grow much faster than mortal children." Which explained her already expanding waistline. "Rather than nine months, they are born in five." She struggled to hold back her tears. If he didn't want to bond with her, then she would have to go to Aidyn. How long should she wait?

"Sweetheart." He bent one knee, still holding her hand. "Will you become my wife? Will you bond with me in the tradition of my people?"

She looked at him, noticed he held his breath while waiting for an answer. "Yes, yes, I will."

He kissed her hand. "You realize what is involved? We will belong to each other for eternity."

She had been schooled already in what the ceremony entailed. She would not lie—it scared her. "I can do anything as long as you're by my side."

He smiled, his eyes softening to a light gray. "I will always be by your side." He reached into his pocket then fisted his hand. "While I'm down here..." He opened his hand to reveal a beautiful pear-shaped diamond. "Will you marry me in the tradition of your people?"

"My god, I never expected this," she gasped.

"I know how important this is to you, and if you want a big wedding, then you shall have it."

"Yes, I will also marry you too." Tears fell like a waterfall as he slipped the diamond onto her left finger. "Marcus, it's the most beautiful thing I have ever seen." A single pear-shaped diamond, set in white gold. The band started at the widest part of the pear and circled around. At the narrow end, another band circled and was encrusted with diamonds.

"It pales compared to you." He pulled her down onto the floor with him and kissed her, his tongue sliding between her lips. She groaned and pressed into his erection, her core boiling with the contact.

"Oh...Oh Christ, get a room, would ya?"

They both stopped to find Daniel standing over them, looking like he was ready to vomit.

"I'm going to kill him," Marcus whispered.

Cassie patted him on the chest. "No, you're not."

He let out a long breath. "As you wish." Then he glared at Daniel. "Count yourself lucky that my female has taken a liking to you."

Daniel lifted his shoulders. "Whatever, dude." Then he looked at Cassie. "He's all talk. He's really just an oversized teddy bear."

"I am no teddy bear," Marcus growled as he reached for the boy's leg. Daniel managed to make a quick escape, but that didn't stop Marcus from yelling after him, "I'll bleed you dry, boy!"

She slapped him on the shoulder. "Stop it, you really are a big teddy bear."

He grinned. "That may be, but I do have a reputation to uphold. Now, back to you becoming my wife. We must perform the bonding ceremony before the marriage. It will ensure your safety. I don't want to wait, would tomorrow be too soon?"

"Tomorrow is perfect."

Cassie was both overjoyed and anxious about the upcoming ceremony, aware of what would take place. Being told about it and living it were two different things entirely. Marcus had gone off to shower while she tapped her nails on the kitchen table, waiting for her sister Jill to answer the phone. One good thing about being back in New York, cell reception.

"Cassie? Everything all right?"

"Yes, I'm calling with some good news."

"You found Marcus?"

"Yes...and he has asked me to marry him." She braced herself for what she knew would come next.

"What? My god! When?"

"Well..."

"Where? We are going to have to go shopping and..."

She rolled her eyes, waiting for her sister's tirade to end so she could get a word in. "Yes, of course, we will shop. I'm not sure when or where yet. Those details haven't been worked out." She wasn't sure she wanted to tell Jill yet that tonight she would actually become a guardian. She'd surprise her later.

"I'm so happy for you. Finally, you'll have what you've always dreamed of."

"Thanks, sis. I have to run, but I'll call soon, and we'll make arrangements for you to come visit."

"Okay. Oh hey, send me a picture of that ring. I can't wait to see it."

She laughed. "I will, love you. Talk to you later." She hit the end button on her phone then set it on the table. Picking up a baby magazine, she started flipping through it, looking at all the cute furniture. She and Marcus were going to have fun fixing up the baby's room. She rubbed her belly and smiled. If things moved along as they should, soon she would experience her daughter's first kick. She looked across the room. Aidyn, Seth, and Gwen sat playing a video game. She smiled. They were like three small children trying to outdo each other. Through the window, she noticed Lucan pass by, he and Garin were outside checking the grounds. She should be safe but still felt vulnerable.

Marcus entered the room, giving her the comfort she had missed. Rising, she moved in his direction, but horror crossed his face as he and the others ran toward her. Sharp pain shot into her back, and she tried to suck in air before she hit the floor.

"Cassie!" Marcus yelled.

"Marcus belongs to me," Eliza screamed.

"Grab her," Aidyn commanded.

Liquid warmth flowed down her spine, and a haze grew over her eyes. Why was Marcus crying? Everyone looked at her with horror on their faces. Blackness covered her in a cold blanket.

"NOOO!" Marcus yelled.

"You can't have her if she's dead. How does it feel to have the one you love taken from you?" Eliza's face lit with joy. She had shoved the dagger deep into Cassie's back. "Now you will watch her die, and your babe will go with her."

Marcus reached for Cassie's limp body and gently cradled her in his lap. He would heal her then take immense joy in slowly killing Eliza. That was if Aidyn or the others didn't get her first.

"Stay with me, sweetheart." Her eyes looked into his. They were so dull, the life draining from them.

"S-so cold."

"I know, baby, it'll be better soon. I promise." He pulled the knife from her back. He hated to hurt her, but it had to be done. His palm covered the bleeding wound, and he closed his eyes. He searched for his power and poured it into his mate.

Nothing happened.

What the fuck? He tried again, nothing. Cassie gasped for breath, her lips blue.

Eliza laughed. "Your power's not working? Funny how demon blood can do that."

"Where the fuck is she?" someone yelled. "Eliza is cloaked somehow."

Cassie's life was fading, and he could do nothing to save her. He was a failure, again. "Eliza, let me save her, and I'll go with you."

She laughed. "I think I'd rather watch you suffer."

"You fucking bitch." Aidyn yelled out. "Where are you?" A burst of energy raged across the room and glass shattered as the king flared out his power.

Marcus concentrated, whatever Aidyn had done worked. His power burst from his soul to his fingertips just as his love took her last breath.

"No. No. No!" The pain too much, he couldn't live without her. His soul fragmented, and the darkness spread. His fangs extended, claws grew from his fingertips. Evil spread through his blood. No longer was he a guardian.

He was now a killing machine.

CHAPTER TWENTY-NINE

CASSIE FLOATED, reached for the light. Happiness waited for her if she could only touch it. Something stopped her, why couldn't she reach the light? She tried harder, willing her body to cooperate. Instead, she moved backward. Farther away from the warmth she wanted so desperately. Her lungs ached, burned. Why did death hurt so much? Maybe she wasn't going to heaven. Maybe the reason she couldn't reach the light was because she was being sucked backward, back to hell.

She took a deep breath as pain seared through her body. She forced her eyes open only to have them fuse shut again. The whiteness was too much, it burned her retinas. She cried out as tears streamed from the corners of her eyes.

"Give it a moment. Your body needs time to adjust."

The voice was male but not one she recognized. It soothed and calmed her nerves though. "Where am I?"

"You are in a place of peace. Come, child, let me help you to sit."

Strong hands grasped her arms and gently pulled. "There, now slowly open your eyes."

She obeyed, looking through slits and letting the brightness invade her. Once she became accustomed, she opened them farther. Moving her gaze up, she saw where the voice came from.

The man was more than six feet tall and wore a linen skirt. His skin deeply tanned and well defined. Eyes, lined with black kohl and the color of the Caribbean Sea, stared at her. His raven hair was pulled back at the nape of his neck.

She blinked. He was stunning.

He smiled. "Hello, Cassandra Jensen. My name is Zarek."

She gasped, recognizing the name. "*The* Zarek?"

He crossed his arms over his chest, raising one eyebrow. "Is there any other?"

Her gaze dropped to the ground. "N-no, I guess not. So I am dead then?"

"Look at me."

She raised her gaze to meet his.

"No, you were dead for a moment, but no longer."

She wasn't sure what that meant. Perhaps in heaven she was alive in another sense. Different than before. Funny... she didn't feel different. Touching her stomach, she asked, "What about my daughter?"

Zarek scoffed as if offended. "Really? Do you think I would save you, to let your daughter perish?"

"Um no, I guess not, but how am I supposed to know that?" *Stupid, probably should not have said that.* "I don't mean to appear ungrateful, I just...well, it's...I guess I'm a bit confused is all."

His eyes softened. "I can understand your confusion, but you must regain your wits and quickly."

"Why, what do you mean?" Now that her vision was finally clear, she looked around. "Where is Marcus?"

"He is why you need your wits. I brought you back from death. Now you must save him from the darkness."

She swallowed, and a thousand nails slid down her throat. "What's happened? Where is he?"

"He is safe for now, I have him locked up. When you took your last breath, he snapped. The darkness spread, and he can think of nothing but killing."

A sob caught in her throat. "How can I help him?"

"He is dark, you are light. Let him drink from your light."

She thought a moment. *What the hell is he talking about?* Then realization hit. "I need to feed him. Will he come back to me then?"

Zarek nodded. "Yes, but he will always struggle with his darkness now. You are his eternal light, you will center him." He reached out and took her hand. "You will bond with him and become a guardian. Together, your healing powers will save many lives in the war to come."

"But I can't heal, not like Marcus."

Zarek flashed his white fangs. "You will become a healer soon enough. Now, your mate awaits you."

"Wait! Why don't you stop Lowan? You can save my people."

"That is what I am doing."

Darkness slid over her and wrapped itself around her like a thick blanket. There was no fear this time, she'd grown accustomed to being flashed. There was also the knowledge that she was going to Marcus, and she would repair his shattered soul.

The cave was dimly lit, a pool of water sent steam rising like ghosts floating through the air. Marcus sat with his back to her, staring into the water.

"Marcus."

His head swung around, damp hair slapping his face. His eyes were no longer like cut steel but more like molten lava. She was not afraid, even though he bared his fangs and hissed. He would not harm her, she believed that.

"I've come to help you." She took a step closer to him. "Do you know who I am?"

He cocked his head to the side then smirked. "You're my next meal. I will kill you then find my way from this hole in the ground. I understand there are more of your kind out there."

MARCUS MOVED TOWARD THE GIRL, but she didn't flinch. *Odd.* She should have been frightened, yet showed no fear. He sniffed. "You're with child. You choose to sacrifice her as well?"

"I sacrifice nothing. I told you, I'm here to help you."

He grabbed her arm to keep her from fleeing. "You're a fool then, but I will let you fill my belly." He bent his head and sniffed her hair, spiced honey. Why did the scent seem so familiar to him? Would her kiss taste the same? He pulled her closer and brushed his lips across hers. She moaned and parted her lips, allowing him entry. Hell, he might as well enjoy the woman before he killed her. He shoved his tongue deep. *Gods, she tastes as good as she smells. More, want more of her.* He palmed her breast, causing her nipple to harden through the thin pink T-shirt.

More.

He maneuvered until she was pressed against the cavern wall, pinned by his weight. Cupping her breast, he rubbed his thumb across her nipple until it was swollen and hard. He had to have her. Grabbed the bottom of her shirt and ripped until her breasts were exposed.

Taste.

Yes, he would. He ran his tongue down the middle of her chest then over to the right breast. Latching onto the rosy bud, he suckled, and she pressed harder into his body. He nearly came undone, his cock throbbing against his jeans. The need to be buried deep inside her filled him. He wouldn't wait a minute longer. Grasping the top of her jeans, he pulled, sending the button flying. Without wasting any time, he removed the offending clothes off her body, leaving her with only a black lace thong. She was beautiful. Her skin kissed by the sun. He ran his hands over the small bump where her child grew and found it sexy. Again, the strange sensation that he recognized her tugged at him.

He removed his jeans and let his erection spring free. The

woman reached out and wrapped her warm hand around his cock, causing him to groan. "Your name, I need to know your name." He didn't understand why it was so fucking important, but it was.

"Cassie," she whispered.

"Cassie." He let her name roll off his tongue. "I'm going to fuck you."

"Yes," she whispered back.

He ripped off her thong, grabbed her ass and lifted her. She wrapped her legs around his waist, giving him access to her wet core. With one thrust, he was buried deep. It felt like home, a place where he belonged. She touched either side of his face and pulled him closer, her kiss nearly had him spilling his seed, but he managed to hold back. He pressed her against the rocks and pulled out of her, stopping when only the tip of his cock remained inside her. She wiggled and tried to impale herself on him, but he held fast, he wanted to tease her, make her beg. "What do you want?"

"You."

"Me what?" His voice sounded full of gravel.

"I want you to make love to me." She pressed her lips against his. "I'm yours, all of me. Heart, body and soul."

"Gods." He couldn't stand anymore. With one thrust, he was again buried deep. He wanted to savor her, but fire burned in his veins, causing him to move faster until he was slamming in and out of her wetness.

She moved her silky hair away from her neck. "Take all of me."

How could he refuse? It's what he wanted, needed and had intended. He suckled the vein, rolling it in his mouth until it was full and plump. His fangs ached almost as much as his cock. Without hesitation, he sank them deep and took long pulls, letting her blood flow down his throat. She screamed as her orgasm overtook her, and he pumped faster, his seed begging for release. He fell over the edge, filling her with his semen. His orgasm seemed as if it would never end and he continued to feed, her blood giving him something no other could.

Life.

Realization hit, as the red haze slowly faded. His mate, this was why she seemed so familiar. He retracted his fangs. "Cassie."

Her eyes opened, and pools of liquid emerald stared back at him before a smile crossed her lips. "Marcus, you've come back to me."

He kissed her, tender now that the urgency was gone. "You brought me back. Gods, I thought I lost you forever. How is it you're here?"

"Zarek brought me back."

He reached down and laid a palm across her swollen belly. "Our daughter is well." A tear escaped and slid down his cheek. "I can never repay Zarek for what he has done. I owe him everything, but today, I will make you mine." He shuddered. "I can never go through that pain again."

His cock still buried deep inside her, he unwrapped her legs and set her feet on the ground. He licked his way to her nipple and flicked across the rosy bud. She gasped, her body shuddered. He moved to the other breast and sucked the nipple into his mouth until it hardened like a pebble. He had to have her again. He turned her around until she faced the cavern wall and bent her over. With a quick thrust, he entered her from behind. Nearly blind with lust, he glided in and out. Her wetness coated him. He reached around and ran his finger over her nub, causing her inner walls to squeeze him tight.

"God, Marcus, don't stop. Please." She placed both her palms on the wall and pushed back against him. "Harder."

He hardly recognized the sultry voice that spoke to him, but he would give her anything she asked.

"Oh yes, baby," she panted. "I'm gonna come again." She screamed, her pleasure echoing throughout the cavern. He quickly joined her. Yelling out his own pleasure as his seed filled her.

They stood still, their bodies coated with sweat and breaths coming in quick pants. He pulled her to his chest and wrapped his arms around her, hands resting on her stomach. "I love you, baby," he whispered in her ear.

She turned her head and placed her hand on his cheek. "I love you too."

He slid out of her then scooped her up in his arms. He was sure her muscles were sore, so he carried her to the steaming pool and waded out until the water was at his waist. Gently he slid Cassie down the front of his body, immersing her into the warmth.

"I need to convert you, today. Now."

She looked up at him. "I know. Tell me about it again."

He sensed her fear and understood. She needed to understand he would protect her, that she would be safe and free from pain. Her body would change in ways she couldn't begin to imagine.

"First, I will take your blood until your heart barely beats. Then, I will feed you my own blood." He brushed his lips across hers. "Once that is complete, I will place you in stasis and submerge you here." He swept his hand across the water. "In the waters, where your body will begin its changes."

Cassie crawled into his arms. "I'm frightened. What about our daughter?"

"She will remain connected to me during your change." He stroked her hair and buried his face in its silkiness. "Don't be afraid, you will feel no pain, and I will be right here until the changes are complete. I will then wake you and feed you." He kissed the top of her head. "I need to know that, while I must go out and fight, you are stronger and better equipped to protect yourself. The others search for Eliza and Odage, but so far, they have been unsuccessful."

She pulled back and looked up at him. "Be warned, when our daughter is old enough, I will fight beside you. Until then, I'll help you heal. Zarek said he needed another healer."

He smiled. "As you wish." He would train her to fight and heal others. Something told him she would excel at both. He knew the future would be filled with war and death. First, they needed to destroy Lowan, then take out his servants.

"I'm ready, Marcus." Her voice pulled him back to the present.

He leaned down and kissed her, his tongue pushing her lips apart. This would be the last time he kissed her as a human. He ran his tongue down her neck then pierced her vein, drinking in her life force.

CHAPTER THIRTY

CASSIE OPENED her eyes and found herself in Marcus's lap, they were both still in the water. She inhaled her first breath as a guardian. Aromas assaulted her. There was Marcus's scent of the ocean breeze. Earthy smells of dirt, rock and water.

He kissed her forehead. "How do you feel?"

She blinked. "Wow, like a million bucks. Seriously." Her senses were overloaded. When she looked across the cavern, she saw the tiniest details in the rocks. Colors were more vibrant, and the dim light was more like a bright sunny day.

Her hand reached for her belly. "Our daughter?"

"Perfect. Reach for her."

"How do I do that?"

"Close your eyes, feel her energy within you. It will be different from your own." He kissed the top of her head.

She gasped when she found the tiny aura, the most vibrant crimson she'd ever seen. "I feel her, I can actually see her tiny body. Ohhh, she's beautiful." Tears of joy filled her eyes.

"With practice, you will be able to check her progress and know her thoughts."

"You mean I can communicate with her?" It seemed surreal. She never thought to be able to actually talk to her daughter while the baby grew in the womb.

He smiled. "Yes, love, you will soon discover our daughter is very strong-willed." He kissed her lips. "Like her mother." He helped her sit up. "Are you hungry?"

She frowned. "I'm not sure. What does it feel like?"

He laughed. "Like hunger."

"Then I guess I am." She found the prospect of drinking his blood appealing but worried she'd be unable to stop. She ran her tongue over her teeth in anticipation. "Ouch!" Shit, fangs.

"Careful, you'll have to get used to working those." He bent down and sucked the trace of blood from her tongue.

She moaned and shoved her tongue deeper into his mouth. Her senses heightened and caused her body to tingle. She needed him inside her right now. "Marcus, I need you."

"I know." He positioned her so she was straddling his lap.

She impaled herself on his shaft in one swift motion, letting out a cry as he filled her completely. Once she got her feet positioned under her, she moved up and down on his cock.

"Oh my god." The sensation tenfold what it had been before, already she was on the verge of an orgasm. When Marcus sucked her nipple into his mouth, she went over the edge. Colors flashed before her eyes as she screamed, her entire body humming. Never in her life had she experienced an orgasm so intense. The desire to take his blood burned in her, taking her by surprise. As if sensing her need, he brought her head to his neck.

"Take what you need, follow your instinct," he whispered in her ear.

She ran her tongue along his neck. His scent drove her insane with desire. Before she knew what was happening, she sank her fangs deep into his skin. Blood ran across her tongue, and she drank.

"That's it, baby, you're doing great." Marcus groaned. "Sweetheart...gods. Baby, I'm going to explode."

She took long pulls, his blood feeding some need deep inside of her. She continued her movement up and down his shaft until she felt him swell.

Yes, love, come with me.

She pulled her fangs free and screamed as another orgasm racked her body. Together they soared into the open night before drifting back to reality.

He leaned forward and licked her chin. "You're a little sloppy there."

A flush covered her cheeks. "Sorry. I...did I do it right?" It was then she noticed the small trickle of blood left on his neck. She reached out and wiped it off. "I guess I am a slob."

He lifted her off of him. "It's all right, sweetheart, you did fine for your first time. It will get easier." He took her hand and led her out into the deeper water. They both submersed and let the warmth soothe their tired muscles.

"Tomorrow, we will perform the binding ceremony. You will pledge your oath to our king."

"I'd like that very much, but isn't it short notice to Aidyn?"

"No, I have informed him. He and the others are already making preparations." A wicked smile crossed his lips.

"What?" Her brows knitted together. "What have you done?"

"Your sister will be there as well."

She gasped and threw herself into his arms. "Marcus, thank you, thank you." It was the best gift he could have given her. She hadn't seen Jill in so long and missed her very much. "I love you." She kissed him long and hard.

"Let's go home. Are you ready to flash yourself?"

"I can do that?"

He threw his head back and laughed. "There are many things you can do. Picture my home in your mind and take us there."

She did as instructed, and before she knew it, the dark vortex sucked them in, and they had left the cave. Marcus laughed so hard there were tears running down his face. When she looked around, she realized they were outside his home, both dripping wet and naked. *Shit!*

She beat him on the chest. "Stop laughing, it's not funny."

"I'm sorry, love, really I am but...oh hell." He broke off into a fit of laughter again. She smiled, then broke into her own laughter.

"Can you help me out and get us inside the house?" In a flash, they were standing inside the bathroom, and Marcus was wrapping her in a large, soft towel. He kissed her on the top of the head.

"It will get easier, I promise. Now get dressed so we can visit the others."

So much had happened over the last twenty-four hours. "It feels like a dream," Cassie said to Gwen and Jill. Both girls were helping her get ready for the ceremony that was scheduled in one hour. Gwen had run her through the entire ceremony and had quizzed her all day. Cassie fretted that she would embarrass herself or worse yet, Marcus. Hell, she was still stumbling through her new skills as a vampire.

"Now do you remember everything I told you?" Gwen asked.

She rolled her eyes. "Like I could forget. I think you've tattooed it into my memory."

Jill stepped next to her and patted her on the back. "Now we don't want you doing something like say...flashing yourself naked into the front yard." Jill and Gwen cackled like a couple of hens, causing her to drop her head into her hands.

"What was I thinking when I shared that bit of information with you?"

Gwen stepped over and gave her a hug. "You'll be fine. Now let's get you into your dress."

Cassie pulled her hands away from her face. She was excited to see the dress Marcus had picked out for her. She had spent last night at Gwen's, deciding that she wanted to at least follow some of her traditions by not letting the groom see the bride. He hadn't been happy to separate from her but caved only on the condition that guards be posted outside the house. Even though his sister was a fit warrior, he wanted the three girls to have fun and relax. Knowing the guards were outside in case something went wrong had given them all relief. No one knew for sure where Lowan, Eliza or even Odage were, and they were still a threat.

"Should I be nervous, Gwen? I mean, is Marcus going to dress me in a burlap bag?"

Gwen giggled. "I don't think so, but let's see."

All three women crowded around the black bag that hung on the back of the bedroom door. Cassie reached up, her hands shaking as she slowly pulled down the zipper. Stunned silence filled the room.

"It's beautiful," Jill said.

"I believe my brother has outdone himself."

She had never seen anything more beautiful. "Hurry and help me get in on." She couldn't wait to see how it looked on her. Jill finished pulling off the black bag and removed the dress from the hanger. Gwen steadied Cassie while Jill held the dress open for her to step into. Once into the dress, Jill pulled it up and helped place the straps over her shoulders while Gwen zipped up the back. Both women took a step back to admire the bride.

"Well?" Her nerves sat on the outside of her skin. She looked down at herself but was unable to get the full effect. The dress fit perfectly and caressed her skin like spun silk. When she looked back up at her sisters, they were both crying.

"What? What's the matter? Do I look fat?"

Both women shook their heads. "You are stunning," Jill replied.

"I don't think even my brother knows how beautiful you are going to be in that dress."

Gwen and Jill stepped aside so she could gaze into the full-length mirror. When she caught her reflection, she gasped and stepped closer. The braided straps held delicate lace that covered the top of her collarbone, leaving her shoulders bare. The front fell into a V-neck, showing off her cleavage. Under her breasts was a wide band of white silk, swathed in lace and crystals. The rest of the dress fell in a straight line to the floor with a small train. Gwen had pulled Cassie's hair into a delicate chignon and wrapped a thin piece of white lace around the top. She stared at herself, unable to speak.

"What do you think?" Jill asked.

"I...I look like a Greek goddess." It was true, and she had never felt more beautiful in her entire life. Marcus had picked the perfect dress, simple yet elegant.

Gwen approached and gave her a kiss on the cheek. "Today, you are a goddess, and I am happy to call you sister."

"Hell, I need a tissue," Jill cried.

Cassie turned to look at her sister. "I think you better bring the box." She smiled and looked at Gwen. "Will you do me a favor and flash us there? I fear I might put myself in the middle of the damn sea."

Gwen extended both hands. "I would be honored."

Her soon to be sister in-law left Cassie inside the small room just outside the throne room, then she and Jill took their places. Cassie paced nervously, waiting for her cue to leave.

Are you ready, sweetheart?

Marcus, his voice sounded like music in her head. *Yes, I'm ready.*

Do you like your dress?

It's beautiful, thank you.

I'm glad you like it. Come now, it's time for our ceremony to begin.

She opened the door and stepped onto the red carpet. Carefully, she walked down the corridor, past the marble columns until the room widened. She stopped for a moment when she spotted every-one. At the top of the dais sat Aidyn on his ornate throne. On his right stood Zarek, then Argathos. On his left were two breathtaking women whom she had never seen before but guessed them to be goddesses. Lined up next to them on both sides of the room were the warriors, including Gwen and a few other females. In the middle, stood Marcus. He was dressed like the other men, wearing some kind of Egyptian skirt and gold bands on his biceps.

After regaining her composure, she began the final steps toward him. She spotted Jill off to the side, blotting her eyes with a tissue. As she walked past each warrior, they moved in behind, until she and Marcus stood inside the circle. She looked up at him, his hair pulled back from his face and his eyes lined with kohl. His sun-kissed body was perfection, and she felt a pool of moisture between her legs. *I'd do you right here, if it weren't for an audience.*

The feeling is mutual, my love. "You are stunning."

Aidyn rose from his throne and stepped forward. "Join hands and kneel before your king and gods." They did as commanded, the marble floor surprisingly warm where they knelt. Cassie experienced the hum in the floor that Gwen had warned her about. It seemed the eye of Ra—which was embedded into the marble beneath them—vibrated with power. The eyes in the statue of Ra that stood behind Aidyn began to glow red.

Aidyn moved back to his throne, and Zarek stepped forward. "Marcus, we have bestowed upon you the most precious gift a guardian can receive. A mate. Do you accept her and promise to care for her?"

"Yes, my lord."

"Then proceed." Zarek stepped back into his place in line.

Cassie watched as Aidyn handed a dagger to the woman directly to his left. She approached, her long sapphire gown complemented her raven hair, she held the dagger across both palms.

"I am Ediva, the goddess of lightning. I bring you the king's dagger." The blade glowed for a moment before Marcus reached for it.

He looked at Cassie. "Hold out your right hand, palm up."

She did, and he made a clean slice across her palm. He repeated the same step on his right palm then placed his over top of hers, his gaze locked onto her. "I bind myself to thee for all eternity. I place your life and happiness above my own. I freely give to you my heart, my soul, and my undying love. I willingly sacrifice my own life to protect you and our children. Should your soul leave this world, I will follow you into the next life."

Warmth flowed through her body, her soul stirred then she felt a sudden connection to Marcus. She knew his every thought and feelings. The feeling of love that flowed through her sent a tear sliding down her cheek. It was his love for her, love that words alone could never express but this...this was more than she could have imagined.

"I give you all that I am, *sia itov*, my love."

Can you feel my emotions too?

He smiled. *I can.*

Then you know how much I love you as well.

Yes.

Ediva picked up the dagger and returned it to Aidyn. Zarek moved in front of Cassie. It was time to receive her gift from him. He placed his hand on the top of her head then white light radiated from his fingers and pain burned across the back of her right shoulder.

Her mark.

She and Marcus now had matching tattoos, the sign of a healer. The only difference was hers had one black wing and one red wing. The red signified her status as a guardian mate. She didn't mind, though, as she looked down at the beautiful diamond on her left hand. He had promised that he would also wear her ring, which she would present him with later.

"Cassandra, you will rise." Zarek took her hand and helped her to her feet. "Do you vow to follow your king and protect all humanity from evil?"

"Yes." She looked up at the towering god.

"Will you help your king keep the peace among all immortals?"

"I will."

"Do you understand that any waiver in your loyalty to him is punishable by death?"

"I do."

He smiled at her, then winked. "Then go to your king."

She moved forward until she reached Aidyn. Kneeling down at his feet, she bit into her wrist and held it up to him.

"Welcome, little one, I am pleased to have you with us." He bent down and took her wrist, drinking the blood that she offered in sacrifice. When he had finished, he rose, pulling her to her feet. "I present to you Cassandra Dagotto, healer and mate to our own guardian, Marcus. May you protect her life as she will protect yours."

Cheers and clapping echoed around the room. Marcus approached, and Aidyn placed Cassie's hand in her mate's.

"Kiss your bride, so we can go drink some champagne," Aidyn said.

"Wife, you're stuck with me for eternity."

She placed a palm on his face. "Husband, I'd have it no other way."

Their lips touched and their souls entwined. Together, they would forge the way to a new world.

A scream filled the air. Warriors scrambled, and weapons materialized from nowhere. Marcus shoved Cassie behind him and yelled to stay put. Eliza stood with a knife to Jill's throat, a vortex opened behind her, and several demons emerged. All encircled Cassie's sister.

Cassie touched Marcus's arm for support. "We have to save her."

His jaw clenched. "I will kill that bitch once and for all."

"How dare you bring your vile pets into my home," Aidyn said, anger rolled off him.

Eliza hissed. "Your home? This is my home. I should be queen!"

Aidyn stepped closer and looked at his sister for several seconds, his emotions in apparent turmoil. Cassie understood what they had meant by being connected. Her heart broke for the warrior. His last living relative stood before him, but she was no longer the sister he knew.

She chewed her lip. Would he sacrifice her sister for his own?

"Let the woman go, Eliza. This is between you and me." Aidyn extended his hand.

Eliza laughed. "Sorry, brother, you would kill me in a heartbeat."

"Sister, I love you, and it saddens me to have to take your life. But I will. You have broken every law a guardian fights to uphold." His fists clenched and unclenched. "You have left me no choice."

Her eyes narrowed. "I'm willing to bargain. Cassie comes with me in exchange for her sister's life."

"No fucking way." Marcus took a step forward.

"What's the matter, afraid of losing your new bride?" Eliza tightened her grip on Jill, and the blade at her neck drew blood.

"No." Cassie pushed Marcus out of the way and ran forward.

Cassie, what are you doing? We will find a way to free Jill.

No, I'm tired of hiding.

"Eliza, I counteroffer. Let my sister go, and I will fight you...to the death."

Marcus moved in behind her and wrapped his arms around her waist. His lips touched her ear. "No." His whisper full of desperation.

Eliza smiled. "I will accept only if every warrior here stays out of the fight and vows *arytissi tiichi*."

Warriors mumbled throughout the hall. Cassie glanced around. Every man clenched his jaw. She looked back at Eliza. "What is that?"

"It means warrior's honor. We must promise to not interfere. To do so brings severe punishment by the gods," Marcus said.

She turned to look at her mate. "What kind of punishment?"

His gray eyes turned stormy. "Death."

She brought her hand to her mouth, then quickly regained her composure. "My sister's life is on the line, you must all take the vow." *Please.*

One by one, each warrior repeated the words. Aidyn stood next to her. "I vow *arytissi tiichi*."

It was now up to Marcus. She looked at him, his eyes were moist. "I can't. You ask too much of me. The world would never survive your death."

She touched his cheek. "You must take the vow."

"I love you."

"Take the vow, for me."

He kissed her hand. "I vow *arytissi tiichi*." He leaned down, and his lips touched hers. "I can't promise I won't interfere." He pulled her into him, and their tongues glided together. She relished every second, since this might be the last time they were together.

"Oh come on already."

Cassie pushed away. "That's it. This bitch is going down." She looked at Aidyn. "Can you contain him?" She nodded at Marcus.

"What? No," Marcus yelled.

"You'll never keep your vow, and I can't have you dying on me."

Lucan slid in and a black mist circled Marcus around the waist. Dozens of tiny hands reached out and latched onto his skin. He fought but was bound tight. His gaze moved to Lucan.

"Motherfucker, I'll deal with you later."

Lucan smiled. "I'll be waiting." He winked at Cassie. "Remember what I taught you."

Cassie strode toward Eliza. "They have all taken the vow, now let my sister go."

"Cassie, don't so this," Jill cried.

She smiled at Jill. "It's already done. Now release her."

Eliza shoved her away, and Gwen grabbed Jill's hand, pulling her into the warriors' fold. It was just the two of them in the center of the room. "Choose your weapon, bitch." Cassie held up her hand and produced a sword.

Eliza laughed and produced a sword to match Cassie's. "Now, to repay you for stealing my mate." She swung, and Cassie matched, metal clanged and sparks flew.

"Your mate? You lost him years ago. He loves me now, and I will bear his children." She lunged and swung, Eliza sidestepped.

Eliza lunged and managed to nick Cassie's arm before she moved out of the way. She heard Marcus growl.

"Damn it, woman, be careful," he yelled.

She ignored him and did her best to remember everything Lucan had taught her before she became a guardian. Now, she had strength and power on her side. *Gods, I hope it's enough.* She felt the babe stir inside her. Resolve rushed through her veins. She had to win this fight. She swung, missed. Flashed behind Eliza, but the older woman was wise to her tricks. Eliza kicked out a leg and sent Cassie to the ground. She jumped to her feet, flashed a dagger into her left hand and threw. It struck Eliza in the thigh.

Eliza screeched. "Bitch!"

Cassie panted, her body tired, not yet used to the changes that had taken place. The wound on her arm healed but had taken a toll as well. She prayed for a miracle, knowing she'd never survive otherwise. Their swords met, Eliza pushed and Cassie stumbled backward.

"Hey, doll. Gotta tell ya, I've been wanting to oust this bitch for some time." Baal had appeared behind Eliza and it was the distraction Cassie needed. She summoned all her strength and prayed this time she got it right. When Eliza turned to face the threat, Cassie flashed, her sword raised and as soon as she appeared, she swung. All her power was thrown into the force of the blade as it connected with Eliza's neck.

Her head rolled and the headless body hit the floor.

"You have no idea how many times I wanted to do that." She looked up at Baal. "Thanks for the help."

He grinned and gave a slight bow. "Pleasure was mine."

Marcus slid in behind Cassie, strong arms wrapped her in a cocoon. "Baal, however you came to be here, I am most grateful."

He snorted. "My friends and I were asked to join the party."

Cassie looked around. The demons who had accompanied Eliza were now turning to ash as Aidyn cleaned up the mess. In their place stood ten large men. Their golden eyes and extreme good looks indicated they were Kothar demons.

"I'm confused. Who asked you to come?" Cassie asked.

"I did." Aidyn stepped beside them. "I may have taken a vow, but it didn't stop me from calling on a friend."

Baal sheathed his sword. "You vampires and your stupid fucking rules. Whoever heard of such bullshit?"

Marcus scowled. "I'm happy you did it, but is that still not interfering?"

Aidyn grinned. "It's a gray area. Cassie still won the fight."

Gabriel strode across the room. "I'm afraid I have some news."

"Please tell me it's good news for a change. I could really use some," Cassie said.

He folded his dark wings close to his body. "I'm afraid not." He looked around. "When Eliza stabbed Cassie, she left with the bloody blade. This means Lowan has her blood, now all he needs is the amulet to open..."

"Hell's Gate." The king's voice rang out.

Everyone turned to look at Aidyn. They all knew what he was thinking. The war had only begun.

ABOUT THE AUTHOR

Award winning and bestselling author Valerie Twombly grew up watching Dark Shadows over her mother's shoulder, and from there her love of the fanged creatures blossomed. Today, Valerie has decided to take her darker, sensual side and put it to paper. When she is not busy creating a world full of steamy, hot men and strong, seductive women, she juggles her time between a full-time job, hubby and her German shepherd dog, in Northern IL. Valerie is a member of Romance Writers of America and Fantasy, Futuristic and Paranormal Romance Writers.

Sign up for Valerie's newsletter and be the first to hear about new releases, receive special excerpts and exclusive contests. http://valerietwombly.com/newsletter-sign/

Follow Valerie
www.valerietwombly.com

ALSO BY VALERIE TWOMBLY

Visit ValerieTwombly.Com

An Angel's Torment (Eternally Mated Prequel)

Fall Into Darkness (Eternally Mated #1)

Veiled In Darkness (Eternally Mated #2)

Bound By Darkness (Eternally Mated #3)

Unleash The Darkness (Eternally Mated #4)

Surrender To Darkness (Eternally Mated #5)

Tempted By Darkness (Eternally Mated #6)

Spanish Nights, A Jinn's Seduction

Sultry Nights, A Jinn's Seduction

Taken By Desire (Demonic Desires #1)

Taken By Storm (Demonic Desires #2)

Passion Awakened (Beyond The Mist)

His Burning Desire (Sparks Of Desire)

Rescue Me (Sparks Of Desire)